THE PRESIDENT SAID KILL HIM

A NOVEL
BOOK FOUR

NORMAN WOOD

BH
bookhouse
PUBLISHING

bookhouse
PUBLISHING

2950 Newmarket St., Suite 101-358 | Bellingham, WA 98226
Ph: 206.226.3588 | www.bookhouserules.com

Red Sword: Book 1, *Thorn: Book 2*, *Checkmate: Book 3*, and *The President Said Kill Him: Book 4* are fictional accounts based on actual events related to Team Thorn of the CIA Clandestine Service and their efforts to protect the United States and stop terrorists from around the world.

10 9 8 7 6 5 4 3 2 1

Printed in the United States of America

Library of Congress Control Number: 2023903390

ISBN: 978-1-952483-70-7 (Paperback)
ISBN: 978-1-952483-71-4 (eBook)
ISBN: 978-1-952483-72-1 (Audiobook)

Editor: Julie Scandora
Cover design: Scott Book
Book design: Melissa Vail Coffman

For more information visit NormanWoodBooks.com

Dedicated to Rollin B. Klink, former Special Agent in Charge, US Customs Service, San Francisco. Rollin was not only my boss but also mentor and friend. Few men come into your life that have a profound and lasting effect on who you become. This man did. Few men are great men. He was. In my novels, he is Robert Klass. Rest in peace, Rollin.

CONTENTS

PROLOGUE

Fish Creek, West Virginia
Noon, Saturday, March 27, 1993

Nathan West turned the metallic brown CJ-5 Jeep down the gravel Fish Creek Road to the cabin a half-mile away. As he slowly drove across the swollen stream from the spring rains, he could see wet tire marks on the creek gravel on the other side.

"Hmmm, someone's here," he said, frowning. Pulling the CJ around to the upper side of the log cabin, he could see a large black Chevrolet Suburban parked there. He glanced at the license plate as he got out of the CJ. It was a government tag, and no one was in it.

"Dammit," he said, carrying the gallon of milk and sack onto the back porch.

Opening the door, he could see two men in dark suits sitting in his living room, both on the blue couch.

"All right, who are you and what the hell do you want?" West asked as he closed the door and walked past the men, glancing at the neatly groomed suits, faces, and hair. In the kitchen, he placed the milk and eggs into the fridge and the bread by the sink.

"Excuse the interruption, Agent West. We are with the Secret Service, and we were asked to come and get you," one of the men said, after they both had gotten up and followed West into the kitchen.

"I'm no longer in the government, fellas. And take me where?" West asked, turning to look at the men.

"The White House, sir. President Crawford would like to speak to you."

CHAPTER 1

WHAT THE HELL'S GOING ON?

PRESIDENT-ELECT BILL CRAWFORD WAS SWORN INTO the office as the forty-second president of the United States on January 20, 1993. Later that same day, CIA Director Robert Gales officially resigned but would stay until a new director was confirmed and sworn in.

On February 5, Roger Wolfe was confirmed as the new director of Central Intelligence. When he arrived at his new office in Langley, Virginia, he found an envelope on his desk. It had the former director's letterhead and was addressed to Director Wolfe. Sitting down at his new desk, he opened the envelope and took out the letter. Unfolding the single sheet of paper he read,

> *Roger, after you've had time to organize the office, give me a call. There's something we need to discuss. I wish you all the luck and good fortune. God bless America.*
>
> *Bob*

I'll do that, Wolfe thought. But first, I've got a lot of things to do with this new youngster of a president. Then in a couple of weeks, Bob can bring me up to speed on what he was working on. Wolfe put the letter back in the envelope and lay it beside the STU encrypted phone on his desk.

TWENTY-ONE DAYS LATER, ON FEBRUARY 26, a car bomb exploded in the basement of the World Trade Center. Within days after the explosion that killed six people, the new president was informed by the FBI the perpetrators were a loose network of ragtag Muslim extremists. The FBI also informed the president the case was solved and the terrorist would be tried in New York federal court. President Crawford was very pleased; he didn't want a big controversy during his first term as president. The disastrous Whitewater Development fiasco had been enough.

CIA Headquarters
1 p.m., Monday, March 15

FORMER CIA DIRECTOR ROBERT GALES WALKED into the office of CIA Director Roger Wolfe.

"Come on in and thanks for coming, Bob," Wolfe said. "I'm up to my ass with this bombing. Looks like the FBI has it pretty much under control. A bunch of dipshit jihadis. I hope we're able to catch them all and tie this up soon. What do we need to talk about? This needs to be quick, Bob. I'm under the gun here."

"Roger, you'll need to cancel any appointments you have for the rest of the day," Gales said as he sat down.

Wolfe stopped writing, lay the pen down, and stared at Gales. "You serious?"

"Yes. Dead serious," Gales said, looking intently at Wolfe.

Wolfe picked up his phone, punched the secretary's line and said, "June, cancel my appointments for the remainder of the day."

"Yes, sir." June McDonald replied and then thought, I knew that was coming.

Hanging up, Wolfe said, "All right. What the hell's going on?"

"Roger, what I'm about to tell you can land me in a lot of hot water. It can ruin my reputation and whatever future career I might have. I have accepted that. Whether I reap punishment will ultimately be your decision."

"Jesus, Bob. Are you sure you want to entrust with me whatever you're about to say?"

"I have no choice. You need to know this. It's vital, especially for President Crawford. It's about the World Trade Center bombing."

"I'm not sure what you're talking about. I realize you've not had our briefings lately, but the FBI has done a good job on this. We have some of the jihadis arrested and looking for more."

"It wasn't jihadis, Roger. It was IIS."

"What? The Iraqi Intelligence Service?"

"Yes, sanctioned by Saddam Hussein himself."

"That doesn't seem possible, and it's against all the facts that I know, Bob. The FBI has arrested several low-level jihadis living here that are from Palestine and Egypt. They're looking for one in Jordan now. None from Iraq."

"They're wrong. It was a false flag operation. Doesn't the date February 26 ring a bell?"

"Yes, of course. Battle of Kuwait," Wolfe replied. "But we have no Iraqi involvement with this bombing."

"I first want you to confirm what I'm about to tell you. This is the truth and you need to verify it. Have June call Spec Ops and get Supervisory Agent Dan Bridger on the phone."

"All right. What do I ask him?" Wolfe asked.

"Ask him how much cyanide he disposed of from the River Wildlife Management Area near Chester, New Jersey. I told him it was a training exercise."

"What are you talking about, Bob?"

"He'll tell you he took 1,764 pounds of sodium cyanide, thirty gallons of sulfuric acid, and 500 pounds of urea nitrate explosives from a black Ford van parked in the shotgun range," Gales said.

Wolfe stared at Gales from across the desk with squinted eyes.

Gales continued, "Saddam Hussein wanted to kill thousands of Americans on the second anniversary of his defeat in Kuwait. He sent two IIS agents that we know of to do the job, Rami Ahmed and another man. Members of my team, at the last minute, took the cyanide. We didn't know about the second bomb. But Ahmed didn't have the cyanide for the explosion, and we saved thousands of lives."

"Dear, God," Wolfe said, picking up his phone and punching McDonald's number.

"Yes, Director?" McDonald said.

"June, call Spec Ops for me and see if Agent Bridger is available."

"Yes, sir," she said, hanging up and dialing Spec Ops.

Wolfe and Gales looked at each other until the phone rang.

"Yes?" Wolfe said, answering the phone.

"Sir, Agent Bridger is on line two."

"Thank you," Wolfe said as he punched line two's button. "Bridger?" Wolfe asked.

"Yes, sir. How can I help you, Director?"

"I'm talking to former Director Gales and he asked me to call you to confirm some details of the River Wildlife Management Area exercise."

"Yes, sir. What do you need to know?" Bridger asked.

"What were the chemicals and how much of each?" Wolfe asked.

"Well, sir. It was as real of a training exercise as you can get. There were almost two thousand pounds of sodium cyanide. I think it was not quite eighteen hundred pounds in five steel drums, to be exact. There was also thirty gallons of sulfuric acid and roughly five hundred pounds of urea nitrate explosives. If that had been detonated somewhere, there wouldn't have been a living thing within a mile radius and five miles downwind. I don't know who put that together, but tell them thanks for keeping the blasting cap and fuse in the glove box."

Wolfe eyes went wide as he listened to Bridger. "Thank you, Dan. Yes, train like it's real," Wolfe said. "Thank you. Goodbye."

"One thing, Director," Bridger said.

"Go ahead. What?" Wolfe replied.

"I just thought it was pretty freaky being on the same day as the Trade Center bombing."

"Yes. Thank God it wasn't part of that bomb," Wolfe said.

"Yes, sir. It would have killed everyone in the towers and anyone in downtown New York."

"Okay, Dan. Thank you. Goodbye."

"Goodbye, sir."

Wolfe hung up the phone, looked at Gales and angrily asked, "Why the hell wasn't this part of my briefing when I took over here?"

"I couldn't tell you this was an ongoing case, just not yet," Gales said. "At the time, I didn't know how all this was going to end. We got lucky, damn lucky. After the explosion, I had to let this settle down some and allow the FBI to do its job, knowing they wouldn't link Iraq to this. Saddam Hussein gets our news. He sees where the bureau over the past few weeks has reported that the terrorist were local jihadis. He now feels safe. We want him to feel safe."

"Why do we need Hussein to feel safe? Don't we want him to feel American heat?" Wolfe asked.

"No. Not yet, and this is why. The cyanide information originated from a deep cover SVR agent that has infiltrated the IIS. He's reporting on Hussein's nuclear program. Hussein is trying to get a nuclear bomb to use on his enemies. That's us and the Russians after they refused to help him in Kuwait."

"Go on," Wolfe said.

"The double agent's cover is paramount. And to keep getting the cyanide assistance from the SVR, I had to agree to their requirement that the double agent's existence be protected at all cost, even if the IIS was able to successfully detonate the cyanide bomb in the US."

"Dear God," Wolfe said. Thinking for a few moments, he then asked, "Did we compromise the SVR source taking the cyanide?"

"I don't think so. I haven't been told otherwise," Gales said.

"All right. I want details," Wolfe said. "Who did this?"

"Are you aware of the training scenario at the farm where they call the people involved the Impossible Mission Team?" Gales asked.

"Yes, I heard it was good work. But I don't know the particulars," Wolfe replied.

"No one does. We had to keep it secret. We had an inside man in the Kremlin."

"This had to do with the Russians?"

"Yes. We saved Gorbachev's ass, and he doesn't even know it. It was called Operation Thorn, and it was deeply buried to protect the Russian colonel who was the source."

"I see. So what does that have to do with the bombing?" Wolfe asked.

"It's the same team almost. It was three of the four men on the original Thorn team. I called this Operation Checkmate," Gales replied. These three were not current CIA employees, and I didn't ask for authorization for the mission. This was a total black op from start to finish. There's no paper trail. No one knows of this except for the men directly involved and the SVR, including Director Primov.

"Dear God," Wolfe said again.

"If we were going to have any chance at all to stop the cyanide. This is how it had to be done," Gales said. "And we were damn lucky it worked out the way it did."

Wolfe thought for several moments and said, "Well, technically, I guess it could be argued you weren't directly in violation of the Intelligence Authorization Act. And from what you've told me so far, I'm still not required to report this to Congress. However, I will advise President Crawford. He must be told."

"Yes. The president must be told what happened, and this must be an eyes-only meeting. Only you and he can be in that room, Roger. The SVR source must be protected so he can continue to advise us on Hussein's nuclear program. The existence of the double agent can never get out because once Hussein gets a bomb, it's very possible it will come to the United States. And he's crazy enough to do it."

"All right. How much of this do you want me to document?" Wolfe asked.

"That's up to you, Roger. My ass is now on your platter."

"Hmmm," Wolfe said, sitting back in his chair. "Damn cyanide. Thousands could have died. It's tragic we lost six souls, but it could have been thousands."

"Yes. We got lucky, and those men are that good," former CIA Director Robert Gales said to CIA Director Roger Wolfe.

"Okay. Give me the Cliffs Notes version," Wolfe said, starting to write on his pad.

"Buddy Hayden from FLETC, Bob Klass, Jack Reynolds, and Nathan West are Team Thorn," Gales stated. "Bob Klass is still the SAC of the Customs Service in San Francisco. He was not part of Checkmate. Only Buddy, Jack, and Nathan stopped the cyanide."

"I know Bob, Buddy, and Jack. Never heard of West."

"West is a rookie. He was recruited by Buddy at FLETC. He's never been to the farm. He went straight to the field and this is why. He's already former law enforcement, a West Virginia State Trooper. And he was able to burn the FLETC CIA training team while he was going through Buddy's program. He set them up, and they didn't know it until it was all over. I've met him. He's a quality operator like Jack, Buddy, and Bob."

"All right. How did they get the cyanide?" Wolfe asked.

"The cyanide came from Uzbekistan. We were able to track it to West Ocean City, Maryland, and then to Jersey City."

"How'd they do that?"

"That's a long story and not part of the Cliffs Notes version. Let me give you the big picture first. Sometime later, we can have a drink, and I can give you the particulars. It was a hell of a case."

"All right. Go on."

"They didn't know there were two bombs. The SVR double agent got info out to where the van containing the cyanide was located in a storage unit in Jersey City. West, with Reynolds backing up, went into the unit and placed a BirdDog on the van to be able to track it. Later, West followed the van to a gas station. There he knocked the driver out, robbed the store, and stole the van carrying the cyanide. He drove it to Chester and the River Wildlife Management Area. That's where Bridger and his team took care of it. We had the assistance of an older SVR agent stationed near New York. Without SVR's assistance, we wouldn't have been able to stop the cyanide, and thousands more would have died."

"Damn, that was ballsy," Wolfe said. "Okay, I want a full report on Operation Thorn so I can pass that information to the president when I inform him of Checkmate. He'll need to speak to you, and he may want to speak to that team too."

"You already have a full report on Operation Thorn. I left it on your computer. Open up your C drive and go to documents. It's listed under OT," Gales said.

"All right. I'll read that later."

"Roger, you'll need to do that before you speak to the president," Gales said. "You and he both need to know Team Thorn and how they successfully completed that mission. It was some of the finest work ever done, and they repeated it with Checkmate."

"All right. Yes, I will," Wolfe replied.

"Okay. Now where does that leave us, Roger?" Gales asked. "Am I going to need to talk to the attorney general? Because I don't think I would enjoy prison food."

Wolfe thought for a moment and said, "No. Hell no," shaking his head. "You men are heroes, Bob. You and those other men are what makes this country great. This will never be passed by me except to the president. I may, however, at some point speak about how I feel Saddam Hussein and the Iraqi Intelligence Service were behind the bombing. But with what the FBI and US Attorney are putting out, no one will ever believe me anyway, so we're good."

CHAPTER 2

He's My Kid Brother

Monday, March 22, 1993

President Bill Crawford's chief of staff, Mack Lawrence, was trying not to piss off the newly elected president. But Lawrence felt this had to be fully understood by Crawford. If not, Lawrence felt it could seriously damage the new president's first term and possibly prevent him from securing a second.

"Your brother's a cokehead, Mr. President."

"Dammit, Mack, he's my kid brother."

"Yes, sir. I understand that. But, now, in your position, you're going to need to distance yourself from him, that is, if you want to have a successful first term and possibly a second."

"It's the damn drug cartel in Columbia's fault. He never used cocaine before going to Medellin with his buddies to party. And that arrest was good for him."

"Mr. President, he's still a cokehead to this day. That arrest did nothing for him. But it did give our enemies ammunition to use against you."

Crawford paced the floor and looked out the Oval Office's window. "What's that drug lord's name? Espanjo or something? You know the one who's on the run now."

"Espinoza, sir. Alejandro Espinoza."

"Yeah, that's it. I need to have the military find him and kill his ass. No, that'd be too obvious. Maybe, I'll order the CIA to kill that prick."

"Mr. President, that's not allowed."

"I'm the president of the United States," Crawford said, turning to Lawrence. "I can do any damn thing I want."

"Sir. Executive Order 11905 signed by President Ford bans political assassinations."

"This is not a political assassination, for Christ's sake," Crawford yelled. "I'm only killing a criminal that's on the run. That son of a bitch is responsible for bringing tons of cocaine into the United States every month, and we can't touch him? If President Gavotti had any balls and wasn't taking hundreds of thousands, if not millions, of dollars in bribes, he'd be hunting his ass right now."

"Yes, sir. What you're saying is true. But President Reagan, with Executive Order 12333, narrowed that language to ban all assassinations. Sir, it doesn't stipulate criminals."

"I don't care, Mack. Randall's my kid brother, and this dirtbag needs to be killed."

Lawrence was quiet for a few moments and said, "All right, Mr. President. May I discuss another issue with you?"

"What is it?" Crawford said tersely.

"CIA Director Wolfe would like to schedule a meeting with you."

"Okay. How about tomorrow? I'm not traveling."

"Yes, sir. That would work. He has a special request for this meeting."

"What?"

"He wants what's called an eyes-only meeting. You and he will be the only people in the room, if you approve, sir."

"Sure, that's not a problem. Go ahead and set it up. And I apologize for yelling at you, Mack. I just get upset over Randall."

"I understand, sir. We go back a long way, Bill. No apology necessary. I know how you can be an asshole at times."

Crawford laughed and said, "Yeah, I guess."

"I'll notify Director Wolfe, Mr. President," Lawrence said.

"Thanks Mack," Crawford said as the chief of staff walked out of the Oval Office. Crawford watched Lawrence close the door as he sat down behind the large wooden desk. Leaning back in the black leather chair, he looked at the presidential seal and said, "I'll still have that son of a bitch killed. I'm the president of the United States."

Alejandro Espinoza was looking down the barrel of his Glock pistol pointed at the man's face who was being held on his knees in the living room of his sparse home.

"Alejandro, I'm sorry. Please, don't hurt my family. They had nothing to do with it," the man pleaded.

"You know the rules, Juan. You steal from me, and you and your family die."

"Please, Alejandro!"

"Kill them," Espinoza said, looking at the men holding the screaming woman and the little girl who was crying and reaching for her father.

As knives slashed the throats of his family, Juan screamed in horror as he watched the blood gush from their necks.

"You were warned," Espinoza said, as he fired the 9mm bullet into the man's head, sending part of the man's skull, hair, and brains against the back wall.

Espinoza walked out of the white stucco home and into the street of the small village outside of Medellin.

"I will kill anyone that steals from me!" he yelled. "If you work for me, I will pay you a fair wage so you and your family can prosper. If you steal from me, I will kill all of you." Espinoza got into the Land Rover parked on the dirty cobblestone street and told the driver, "Take me home before General Marquez shows up."

"Yes, sir," the bodyguard said as he pulled out and headed towards Medellin.

The man's body was dragged out of the house into the middle of the street. Leaving it there, the blood ran down the stones as the Medellin Cartel enforcers got into their own Land Rover and pulled out. They followed the richest and most dangerous drug lord in the world back to his hideout.

One year before, Espinoza had worked out a deal with the corrupt president of Colombia, Sancho Gavotti. If Espinoza stayed in his self-made prison for five years in Medellin, called the La Catedral, he would not be extradited to the United States to stand trial for cocaine smuggling.

But in 1992, with increasing pressure from the United States and President George H. W. Bush with the War on Drugs, Gavotti ordered Espinoza to be arrested and taken to a Colombian prison. The only problem with that was most of the local cops were also on Espinoza's payroll. When Espinoza learned of the arrest order from the cops, he simply walked out his front door in Medellin and went into hiding. The cops knew he now lived in the Los Olivos neighborhood of Medellin, right under their noses. He had simply moved across town to his old neighborhood. But Espinoza was too powerful and dangerous for the police to even attempt an arrest. If anything, you would have to kill him, or he would kill you and your entire family. He was untouchable, and the local Columbian police knew it.

However, there was one man Espinoza feared, General Hugh Marquez. General Marquez was the commander of the National Police special unit called Search Bloc. This unit was formed by the former president of Colombia, Virgilio Vargas in 1986 with the express mission of curtailing drug trafficking. It was General Marquez, through his dogged pursuit of Espinoza, that forced him to reach the five-year deal with current President Gavotti.

Now that Espinoza was on the run again, he knew there was only one man in Colombia to fear, General Marquez.

CHAPTER 3

I Want That Bastard Dead

Tuesday, March 23, 1993

CIA Director Roger Wolfe walked into the Oval Office and shook hands with President Bill Crawford. "Good afternoon, Mr. President."

"Welcome, Director Wolfe. Please have a seat."

"Will you need anything else, Mr. President?" Chief of Staff Lawrence asked.

"No, we're good, Mack. I'll let you know when the meeting's over," President Crawford said.

"Yes, sir," Lawrence replied and closed the Oval Office door behind him.

"So how are things going at Langley? You getting all the cooperation you need?" asked Crawford.

"Yes, Mr. President. There're some really fine people who work there, and it makes my job easy."

"Wonderful. This's a dangerous world with all these crazy jihadis and drug dealers. I need you to keep a tight ship over there, Roger. We don't need any more bombings. Those crazy bastards all need to be killed."

"Yes, sir. I agree. I'll make sure we keep an eye out for any chatter that may point in the direction of some bad people wanting to do us harm," Wolfe replied.

"Okay, Director. What's this all about? I never even knew what an eyes-only meeting meant until Mack told me."

"Yes, sir. In this instance, it's more ears only, but it's the same thing."

"Yes, I guess. So what's so important?" Crawford asked.

"Sir, the World Trade Center bombing was ordered by Saddam Hussein and carried out by his intelligence agency."

"What are you talking about? I've been briefed by FBI Director Short multiple times, and he says the bombers were a loose network of Muslim extremists."

"That's exactly how I reacted to former Director Gales when he told me. But it's true, Mr. President."

"Now I know why the eyes-only," President Crawford said. "Explain. I want to understand this completely."

"Yes, sir. February 26 was the two-year anniversary of Hussein's defeat in Kuwait by coalition forces led by us. He wanted revenge. He also wanted thousands of American citizens to die in the bomb blast."

"How would that have even been possible?" Crawford asked. "The FBI says with the amount of explosives, the most that could have been killed would have been a couple of dozen. We lost six."

"Yes, sir. What you're not aware of is he had almost two thousand pounds of cyanide that was to be included in that explosion. If detonated, that would have killed tens of thousands, probably everyone in the towers and most of the people downtown New York."

"Jesus. Cyanide?"

"Yes, sir. I have confirmed that he had almost 1,800 pounds of sodium cyanide and members of a CIA team stole it before it could be used. Director Gales called this mission Operation Checkmate."

"That dirty bastard. Why wasn't I informed of this by the FBI? They're running that investigation."

"Because they've never been told, and they can never be told."

"What the hell are you saying, Director?"

"Mr. President, for us, the CIA, to be able to have a chance of interdicting the cyanide, we had to reach an agreement with the

Russian SVR who was providing the intelligence on this. They have an inside man with Hussein, and his identity must be protected at all cost. That was our agreement, not to do anything that would compromise their agent in Baghdad."

"Why is that?" Crawford asked, squinting his eyes.

"Because Saddam Hussein is developing a nuclear bomb to use on us or the Russians and this agent is providing and will continue to provide us with intel on that development."

"That murdering bastard."

"Yes, sir. And he is crazy enough to do it."

Crawford sat back in his chair and asked, "So if we're not willing to go to war with Iraq now, we'll need to wait until we can wait no more?"

"Yes, sir. Those are our only options."

"If I start a war, I'll not be re-elected for a second term."

"Sir, if we do anything, it will have to be all-out war. Anything short of that and Hussein will know we are aware of his nuclear program, and he will start torturing and killing his own people to figure out who told us. We can't risk that, sir. We must have that SVR source secure in Hussein's camp."

"Yes, I see that. How soon will he have the capability to have a nuclear device?"

"From my understanding, sir, five to ten years. He was very close before invading Kuwait, possibly only one year away from having a nuclear device. But this defeat has set him back, and we now feel it will be five to ten years. And that is exactly why the SVR source is so valuable."

"Christ, I hope this takes him at least eight. I don't want anything to do with invading Iraq. So we have some time?"

"Yes, sir. We do."

"Okay, tell me about the men that pulled this off. Perhaps, I can have a secret awards ceremony to congratulate them."

"Sir, I don't think that would be a good idea. These men know this can never be spoken about. If you told them to attend an awards ceremony, I doubt if any of them would show up."

"Yes, I guess, you're right. Bad idea. Okay, who are they?"

"They are all former CIA personnel. But I need to start this story six years ago when these men worked together for the first time," Wolfe said.

"Okay, what did they do?"

"They saved Soviet General Secretary Mikhail Gorbachev's life, brought about the fall of the USSR, and ended the Cold War."

"WHAT?"

"Yes, sir. It's true. This case started under President Reagan and CIA Director Casto. It was called Operation Thorn, and there were four agents involved—Buddy Hayden from FLETC in Georgia, Jack Reynolds from Maine, Bob Klass, SAC for Customs in San Francisco, and a rookie by the name of Nathan West who went by the undercover name of Tony Davis. The Russian military and the KGB were smuggling hashish into the West Coast to raise money for the coup of Gorbachev in 1989."

"Drug smugglers. Go on," Crawford instructed.

"Yes, sir. Operation Thorn was able to stop the shipment of fifty-six tons of hashish in San Francisco in '88 and prevented the conspirators from receiving almost fifty million dollars. Without the money to bribe more Russian generals, they postponed the planned coup in '89, and then it failed in '91 for the same reason. They didn't have the money to bribe enough of the military."

"I remember hearing about that drug bust but didn't know it involved Gorbachev. And of course, the whole world knows about the failed coup."

"Yes, sir. No one knows it involved Gorbachev because, again, they had an inside man to protect, a Russian colonel. We let it be reported that the drug seizure was by a rookie Customs agent, and he just got lucky."

"I see. This rookie, I guess he was good at sniffing out these drug smugglers?" Crawford asked, showing an interest.

"Yes, sir," Wolfe said. "From the report I read, created by former Director Gales, he and the others did an amazing job."

"Hmmm. We do have a problem with drugs in this country.

Especially cocaine from Colombia being sent by the Medellin Cartel and their boss, Espinoza. He needs to be killed."

"Well, sir, maybe we can do something about that at some point. Now to continue, sir, one of the SVR agents involved with the investigation of the cyanide knew Jack Reynolds. SVR Director Primov then demanded his agents work only with members from Operation Thorn since they knew Reynolds was on that team. And if Team Thorn was good enough to protect Gorbachev, Primov felt they could be trusted. If Director Gales didn't agree, the SVR was going to walk away and not provide any more information on the cyanide from their Baghdad source. Sir, the SVR source is what made this mission possible and prevented thousands of deaths."

"I see," Crawford said. "You said they were former CIA. How did that work?"

"Sir, Jack Reynolds was the only active member when he was contacted by the SVR agent that knew him. It was a woman; he had lived with her in Moscow when he was on non-official cover, a NOC, sir. Hayden was retired from FLETC. Klass and West worked for Customs. Gales had Reynolds retire before this got started so he wouldn't be forced to report Checkmate as an active CIA mission under the Intelligence Authorization Act. He couldn't. Director Primov demanded that operational information remain very tightly controlled by the SVR. Gales had no choice if he wanted to stop the cyanide. This was a non-sanctioned operation, a black op from start to finish, sir."

"Damn, a big can of worms," Crawford said.

"Yes, sir. And it was successful, at least most of it. They stopped the cyanide, but they had no way of knowing or to even being able to stop the other bomb that exploded in the WTC."

"Wow, I understand. That murdering bastard Hussein. I'll not forget this, and I'll not mention a word of this to anyone to protect the SVR source. But, if I can, I'm going to strike that son of a bitch as soon as I get the chance as long as it doesn't jeopardize the SVR agent."

"Yes, sir. We need to keep that agent in mind with whatever we do in the future."

"All right, I'll put that on the back burner for now. How good are these guys in stopping drugs from being smuggled into the country? This is one of my primary concerns right now."

"From the report on Operation Thorn, it was mainly Reynolds, Klass, and West as undercover Special Agent Tony Davis for the Customs Service who was in the ditches. He was out there spearheading the interdiction efforts and being supported by Reynolds and Klass. West may have been a rookie, but he pulled it off. And they did it again with the cyanide in Operation Checkmate. West knocked out the driver of the cyanide van at a gas station when the van was heading to the WTC. He then robbed the store to add more cover and stole the van. Drove it out into the countryside where the CIA Spec Ops team recovered it."

"Damn, that took guts. They sound like the men I need for another mission. This one will be authorized by me, and fully within IAA guidelines," Crawford said.

"What are you thinking, sir?"

"Alejandro Espinoza is smuggling tons of cocaine into our country every month. It's making us a damn addicted country with rising crime and killing our people with this poison. Alejandro is now a wanted man in Colombia, but President Gavotti isn't doing shit to catch him. That piss-poor excuse of a president is being bribed by Espinoza and is looking the other way while Espinoza continues his smuggling operations."

"Yes, sir."

"I want to meet the men involved in taking the cyanide. I'm going to send them to Colombia to stop Espinoza. I want that bastard dead."

"Yes, sir. I'll set it up."

CHAPTER 4

Who the Hell Are You?

Noon, Saturday, March 27, 1993

Nathan West had been at Greg's Market in Cameron, West Virginia, and was returning home after picking up some groceries. He had the soft-top plastic window folded down to the inside on the CJ and was enjoying the warm spring scents and the deep-blue sky. Glancing at the spice bushes along US Route 250 as he drove, he could see the red buds sprouting out. He smiled. Spring was here. He was in paradise and took deep breaths of the pure West Virginia air. West drove the winding road the seven miles towards his cabin on the family farm where he had grown up. He grinned as he listened to the headers roar and the tires squeal as he came out of the many turns gunning the 360 engine. "This baby can scream," he said as his smile suddenly contorted to a look of despair.

Baby, he thought. His heart was heavy, and he still grieved. In his mind, he could see the yellow Ryder van pull out of Easy Storage in Jersey City an hour before it exploded in Level B-2 of the World Trade Center on February 26. "Those bastards," he seethed under his breath. Monica Smith was seven months pregnant when her office on Level B-2 was incinerated when the 1,500 pounds of urea nitrate was detonated in the yellow Ryder van just feet from her desk. The death of the her and her baby haunted West.

Shaking his head to remove the image he knew it must have looked like, he turned his concentration to the winding road and gunned the engine once more.

"You're out, dammit," he said as he fought tears and tried to think of his now peaceful world and the new upcoming career in medicine. As far as he was concerned, he was out of the game. He was done with the government and had put in his request for inactive status. After stealing the cyanide that Saddam Hussein had intended for the World Trade Center bombing the month before, he had said, a silent prayer in the Saint Lawrence Catholic Church in Chester, New Jersey. He had thanked God for allowing him and Jack Reynolds to survive that mission. He told God he would do his bidding. If he was accepted into medical school, he would leave the government. If not, he would stay in the CIA Clandestine Service and kill bad guys with Jack Reynolds and Buddy Hayden.

When West had returned to his cabin on Fish Creek after stealing the cyanide, an acceptance letter from the West Virginia School of Osteopathic Medicine had been waiting for him in his mailbox. So God had made the decision for him. He now looked forward to beginning his new life as a physician. He would be the fifteenth physician in his family. He knew he had big shoes to fill, and maybe he could do some good. He would start medical school in Lewisburg on August 9.

West slowed as he came down Belton Hill and turned the brown CJ-5 down the gravel Fish Creek Road towards the cabin. The spring rains had made the stream full but not too high to keep him from crossing in the Jeep. Getting to the other side, he could see wet tire marks on the creek gravel. "Hmmm, someone's here," he said, raising his brow. Pulling up the bank and around the cabin, he could see a large black Chevrolet Suburban parked there. He glanced at the license plate as he got out of the CJ. It was a government tag, and no one was in it. "Dammit," he said, carrying the milk and sack onto the back porch.

Opening the door, he could see two men sitting on the blue couch. "All right, who are you and what the hell do you want?" West asked as he closed the door and walked past the men, glancing at them as they stood up. Walking into the kitchen, he placed the milk and eggs into the fridge and a loaf of bread by the sink.

"Excuse the interruption, Agent West. We are Secret Service, and we were asked to come and get you," one of the men said as they both stood in the kitchen.

"I'm no longer in the government, fellas. And take me where?" West asked, turning to look at the men.

"The White House, sir. President Crawford would like to speak to you."

"I voted for the other guy. Do you gentlemen have names?" West asked, looking at both of the tall men standing next to the big wooden table.

"Yes, sir. I'm Agent Smith and this is Agent—"

"Don't tell me . . . Jones," West said without smiling.

"No, sir," Smith said with a chuckle. "This is Agent Montgomery."

"All right, Smith. Do you know what this's about?"

"No, sir. That's above my pay grade. But you'll need to come with us, sir. The president was, let's say, forceful in his instructions."

"Hmmm." Looking at the other man, West asked, "Montgomery, can you speak?"

"Yes, sir," Montgomery replied.

"Who else does the president want to speak with?"

"A Mr. Hayden and a Mr. Reynolds," Montgomery replied.

"Hmmm," West said again. "You guys bringing me back here?"

"Yes, sir," Smith said. "We were to come and get you today. Hayden and Reynolds will already be at the InterContinental Hotel when we get there this evening. The president wants to have the meeting tomorrow. We're then to bring you back later tomorrow afternoon or the next day, whatever you prefer."

"You guys know Dave Lewis or Jimmy Douglas?" West asked.

"Yes, of course," Smith replied. "They're still on the presidential detail as drivers. Dave is chief driver now. How'd you know them?"

"I rode with them at FLETC," West said. "It's been a while. Give me a few minutes, and let me grab my stuff."

West walked past the men to a flag case of the thirteen original Colonies hanging on the wall in the living room. As he pulled it down, a variety of weapons could be seen—pistols, knives, handcuffs—and an old Oregon driver's license. West picked up his Smith and Wesson, Model 39, 9mm, and racked the slide hard, placing a hollow point cartridge into the chamber. After sliding the weapon into a holster he now held, he closed the case.

"That's pretty nice," Smith said.

"Yes, I like it," West replied, as he walked into the bedroom. West pulled out his travel bag and was packing it when he heard the STU-II in the kitchen start to beep.

"Is that what I think it is?" Montgomery asked as West walked out of the bedroom and towards the kitchen.

West didn't answer but motioned with his hand for both men to follow him. Reaching underneath the oak cabinet on the wall, West pushed a hidden button that opened a lock on the cabinet door as it automatically swung open. Sliding the bottom oak shelf out, he picked up the STU receiver and said, "Hello."

"Nathan, it's Buddy. Do you have company?"

"Yes, two guys in suits."

"All right. Don't give them any grief, and don't tell them shit. I'll see you tonight in DC."

"Roger that. I'll see you later," West said, hanging up and closing the cabinet until he heard the lock click.

"Who the hell are you?" Montgomery asked.

"I'm just one of the good guys. I'm ready to go, fellas. Let's hit the road," West said as he picked up his bag and headed out the back door.

West climbed into the rear of the black Secret Service vehicle, place his bag on the seat, and thought, What the hell am I getting himself into? I need to be in school. Dammit! I'm not telling the president a damn thing.

Bogota, Colombia

The barmaid was the reason most of the guys now visited the Taya Night Club in Bogota. Normally many beautiful women were there, but everyone agreed Sanita Perez was on a whole new level all by herself. She was not only beautiful with jet-black hair but also had a sensuous personality that oozed from every seductive pore. Men adored her. She would look at the customers with those big dark eyes, and the men would all fall in love with her. She didn't even have to smile. A lot of the women hated her guts because she was so beautiful, but that was okay with her. She got what she needed. All the big movers and shakers in Bogota knew her, especially the men who ran the Medellin drug smuggling and distribution networks for Alejandro Espinoza.

She'd never met the big boss, but she had flirted with many of his lieutenants and knew more about the drug smuggling operation than just about anyone in Colombia. After all, that was her job.

Undercover Special Agent Angelina Lopez was the star of the US Customs Service in Colombia. But her identity and cover were so sensitive to the Customs Service and the War on Drugs that the regular Customs field special agents with top secret clearances didn't know much about Lopez, if anything at all. US Customs SAC Dale Wilson in Bogota wouldn't speak her name, referring to her only as Agent One, never giving a name or gender, even to his own people. Wilson was not taking any chances; loose lips could get Lopez buried alive. There was just too much money to be made by informing for the Medellin drug cartel, and many of the best informers wore a uniform and badge of the Colombian local police. And these crooked cops tried to get information from Customs agents on a daily bases. No, Wilson wasn't taking any chances with Lopez.

CHAPTER 5

I Know What He Looks Like

Noon, February 24, 1993

Twenty-four-year-old Angelina Lopez was born in Mexicali, and her parents migrated to San Diego when she was twelve. Her father become an inspector for the Customs Service and worked at the port of entry in San Diego. She admired him for that. Her older sister, Danielle, however, fell into the wrong crowd and became a victim of the cocaine trade. She became a coke whore, selling her body to get the next snort. Her parents found Danielle's murdered and mutilated body in a rundown apartment complex used by other prostitutes. She'd been dead for days, and the rats had eaten their fill. Angelina's heart was broken, not only over her sister's death but also from watching the grief her mother and father went through. From that day, her hatred of the drug dealers in her neighborhood intensified to the point she made it her mission in life to know everything she could about them and their trade and do what she could to stop them. To remember her sister, she had an upside-down red rose tattooed to her right ankle, a sign of continual grief.

After high school, Angelina enrolled in San Diego State University where she received her bachelor's degree in criminal justice. Following graduation, she joined the US Customs Service as a special agent. She was a natural. Smart, soft-spoken, and shy by nature, she could easily fit in anywhere. Loud-mouthed people don't make good undercover operatives and usually have to be rushed out of a situation to keep them from being killed if you can get to them at all. Her rare beauty was a big plus too; men wanted her around just to look at.

In 1990, her duty assignment was in Philadelphia as undercover operative Mariana Garcia. While there, she was able to infiltrate the East Coast's largest Colombian cocaine smuggling and distribution network—dangerous people who thought nothing of cutting someone's throat or putting a bullet in your head. She worked those people for two years before the Customs SAC in Philadelphia, Margaret Cutter, and the United States attorney determined they had enough evidence to bring down the entire organization. After those arrests, Angelina's identity and role were still kept a secret. She was rushed out of the area and excluded from testifying in court by the United States attorney to further protect her undercover status. No one knew she was a Customs special agent.

The roundup of perpetrators of the drug ring was almost complete with very few eluding the dragnet created by the Organized Crime Drug Enforcement Task Force. Law enforcement had planned this for months, but Alex Sanchez, a very low-level player, did slip through. Few in the task force gave him much notice. Lopez had met him a couple of times, and he seemed to be a nice quiet man of little importance in the organization. No one knew, not even Lopez, that Sanchez was the eyes and ears, as well as the cousin, of Alejandro Espinoza. Sanchez was the counter surveillance undercover operative, as well as the intelligence officer for the Medellin Cartel in Philadelphia. He had been highly trained by former Israeli Mossad commandos to keep a low profile.

After Philadelphia, Lopez was visiting her parents in San Diego when her pager went off. Looking at the readout, it displayed the number 100, the code to call Customs SAC Margaret Cutter.

"Mom, I need to go to my room and use the phone. I'll be back down in a few minutes," Lopez said.

"Okay, Angel," her mother replied as Lopez climbed the stairs to her childhood bedroom.

Angelina picked her bag phone up off the floor and laid it on the bed still covered with the red-rose blanket her mother had made for her as a child. Lopez called the SAC number in Philly.

"US Customs Service Office of Enforcement, how can I help you?" the operator said.

"This is Agent One," she said. "I need to speak to SAC Cutter. She paged me."

"Yes, Agent One. She told me you'd be calling. Hold on and I'll put you through."

"Thank you," Lopez replied.

The phone was answered, and Lopez heard Cutter say, "Where are you?"

"San Diego, visiting my parents."

"The commissioner wants to meet with you."

"What's this about?"

"I don't know. It's hush-hush so far," Cutter said. "We'll fly to you. I'll get us a room at the old Coronado Hotel and let you know when we arrive."

"Yes, ma'am. When you flying in?"

"Gary wants to leave in the next hour, so we'll be there sometime tonight."

"Okay, page me with the room number when you arrive."

"Will do. I'll see you this evening."

"Yes, ma'am," Lopez said, hanging up and starting back down the stairs to sit with her parents. She wondered why the commissioner of Customs was in a rush to meet her.

At 10:15 p.m., Angelina Lopez's pager went off as she sat with her parents in the living room, watching the new series *Beavis and Butt-Head*. Her mother and father were belly laughing when Angelina looked at the pager and said, "I need to go out for a while, but I'll be back."

"Okay, sweetheart," her father said.

"Be careful," her mother added.

Both knew she was a special agent for Customs, but neither knew of her deep cover or the extreme danger she lived in.

Thirty minutes later Angelina arrived at the Old Coronado Hotel. Walking to the entrance, she could see the gas fireplaces lit on the beach near the wine bar. It was crowded on this warm evening. Going to the fourth floor, she knocked on room 410's door. As it opened, she could see SAC Cutter.

"Good evening, Angelina," Cutter said as she moved out of the way for Lopez to enter the suite.

"Good evening, ma'am," Lopez replied as she glanced around the luxury room at the two men sitting on the couch and Commissioner Gary Williams standing in the middle of the room.

"Hello, sir," she said, shaking hands with the commissioner.

"Hello, Agent Lopez. Please have a seat here," Williams said, pointing to a chair facing the couch.

Sitting down, she nodded at the two men who hadn't spoken yet. They nodded back in return still without speaking.

Cutter shut the door and started talking as she walked to the middle of the large room. "Angelina, this is Customs Special Agent in Charge Dale Wilson, stationed in Bogota," Cutter said, as the man she was pointing to stood up from the couch.

"Nice to meet you, Agent Lopez," the tall slender man said, shaking hands with Lopez after she also stood up. Wilson sat back down as Lopez continued to stand and look at the other man.

"This other gentleman is General Hugh Marquez of the Colombian National Police. He's in charge of the task force to capture or kill Alejandro Espinoza. The task force is called Bloque de Busqueda, or Search Bloc," Cutter said as the man remained seated and nodded to Lopez.

"Hello, General," Lopez said.

General Hugh Marquez started speaking to Lopez in Spanish. "Where are you from, young lady?"

"San Diego, sir," she replied also in Spanish.

"No, where are you originally from?"

"Mexicali, Mexico," Lopez replied.

"You never say you're from San Diego. You're from Mexicali, and you never say sir."

Lopez didn't reply and looked intently at the general.

"Have you killed anyone?" the general asked, still speaking in Spanish.

"No."

"Are you afraid, little girl? You look like a scared little bitch."

Lopez pulled her Sig Sauer P226 from the small of her back and pointed it at the man sitting on the right end of couch. "Do I look afraid now, asshole?" she said, still speaking in Spanish.

"Stand down, Angelina," Cutter said tensely.

General Marquez stood up and walked toward the pistol until it was touching his chest.

Lopez didn't move, gazed at Marquez, and shoved the pistol harder into his chest.

Looking into Lopez's eyes, he said in English, "No, you're not afraid. She'll do. You can put the Sig away for now and then get rid of it."

The general turned to sit back down as Lopez placed the gun back into the waist belt in the small of her back.

"Agent Lopez," Commissioner Williams said, "I'm sending you to Bogota, and you're going to help us find and arrest Alejandro Espinoza."

"All right," Lopez replied. "Why Bogota? Isn't Espinoza working out of Medellin?"

"Yes, but his family is being kept in Bogota under protective custody while the cartel leader is on the run. That's where you start your hunt."

"Yes."

"No one in Bogota will know who you are other than the four of us. You'll be on your own—no backup, no support. The general will be your only contact, and he'll not be close." Handing a piece of paper with a number on it to Lopez, he said, "That's the general's mobile number. Memorize it and burn the paper. His command center's in the Carlos Holguín School, an old police academy in Medellin. But never go there; it's watched by the cartel. You'll have to contact

Customs yourself if needed. No one will know you exist other than us. Do you think you can handle that?"

Lopez turned to the general and asked, "Why dump it?"

"Not many people carry Sigs in Colombia," the general replied. "Get something cheap, a Taurus or something similar. That Sig will make you look like an agent."

Lopez nodded to the general, turned to Williams, and asked, "When do I start?"

"Tomorrow. This is who we're going after," Williams said, laying down a picture of Espinoza.

"Yes, I know what he looks like."

5 p.m., Saturday, March 27, 1993

After a four-and-a-half-hour drive, Secret Service Agent Smith pulled the Suburban up to the InterContinental Hotel entrance. West had been lying on the back seat and trying to sleep the entire trip. No need to make an excuse not to talk.

"Agent West, we're here," Montgomery said. Turning in his seat, he handed the key to room 517 to West. "Mr. Hayden and Reynolds are in rooms 519 and 521.

"Fellas, I'd appreciate it if you'd just call me Nate."

"That's not a problem," Montgomery replied. "Nate, we're to pick you, Hayden, and Reynolds up in the morning at 0900 hours. And one more thing, don't be carrying."

"I'll leave it here. Thanks. See you guys in the morning," West said as he got out of the Secret Service Suburban with his bag.

West walked into the hotel and went to the elevator. After arriving on the fifth floor, he walked to 517 and entered the room. Throwing his bag on the bed, he knocked on the connecting door to room 519.

"What's the pass phrase?" he heard Reynolds ask through the door.

West chuckled and said, "Is a frog's ass watertight."

The door opened as West could see Jack Reynolds laughing.

"That was perfect," Reynolds said. "And no shit, that's our code phrase if everything's okay."

"Sounds good to me," West replied, shaking hands with the legendary CIA agent.

"Hi, Nathan," Buddy Hayden said, as he came out of the kitchen carrying a bottle of Lagavulin Scotch and three glasses. Setting those down, Hayden and West shook hands.

"Hi, Buddy. How's the hip?" West asked.

"It hurts like hell," Hayden said as he poured the glasses half full of the finest whiskey to come out of Scotland.

"Cheers, gentlemen," Hayden said, holding up one glass.

"Cheers," Reynolds and West said, as they picked up a glass and the three men clicked them together.

Taking a sip, West said, "I don't know, but I may be starting to like this cow piss."

"Yeah, it grows on you," Hayden replied.

"Okay, Buddy. What the hell's this about?" Reynolds asked as the men sat down at the table.

"I haven't told Jack anything yet, Nate. I wanted to wait until you got here. All right, I've tried to reach Gales and can't. I'm in the dark just as you two are," Hayden said, looking at West and Reynolds. "But if I was to guess, I'd say this is about Checkmate."

"Well, unless I talk to Gales, I'm not saying shit to anyone. Not even the president," Reynolds said. "I'm the one that told the Russians about Thorn. I'm not going to prison if I can help it."

"I'm with Jack," West replied. "Checkmate was a non-sanctioned op. I don't have the authorization to talk to anyone. I don't think any of us do. Gales will have to be in the room before I'm opening my mouth. But when I do, I'm telling the president Jack told the Russians about Thorn."

Hayden laughed as Reynolds said, "You little prick."

"Jack, you know, I wouldn't say shit," West said with a chuckle.

"All right," Hayden said, "so this is the plan. I'll do most of the talking. You two just nod your heads and say, "Yes, sir" and "No, sir." And we don't admit to anything unless we can find Gales."

CHAPTER 6

Sanita Perez

9:30 a.m., Sunday, March 28, 1993

Hayden, Reynolds, and West arrived at the White House and were escorted by Secret Service Agents Smith and Montgomery to the Oval Office. At the Oval Office door, they were met by chief of staff, Mack Lawrence.

"Hello, gentlemen. Welcome to the White House. President Crawford called this meeting to express his gratitude for the successful conclusion of Operation Thorn."

"Hmmm," Reynolds said under his breath and shuffled his feet like he was preparing to run.

Clearing his throat, West tried not to laugh as he glanced at Reynolds staring at Lawrence.

Lawrence continued, "I'll not be in the room, but CIA Director Wolfe will be in attendance and is already here. Do you gentlemen have any questions before you go in?"

"Yes," Hayden said. "Will former CIA Director Gales be here?"

"No, I don't believe so," Lawrence replied as he turned and opened the door. Standing in the doorway, he said, "Mr. President, I have the gentlemen you requested."

"Yes, let them in, Mack," President Crawford said in his Arkansan accent.

Opening the door all the way, Lawrence said, "Please, go on in, gentlemen," motioning with his hand in a sweeping gesture.

Hayden glanced at West and Reynolds, and the three filed into the room as Lawrence stayed in the hall, closing the door behind them. President Crawford got up from behind the presidential desk and began to shake hands with the CIA operatives. Coming to Hayden first, he said, "You must be Buddy," shaking his hand.

"Yes, sir. Was the hip a giveaway?"

"Yes, I am afraid so. It was mentioned you had an accident and it sent you to FLETC as an instructor," Crawford said.

"Yes, sir. I was at FLETC for ten years before I retired."

"Well, I've heard you did an incredible job there."

"Thank you, sir."

The president next stepped to West, shook hands, and said, "And as I understand it, you must be Mr. West."

"Yes, sir."

"And Mr. Hayden recruited you."

"Yes, sir."

"Did you enjoy stopping those drugs? Because we're having a big problem with that now in our country."

"Yes, sir," West said, nodding his head."

Stepping to Reynolds, the president shook his hand and said, "You've got to be big Jack Reynolds."

"Yes, sir," Reynolds replied, nodding his head.

"You've got quite a dossier. But, frankly, you all do." The president turned to the short man with thinning gray hair standing off to the side and said, "Gentlemen, this is CIA Director Roger Wolfe."

"Director," Hayden said, as he nodded.

"Sir," Reynolds and West each said.

"Gentlemen, you guys take the couch, and Roger and I will sit in the chairs. Please have a seat," the president directed.

Sitting down, the president said, "I've asked you to come here today for three reasons. First, I want to congratulate you on the superb job in Operation Thorn. What you men did was absolutely amazing. And in all sincerity, you three and Bob Klass changed the course of history, probably saved Mikhail Gorbachev's life, and brought about the end to the Cold War with Russia, not to mention the outcome of the failed coup with the collapse of the USSR. An astonishing achievement by any measure."

"Thank you, sir," Hayden said as Reynolds and West nodded their heads.

"The second thing I want to do is congratulate you on Operation Checkmate. The interdiction of the two thousand pounds of cyanide saved thousands of American lives while putting you in grave peril in its removal. Sadly we lost six wonderful people, but I realize the enormous tragedy that was averted. And in that, I hope you can quietly receive my admiration as your president. Know that I will always cherish the heroic efforts you three put forth. While at the same time, you must quietly accept that no American will ever hear of this outside of this room."

"What cyanide, sir?" Hayden asked.

Reynolds shifted in his seat and swallowed hard.

West stayed mute.

The president of the United States stared at the three men as CIA Director Wolfe said, "Gentlemen, I have been briefed by former Director Gales. You can speak freely."

"Director, we're not sure what you're referring to. What cyanide?" Hayden asked again.

"What? Was this all some made-up story by you, Roger?" the president asked.

"No, Mr. President. This is the truth," Wolfe said. Turning to Hayden, he smiled and asked,

"Okay, Mr. Hayden, what would you recommend we do?"

"Sir, perhaps if you could find former Director Gales, he may be able to spread some light on this," Hayden replied.

"Reynolds, West, what do you fellows know about Operation Checkmate and the cyanide?" President Crawford asked.

"Sir, I think Buddy has the solution," Reynolds replied.

"West?" the president asked.

"Sir, you're talking about cyanide, the stuff that makes you sick, correct?" West asked.

"Jesus Christ!" the president yelled. "Wolfe, if this is some kind of joke, I'm going to have your ass."

"Excuse me, Mr. President. I need to use the phone," Wolfe said, walking to the wall where a phone rested on an old oak end table that had belonged to Abraham Lincoln. Picking up the phone, he dialed a number.

"Hello," Robert Gates said.

"Bob, I need you at the White House right now."

"I'm pulling in as we speak. Be there in a couple minutes."

Wolfe hung up the phone and said, "Mr. President, former Director Gales will be here momentarily."

President Crawford looked at Hayden, West, and Reynolds and said, "With you three monkeys, one of you needs to cover your mouth, the next cover your eyes, and the last cover your ears."

West chuckled as Reynolds elbowed him to shut up.

"I sure as hell hope you gentlemen are enjoying this because, as your commander in chief, I'm getting damn pissed. West, do you think this is funny?" the president asked.

"No, sir. I apologize sir. It's just that Jack is deaf anyway, and I think he should be the one that covers his ears."

Wolfe tried not to chuckle as the president gazed dumbfoundedly at West.

The president was getting ready to say something when the door opened and Bob Gales walked in.

"Hello, Mr. President. Sorry, I'm late. Got tied up in traffic."

"Good morning, Bob. I hope the hell you can straighten out this can of thick gumbo," the president said.

"I'm sure I can, Mr. President," Gales said. Shaking hands with Hayden, West, and Reynolds who stood up when their former boss walked into the room, Gales said, "Good morning, gentlemen."

"Good morning, sir," all three replied, shaking his hand.

Gales turned to Wolfe and asked, "They not talking?"

"Not a peep. You've trained them well," Wolfe said.

"I never trained them. He did," Gales said, pointing at Hayden.

Turning to Hayden, West, and Reynolds, Gales said, "Gentlemen, speak freely here. I've already fully informed Director Wolfe, and he has relayed that information to the president. They already know, so answer whatever questions they may have of Checkmate."

"Yes, sir," the three replied.

"Mr. President," Hayden started, "I speak for all of us when I say, we deeply regret appearing ignorant about Operation Checkmate. But we wouldn't be the best team the CIA has if we couldn't keep a secret. We are bound by secret CIA policies and regulations. Plausible deniability is critical in our line of work. If we didn't operate this way, we wouldn't be successful and the United States would be more at risk. What would you like to know about Operation Checkmate, Mr. President? We'll answer any questions you have."

Three weeks prior, Customs deep cover Special Agent Angelina Lopez had arrived in Bogota, Colombia. She wore old clothes and carried an old suitcase as she got out of the taxi at Hotel Tequendama in central Bogota.

Going to the check-in desk, she asked the elderly lady behind the counter, "Where can I get a job?"

"Looking at the beautiful woman, the clerk asked, "What are you willing to do? Someone with your looks can bring in many pesos."

"I'm not a whore, but I've worked in clubs before."

"The Taya Night Club is hiring. I think they would snatch you up in a hurry."

"Where's it located?" Lopez asked.

"It's within walking distance, about four blocks away on Carrera 16."

"Thank you. I don't have a car. I left it with my deadbeat ex in Mexico. To hell with him; he'll never find me here."

"Oh, I'm sorry."

"Thank you. I need a room until I can find a place to stay. What do you have that's cheap?"

"I have a small room in the back. This floor. I can rent for two thousand pesos a month, but I can do that for only one month, maybe two," the lady said.

"Thank you, *veija*. Right now I need help," Lopez replied.

The older lady nodded her head and said, "You remind me of me when I was your age. I will help you as much as I can."

"Thank you."

Lopez filled out the registration in the name listed on the *matricula consular*, the Mexican ID card she carried: Sanita Perez.

CHAPTER 7

The President Said Kill Him

10 a.m., Sunday, March 28, 1993

"YOU THREE HAVE SOME BALLS," President Crawford said. "Now, let's start this over. Fill me in on what happened in Operation Checkmate. And I want to hear it all. Hayden, you start."

"Sir, if I may, you need to hear how this started, and that directly involved Agent Reynolds."

"Okay, Reynolds, you start."

"Mr. President, a year ago while at my home in Maine, I was contacted by a Russian SVR agent that I know. She'd been shot and warned me of a load of cyanide coming to the United States to be used in a bomb. She called me as she was collapsing with a bullet in her chest. I just happened to be near the phone to take the call. She lived and is now doing well. The cyanide came from Uzbekistan. After getting this information, I passed it on to Buddy."

"The Russian SVR?" Crawford asked.

"Yes, sir. Without their help, the interdiction of the cyanide would not have been possible," Reynolds replied.

"All right. Hayden, pick it up from there," the president instructed.

"Yes, sir. Again we apologize. Checkmate was one of the most difficult missions I've ever been associated with, not because of the overall task but because we had virtually no information to go on other than cyanide was coming to Baltimore. If God ever intervened in anything devised by man, he did so here. Every commercial vessel that entered the East Coast was searched by Customs, and they didn't find anything. That was because the vessel stopped at sea and unloaded the cyanide to a fishing boat that took it to West Ocean City, Maryland."

"My God, a needle in a haystack," the president said.

"Yes, sir. And this is where God intervened. I sent Reynolds and West to Baltimore Harbor to see if they could find out any information. And again, we knew nothing other than the location. Nathan and Jack were barhopping, and late at night, Nathan overheard a drunk talk about being left behind by the vessel *Bayram*. He also mentioned it had stopped for a fishing boat out at sea and unloaded five steel drums of oil. We would later learn the fishing boat's name was the *Little Dave*."

"Dear God, what are the odds of hearing that?" the president said. "Agent West, how'd that make you feel?"

"Mr. President, have you ever pissed on an electric fence?"

"Jesus, Nate," Reynolds whispered and elbowed him again.

"Agent West, you'll be surprised by this, but I grew up in rural Arkansas. Yes, I have. Did it feel like that?" the president asked.

"Yes, sir. Every hair on my body was sticking straight out. It was a surreal experience, sir."

"So that's how you men got on the track of the cyanide. Superb, gentlemen. I understand that you, Agent West, knocked the driver out, robbed a store, and stole the van containing the cyanide and bomb."

"Yes, sir. I got lucky. The opportunity presented, and I took advantage of it."

The president got up from his chair and began to clap. Wolfe and Gales did the same as Hayden, West, and Reynolds stood and nodded to the acknowledgment.

"You men are true heroes, and I'm adding former Director Gales in that as well," the president said. "You men have done an incredible service to this country, not once but twice. I've never been more impressed by such fine patriots. Please, gentlemen, sit back down. I have another mission for you."

ALMOST THREE WEEKS PRIOR, SANITA PEREZ had walked into the Taya Night Club wearing a red-rose-print, strapless sundress with white low-heel pumps. It was almost 9 p.m., and the place was packed. The woman behind the bar wearing a black miniskirt and white silk top was the only one working. With sweat forming on her forehead and running down her back, she was struggling to keep up with all the customers as she kept brushing the long dark hair out of her face.

Seeing this, Sanita walked to the end of the bar that was open and went behind it. Coming to the first customer, she asked, in Spanish, "What can I get you?"

"Double Aguardiente on ice."

Looking on the shelf, she turned to the man and asked, "Antioqueno good?"

"Yes, perfect," the man replied.

Sanita picked up a glass from under the bar, dipped it in the ice bucket, and reached for the bottle of Antioqueno Aguardiente.

"Hey, you can't be back here," the barmaid said.

"You want help or not? I know what I'm doing," Sanita replied.

"Miguel, can she help me?" the barmaid yelled to a large man standing in the corner wearing a suit.

Miguel, the Taya floor manager and bouncer, walked over to the bar, looked at the raven-haired beauty, and said, "Keep serving. I want to watch you."

Obviously very experienced, Sanita quickly served several more patrons.

"You want a job?" Miguel asked.

"Yes," Sanita replied as she continued to work.

"You're hired," he said, smiling at his good fortune in hiring another barmaid and one that was drop-dead gorgeous.

IN THE OVAL OFFICE, THE PRESIDENT SAID, "Gentlemen, we have a cocaine epidemic in this country. Most of it is coming from Colombia and the Medellin Cartel run by Alejandro Espinoza. He was under house arrest but has now gone into hiding. We almost had President Gavotti under enough pressure to turn him over to us, but Espinoza was informed by who we suspect was the police, and he escaped. Gavotti is a worthless corrupt politician. The NSA has intercepted phone conversations between Espinoza and Gavotti. The bastard's taking money. The local police are all on the take as well. None of them can be trusted."

"I have the US Customs setting up an operation in Colombia that may locate Espinoza. It's being run by the SAC in Bogota, Dale Wilson, and members of the Colombian National Police under General Hugh Marquez. General Marquez is the only police officer in Colombia that I trust. Espinoza tried to kill him with a car bomb and failed. But, his daughter and several of his officers died in the attempt. Marquez wants Espinoza dead or behind bars. Marquez and the National Police can't be touched by Gavotti or any president due to laws passed by the Colombian Congress. No one tells General Marques what to do. No one."

"I understand, sir," Hayden said.

"What I'm asking is this," the president said. "With your experience in drug smuggling and achieving amazing results, will Team Thorn go to Colombia and assist in apprehending Espinoza? Agent Hayden what do you say?"

"Mr. President, I'm long past fieldwork. But, if needed and if Jack and Nathan would be willing to do this, I could work the communications from FLETC."

"Agent Reynolds?" the president asked.

"Mr. President, I'm a soldier and will go wherever asked. I'm not speaking for Nate, but he has plans, sir, that are coming up soon. And frankly, sir, I'm not going anywhere without him."

"I see. Well, Agent West, what's your decision? You worked for Customs."

"Mr. President, yes, sir, I did. But I've been accepted into medical school, and it starts August 9. I'll be in that class, sir."

"I see. Well, congratulations. That's quite a feat in itself. I thought about medicine at one time in my life, but I decided I couldn't be a DeBakey, so I went into politics. I think I made the right choice."

"Yes, sir. It would seem so," West replied.

"Roger, how long would this operation take to capture Espinoza?" the president asked.

"No way to know, sir. Could take a couple months or a couple years. All depends if we get lucky," Wolfe said.

"Well, we're almost into April," the president said. "West, would you be able to give four months, up to the end of July if needed?"

West looked at Reynolds and said, "You weren't kidding in Newark, were you?"

"No, Nate. It never ends."

West thought for a few moments and said, "Yes, Mr. President. I'm in, at least until I have to start school."

The president of the United States turned to CIA Director Wolfe and said, "Whatever they need, they get. You make it happen, Roger." Getting up out of his chair, the president continued, "Gentlemen, it has been my great honor in meeting you and realizing the metal you are made of. Now, if you will excuse us, Mr. Gales, Director Wolfe, and I have a couple of things to discuss in private."

Hayden, West, and Reynolds got up from the couch, shook hands with the president, and left the room. Once in the hallway, Reynolds asked, "Now, what do you think he's saying?"

"I honestly don't know," Hayden replied.

In the Oval Office, President Crawford asked Director Wolfe, "What are our chances?"

"Thirty, maybe 35 percent tops," Wolfe replied. "They're way down on the probability scale."

"Bob, what do you think?" the president asked.

"Mr. President, I gave them 20 percent chance in stopping the cyanide. They've been proving their bosses wrong for the past five years. I won't bet against them; they're that good of a team. If they don't run out of time with West, I would bet big bucks they pull this off."

"Hmmm," the president said. "All right, this is what I wanted for your ears only, but I expect you to pass this sentiment on to those men. I don't want Alejandro Espinoza arrested. I don't want him sitting in a prison in Colombia that looks like a luxury resort. I want that bastard dead. You tell Team Thorn to kill him. *Kill him!*"

Hayden, West, and Reynolds were waiting in the hall when Gales and Wolfe came out.

"Walk with us, gentlemen," Wolfe said as he and Gales led the way out of the White House, followed by six Secret Service agents.

Stopping near the Secret Service cars, Wolfe said, "We meet at Langley in seventy-two hours. From there, Jack and Nathan are on their way to Bogota."

"Why Bogota and not Medellin? Espinoza operates out of Medellin," Hayden asked.

"Yes, but his family is being kept in a hotel in Bogota. He won't be far from them. Gentlemen, I'll see you at Langley," Wolfe said as he got in a car driven by a CIA agent.

After watching Wolfe leave, Hayden said, "What do you think, Director?"

"What I think's not important," Gales said. "But, Jack and Nathan, you guys keep your heads down while you're in Bogota. That cartel is nothing but butchers. It's a different world down there, and they love killing cops and agents."

"Yes, sir," Reynolds and West replied.

"Thanks for coming, fellows, and Godspeed with this mission," Gales said. After shaking hands, he started towards his own car.

"Director, one last thing," Reynolds said. "What did the president say after we left the room?"

Gales turned to face the men and said, "The president said kill him."

The Secret Service took Hayden and Reynolds to Reagan Washington National Airport to catch their flights home in Georgia and Maine, respectively. West slept on the back seat of the Suburban during most of the four-and-a-half-hour drive back to West Virginia.

"Where we at, fellas?" West asked after waking and still lying on the back seat.

"We're almost to Morgantown on 68. Should we go to Route 7 and down or go to Fairmont and turn west on Route 250?" Montgomery asked.

West sat up and said, "Turn south on I-79 to Fairmont. Get off there and then take 250 towards Mannington. Better roads, Route 7's a bitch."

An hour and twenty minutes later, the Suburban drove across Fish Creek and pulled up to the cabin.

"Gentlemen, it's been a pleasure," West said as he grabbed his bag and started out of the car.

"Nate," Montgomery said, "likewise, you're a cool customer."

West nodded.

"Whatever this is about, you be careful," Smith said.

"Thank you," West replied. "And you guys always watch their hands."

"Yes, sir," both Secret Service Agents replied.

West shut the rear door, and the Suburban pulled away.

CHAPTER 8

Going Live in Forty-Eight Hours

Two weeks prior at the Taya Night Club, Sanita was starting to be a big hit, and many men came to the club to flirt with her and order their drinks. Carlos Rodriquez, the owner of Taya, stood and watched Sanita through the one-way glass in his office above the bar. Yes, he thought, she's a keeper. As he was watching her, a tall man in an expensive suit walked into the club and proceeded to the bar.

"She'll have no idea whom she's talking to," Carlos said as he took another drink of Aguardiente and watched.

Sanita enjoyed the attention as she kept her eyes and ears out for any information that would lead to Espinoza. She flirted back with them all and was beginning to learn not only their names but also what they did for a living. Most were working people, but occasionally, she would meet a member of the cartel. The fancy clothes, expensive jewelry, large rolls of hundred-dollar bills were dead giveaways. None of those men carried pesos; it was all Benjamins. And the more she flirted with the cartel members, the bigger the tip and the more they opened their mouths.

"What can I get you?" Sanita said to the man leaning against the bar and looking the other direction at the dance floor. He was slender and tall, wearing a shiny, blueish-gray sharkskin suit.

Turning he said, "You to start," and then smiled with a big mouth of pearly white teeth set against high cheekbones and black hair to his shoulders.

She smiled back and said, "That's not going to happen. So what do you want to drink?" as she moved to the next customer.

"You're new here, I heard," he said inquiringly.

"So you've been checking up on me? she asked, setting a bottle of Dorada Pils on the bar in front of a prostitute that worked the area.

"I always want to know the most beautiful women, Sanita," he said.

Sanita looked at the man. She was almost sure now and said, "Thank you. You know my name. What's yours?"

"Rafael," the man replied, extending his hand across the bar.

Sanita smiled, her suspicions confirmed as she shook hands with Alejandro Espinoza's brother, Rafael Espinoza, the Medellin Cartel's accountant.

9 a.m., Wednesday, March 31, 1993

West pulled his CJ up to the security checkpoint at Langley. "Nathan West to see the director," he said, handing his West Virginia driver's license to the CIA officer.

"One moment, sir," the officer said as he checked his computer screen for authorized visitors. Looking at the screen with a picture, the officer compared the photo to the driver's license and then looked at West. "Agent West, you'll need to lay this placard next to your windshield and park in one of the reserved spots next to the building. Also put this visitor pass around your neck."

West took the small sign that said Authorized, stuck the end down in the window vent so it could be seen from the outside, and put the visitor pass lanyard over his head. "Thank you," he said as he drove away. At the large white granite building, he pulled into a reserved parking spot and turned off the CJ. Two vehicles down, he could see a powder-blue Jaguar next to a cranberry F-150 pickup.

"They beat me," West said as he started into the building. After getting through the magnetometer, he walked into the elevator and pushed the button for the seventh floor. As the elevator door opened on the seventh floor, two agents stood there.

"Name, sir," one of the men in a gray suit asked.

"Nathan West."

"Yes, sir. The director and the other men are waiting for you in his office."

"Thank you," West said as he walked to the office. At the door, two more agents held the door open for him.

"Thank you," West said as the men nodded.

Walking into the front office, he could see June McDonald sitting at her desk.

"Hi, June. How have you been?" West asked.

"Well, if it's not the legendary Nathan West," she said, getting up from her desk and walking around to give West a hug. "I'm good, and you?" she asked.

"I'm good. Nice seeing you, June," West replied, after hugging the lady.

"You too, Nathan."

"I saw Buddy's and Jack's vehicles outside."

"Yes, they're already in with the director. They're waiting for you."

"Just go on in?" West asked.

"Yes. Knock first."

West knocked on the director's door and then opened it. He could see several men in the room.

"Come on in, Nathan," Director Wolfe said.

Hayden and Reynolds were standing at a table off to the side, looking at satellite photos of Medellin and Bogota, Colombia.

"Come here, Nate," Reynolds said.

Walking up to the table, West said, "Hey, fellas."

"Hi, Nathan," Hayden said.

Reynolds was still looking at the photo of Bogota and pointed his fingers at a building that was tagged Hotel Tequendama.

"This is where Espinoza's family is being kept. They're in protective custody while Alejandro is on the run." Looking at West, Reynolds asked, "What would you do?"

"I'd visit the hotel somehow or at least get as close as I can," West replied.

Reynolds nodded his head and said, "And he will too."

"Familiarize yourself with these photos," Hayden said as he pointed to several lying on the table, all with names on the bottom. "These two are the most important," he said, continuing to point. "This is Alejandro Espinoza, and this is his older brother Rafael Espinoza. Rafael is the accountant for the Medellin Cartel. Where you find one, you'll find the other."

"Roger that. What's our cover?" West asked.

"You and Jack work for Dominion Energy out of Richmond, Virginia," Director Wolfe said, approaching the table.

"We're sending you to Bogota to determine if a joint venture would be profitable with Central Gas Investments located there in the capital city. You guys are basically researching natural gas volumes in Colombia. All your identification will be from Dominion Energy. We have personnel at Dominion who are creating your employment histories. Jack has been with the company eight years and you, Nathan, for two."

"If I only have two years in, why would the company send me?" West asked.

"Because you know more about natural gas than almost anyone in this room. You do own a natural gas well, don't you? Wolfe asked.

"How'd you know that?"

Wolfe smiled and said, "We're the CIA."

"Yes, there's one on the family farm. I grew up around natural gas and have worked with it a lot."

"How deep do you have to go to find natural gas?" a barrel-chested man asked West as he walked to the table.

"Who are you?" West asked.

"Gentlemen, this is Greg Jerold. He's one of the managers at Dominion Energy," Wolfe said.

"A thousand to ten thousand feet," West replied.

"How many pounds of pressure do you need to supply a home?" Jerold asked.

"You don't. One pound will supply three or four homes if you have the volume."

"What's drip gas?"

"It's the moisture that collects in a gas line. If you can get it out, it'll run a car engine, sorta."

"He's good," Jerold said and walked away.

"That's why you're going," Wolfe said.

Reynolds and Hayden smiled at West.

"Nathan," Wolfe continued, "you can use your West Virginia driver's license, and Jack will have a Virginia driver's license. Credit cards and IDs are from Dominion Energy and will be in your names. There's no limit on the cards. The CFO for Central Gas Investments in Bogota has done contract work for us in the past, so your cover will be solid and documented at CGI. His name is Lando Hernandez. You'll need to meet with him on a few occasions to keep your cover solid. The rest is up to you guys. Use your instincts, experiences, and knowledge on how to do this. Just keep in mind Hotel Tequendama is the center of the bullseye."

West looked at the map again and the tag for Central Gas Investments.

"What do you think, Jack?" West asked.

"I'll take the Hotel Tequendama. I've had more combat experience, and there's a real possibility that Espinoza and crew just might show up there one day."

"What weapons will we have, Director?" West asked.

"MP5s and your choice of sidearm."

"That'll work," West replied. "Okay, if you'll take the night clubs around Tequendama, I'll go north of Central Gas and get a room at Santafe Suite," West said, running his finger up the photo and tapping on a building. "I'll be close to the night clubs over on that side and just a few blocks north of Central Gas."

"That sounds like a good plan," Hayden said. "Damn, wish I could go, men. But I'll be at FLETC working the coms."

"It's another needle in a haystack," West said, looking at Hayden, Wolfe, and Reynolds.

"Yes, but we're 2 and O," Reynolds said. "Let's keep the winning record going."

"Roger that," West said.

"Do you men have it worked out?" Director Wolfe asked.

"Yes, we're good," Hayden said.

"Okay, Jack, you and Nathan fly out tomorrow. Buddy, get back to FLETC. We go live in forty-eight hours," Wolfe said.

Bogota
6 p.m., April 1, 1993

Reynolds and West landed in Bogota on a commercial jet. Both talked about natural gas the entire flight and as they walked to the carousel to get their luggage. Wearing Dominion Energy Company blue slacks and white shirts embroidered with their names, they carried briefcases with Dominion Energy stickers on both sides. Getting through Colombian Customs took only a few minutes, and afterwards, they made it to the sidewalk where a taxi pulled up.

The black driver got out and asked, "What's your mother's name?"

"Roger," Reynolds replied.

"Okay, throw your stuff in," the driver replied as he unlocked the trunk.

"Luis Aguilar," the driver said, extending his hand.

"Jack Reynolds," Reynolds replied, shaking hands with the man, "This is Nate West."

West nodded to the man as he threw his luggage into the trunk next to Reynolds'.

West and Reynolds got in the back seat as Luis got back in behind the wheel and pulled out.

There were two small black zippered bags on the backseat between the two men, one with a blue tag.

"What are these?" Reynolds asked.

"The blue tagged one's yours," Aguilar replied. "Your Beretta,

MP5, extra mags, two Nokia phones, recharger, flex-cuffs and the room key for Hotel Tequendama. Agent West's bag has his S&W, MP5, extra mags, two phones, recharger, flex-cuffs, and the Santafe Suite room key. The phones have been pre-programed with each other's phone numbers in the memory. You only have to select number one or number two. If you call 911, that goes straight to me. If you think a phone's been compromised, destroy it and dump it. I'm pretty much your only backup from the agency here. We don't communicate much with Customs or DEA if we can help it. It's too risky. The cartel has eyes everywhere. So basically, you're on your own. If you need me, I'm probably an hour from getting to you. A lot can happen in sixty minutes."

"What's your background?" West asked as he and Reynolds were taking their pistols and room keys out of the bags.

"SEALs."

"All right," West replied. "Just remember if we call you, the shit has already hit the fan. So come with extreme hate."

"Roger that," Aguilar replied.

Racking a live round into the 9mm, West slid it into the front of his waist belt and covered it with his shirt. Reynolds did the same with the Beretta.

"Agent Reynolds, I'll drop you off first at Hotel Tequendama. Be extra careful. With Espinoza's family being kept there, he has multiple eyes watching the place. He has his own people working there masquerading as an attorney group representing his wife. They are the only people allowed to come and go. A bribed judge ruled they could do this. The Espinozas have the entire fourteenth floor. You must have an elevator key to get on that floor, and all the stairway doors are locked from the inside with guards. Your room is 217. It's in the corner so you're close to the stairs. There's a good bar and restaurant on the first floor."

"Roger that," Reynolds replied.

"Agent West, you're in room 302, and it's also near the stairs. I have to warn you; Santafe is a shithole—no bar or restaurant, plenty of whores and dealers, and that's about it."

"As long as it has a bed and bathroom, I don't care," West replied. "Where is a good bar with food near there, someplace the cartel would visit?"

"The Taya Night Club is about two blocks up the street from you. It's a regular cartel hangout. You'd better have your A-game on if you visit that place," Aguilar said.

"Always," West replied.

As the taxi pulled up to the Hotel Tequendama, West said, "Jack, pick a phone and call me when you get to your room. Be careful."

"Will do. Remember our all-clear phrase," Reynolds said as he got out of the taxi with the small black bag.

"Got it," West replied.

Aguilar got out of the taxi and opened the trunk for Reynolds to get his suitcase. West watched Reynolds walk into the hotel as Aguilar got back in.

"He's a big man," Aguilar said as he started the taxi towards Santafe Suite.

"Yes, and he's meaner than a snake if he has to be," West replied.

CHAPTER 9

No, This Is Bogota

Bogota
2:30 a.m.

THE WEEK BEFORE, LOPEZ WAS GETTING BACK to her room at the Hotel Tequendama after a late night working at the Taya Night Club. Rafael had been coming in every few days, and she felt for sure a relationship was developing. But she continued to act coy and reel him in slowly. Opening the door to her room, she found an envelope on the floor where it had been slid under the door. She picked it up, closed the door behind her, locking the two locks, and read the letter:

Scared little girl, you put the pistol against my chest. Leave now and walk to the corner of Calle 25 and Carrera 13. It's behind the triangle across the street. Walk to the end of Calle 25. Now burn this letter.

I wonder what the general wants, Lopez thought as she placed the letter back in the envelop. Taking the lighter out of her pocket she used to light patrons' cigarettes, she lit the envelope and dropped it in the sink to burn. She locked the door behind her as she went back out of the room and proceeded across the street and into the dark alley of Calle 25. "I need a gun," she said as she walked through the darkness. She had done what the general had said to do and left the Sig at her parents' home, under her old bed in her childhood bedroom in a red-flowered shoebox in San Diego. At the end of the alley at Carrera 13, headlights flashed from a car parked in the dark to the right.

Lopez walked to the dark sedan and got in the back seat where General Marquez was seated. "General," she said, nodding to the big man in the dim light.

"Ninita, have you learned anything?"

"Why do you call me little girl?"

The general took a deep breath and said, "Because that's what I called my daughter before she was killed. You remind me of her. Now, have you learned anything?"

"How did she die?"

"She was killed in a car bomb intended for me. Espinoza killed her. Now, what have you learned?"

"I'm sorry," Lopez said, paused, and then continued. "I've met Rafael Espinoza, and he seems to be romantically interested."

"Rafael? You sure?" asked the general. "Describe him to me."

"Handsome, early forties, black shoulder-length hair, five eight, one sixty, big set of white teeth."

"Hand me my briefcase," the general said to the driver.

The driver picked up the briefcase off the front seat and handed it back to the general in the dark. Laying the briefcase on his lap, he opened the tabs and took a penlight out of one of the pockets.

"Watch for someone," he said to the driver.

"Yes, sir," the driver replied.

Marquez turned the penlight on and put it in his mouth as he took a folder out of the briefcase and opened it. Thumbing through several pictures, he pulled one out and handed it to Lopez.

"Him?" the general asked after taking the light out of his mouth.

Lopez looked at the picture and said, "Yes, that's him."

"Yes, that's Rafael Espinoza, Alejandro's older brother," the general said. "He's the accountant for the Medellin Cartel."

Handing the picture back to the general, Lopez said, "Yes, I know. I'm locked on."

"Stay close to him. He'll eventually lead us to Alejandro."

"I will," Lopez said.

"I don't need to tell you what to do," the general said. "You know."

"Yes, general. I need to get back."

"Here, I brought you something," the general said, pulling a small black Taurus .380 caliber pistol out of his coat pocket. Handing it to Lopez, he said, "I've shot it several times; it works well. And there's one in the chamber. Also, I want you to call me once a week to give me an update. If I need you, I'll leave another letter."

"All right and thank you," she said.

"You still remember my number?"

"Yes."

"Okay, be careful," the general said.

Lopez nodded and got out of the car, placing the pistol in her back pocket. As she walked back to Hotel Tequendama, she patted the pistol with her hand. She liked how it felt.

As the sedan pulled out and headed down Carrera 13, the driver asked, the general, "Do you think she can do it?"

The general looked at the lights of Bogota and said, "No, this is Bogota. The Espinoza brothers or someone will figure out who she is, order her to be kidnapped, gang-raped, and then they'll bury her alive. I only pray it's fast for Ninita."

The driver nodded and continued to the Carlos Holguín School.

"I FEEL THE GENERAL GETTING CLOSER," Espinoza said to the man.

"Anything specific?" the man asked.

"No, just a feeling. Nothing I can put my finger on. I need you to double-check everything and everyone. I know they're near me, but I don't know where they are."

"I'll take care of that," the man said. "You can rest easy."

"I'm glad you're back home, Alex. I know I can trust you. I need to be able to close my eyes but feel I can't."

"I'll start at the Tequendama and then go to the clubs. Nobody knows who I am, do they?"

"No, only Rafael and our men. No one on the outside knows who you are or what you do."

"Good, I'm more effective that way. I don't want to be associated with the cartel. I need to be able to fit in anyplace without the looks."

"Yes, we need to keep you in the background."

"Is Raya still at the Tequendama?" Sanchez asked

"Yes, she's in charge of the whores for the men and police."

"How's your family?"

"They're good. Raya says they're being treated well."

"Let's hope it stays that way. If she keeps the whores available for the men, it should."

"Yes. I have questions about Philly. How did Customs find out?" Espinoza asked.

"An undercover agent had to be there somewhere. But the US attorney kept him hidden. He never exposed himself and was never called to testify. From what our attorneys told me, they still have no clue who it is."

"That bothers me. Maybe we can find out and kill that bastard someday."

"Perhaps. But let's concentrate on you here now. We must keep you hidden and safe. I'll get someone to speak to President Gavotti. With your approval, I'll increase the amount we pay him from five million to ten million a year. I don't think he'll pass up the money. President Crawford doesn't have that much control over him."

"All right. Yes, get him the money. I want to be able to go back to La Catedral. Make that happen, Alex."

"I'll make that happen sometime this year. If I can't, then that means we're both dead," Alex Sanchez replied.

After getting out of the taxi, Reynolds entered Hotel Tequendama and avoided everyone by walking up the stairs to the second floor. Opening the door to room 217, he said, "Wow, what a nice place," as he looked around at the plush furniture, expensive drapes covering the windows, and the two king-size beds with a white silk comforter on each. He set his suitcase on the floor, laid the black bag on the first bed, unzipped it, and took out the MP5. Racking a live 9mm round into the chamber, he placed the safety on and shoved the machine gun under the mattress. "I want that close," he said as he pulled the comforter back down over the edge of the bed.

Next he picked up one of the phones and called the first number listed in the memory.

Aguilar was almost to the Santafe Suite when one of the phones in West's bag began to ring.

"Hello."

"Nate, it's Jack. That's your number one phone."

"Got it. I'll call you after I get in the room. We're here now," West said, hanging up and sliding the phone into his rear pants pocket.

It was starting to get dark as Aguilar pulled the taxi up to the front of Santafe Suite. The street side of the sidewalk in front of the rundown, gray-walled hotel was lined with prostitutes with low-cut blouses, miniskirts, black fishnet stockings, and high heels. Against the building on the other side of the sidewalk were drug addicts sleeping against the wall. To walk down the sidewalk, you had to run the gauntlet of hookers, dealers, and addicts in the dim light.

"You're right; it's a shithole," West said, looking out the rear door window. "You say up the street a couple of blocks is the Taya?"

"Yes, back that way," Aguilar said, motioning with his thumb. "It's a nice club. High-class whores. These women here," he said, nodding at the girls on the sidewalk, "aren't allowed in there."

"Well, I guess that's saying something," West said, reaching his hand across the seat and shaking hands with the cabbie. "Thank you."

"Stay tight," Aguilar replied.

"Watch their hands," West said, getting out of the taxi with the black bag.

After Aguilar opened the trunk, West took his suitcase and said, "*Gracias*."

As he walked into the hotel, he began to get catcalls from the working girls on the sidewalk. He smiled back at them and walked on, past the front desk on the right, nodding at the young man behind the counter, who nodded back. The hotel was full of smoke, with beige, dingy plastered walls that needed replastering ten years ago. The broken multi-colored tile floor must be fifty years old, West thought as he pushed the upper button to the elevator on the other side of the check-in desk. There were only two buttons and neither had any markings.

He stepped into the elevator, and the stench of urine and feces hit him like a sucker punch from a heavyweight boxer. "Jesus Christ," West said as the door closed and he pushed the third-floor button, deliberately not leaning back against the wall and trying not to breathe. I'm taking the stairs from now on, he thought. The door opened to the third floor, and he let out the held breath and gasped another one. Turning left out of the elevator, he walked to the end of the hall and used his key to open room 302. The stairs were the next doorway down the hall.

As he walked in, he was pleased the room didn't smell like urine, although it did smell like smoke from a thousand cigars. "Well, this is tolerable," he said, dropping his suitcase next to the closet and placing the black bag on the bed, covered with an old brown blanket. Walking back to the door, he closed it and locked the deadbolt. As he looked around the room, the walls appeared to have been painted white sometime in the past year, and the green carpet was stained but appeared to be clean. The bathroom was, well, a cheap hotel bathroom. But it would do.

Pulling the phone out of his pocket, West sat down in one of the chairs next to a small table against the wall and hit the first number in the memory.

"Hello," Reynolds said.

"Jack, it's me. I got in the room."

"How is it? This one here is nicer than the Marriott in Baltimore Harbor," Reynolds said.

"This is a shithole, Jack, a literal shithole, but that's okay. It will push me to be outside more than I normally would be inclined to be. So that's good."

Reynolds laughed. "If you can't find me, come knock on my door and wake me up from my nap after eating my room service meal."

"Kiss my ass."

"What are you doing tonight?" Reynolds asked.

"I'm going to sleep for a couple of hours, and at twenty hundred, I'm going to the Taya," West replied.

"All right. I'm going downstairs and will hang out in the bar. Get something to eat and look at the classy Colombian women."

"Eat shit," West said. "I just hope to see a good-looking prostitute at the Taya. They'll probably be all hard-looking used-up women. The sidewalk was full of them when I came in."

"Okay. Remember our cover. The reason we're not in the same building is because we got in an argument, and you wanted to be closer to Central Gas."

"I've been thinking about that, Jack. I think I'm going to say you propositioned me and I didn't feel safe sleeping in the same building; I didn't know you were a pedophile, or I wouldn't have agreed to this trip."

"You asshole."

West laughed and said, "I really think that sounds more logical. And when people look at you, they probably naturally think, Oh yeah, that big bastard with the bald head is probably a pervert."

"I'm going to stomp your ass," Reynolds said.

Trying to stop laughing, West said, "Especially in that Dominion Energy outfit, people look at you and think, oh yeah, he likes kids."

"Nate, you need to stop right now, or I swear I'm going over there and I'll pummel you to death."

West finally stopped laughing and said, "Okay, Jack, okay. I'll look over my hardware and then get some shuteye. I'll call you later after I get back in."

"You little bastard. All right," Reynolds said and hung up.

West was still chuckling as he laid the phone on the nightstand next to the bed. Opening the black bag, he took out the phone charger and placed it on the nightstand after plugging it into an outlet beside the bed. Next he pulled out the MP5 and one of the magazines, put the safety on, and locked the bolt open. After looking at the rounds in the magazine, he inserted the mag all the way up and pulled it to the rear, locking it in place. He slapped the bolt back and down, and it closed, chambering a live 9mm round. West then pulled the magazine out again, looked at the rounds to make sure the top round was on the opposite side as before, indicating a round had been chambered. Inserting the mag once more, he pulled it to the rear and again locked it in place.

West walked to the other side of the bed, pulled the mattress up, and slid the weapon underneath it. If I have a shootout in this room, he thought, they are probably coming through that door and I want that bed between me and the shooter. I'll make sure they walk into a meat grinder. Picking up the black bag, he slid it underneath the bed. He then lay down on the bed and closed his eyes with one final thought, I need sleep.

CHAPTER 10

I Think My Heart Stopped

Thursday, April 1, 1993

Lopez arrived at the Taya at 6 p.m. to start her shift until 2 a.m. when the club closed. Dressed in a pink-flowered sundress, the five-foot-two-inch, 120-pound beauty was breathtaking. Her long black hair she kept pulled over her left shoulder and her big black doe eyes mesmerized the male patrons and they loved her.

So did Carlos Rodriquez, the owner of Taya. He would stand in his office and watch her through the one-way glass for hours. The sensuous beauty was good for business, and he lusted after her. I need to get her up here in my office, he thought, rubbing his crotch. He was sure she would want to make some extra money. Most of the girls that worked there did, and he enjoyed them all. It was a win-win—the girls got extra cash, and he didn't have to have sex with that bitch of a wife at home.

The only reason he hadn't taken advantage of her already was Rafael Espinoza who was showing an interest in her, and Rodriquez wasn't about to take the chance of pissing him off. The cocaine that Rodriquez peddled for the cartel was significant cash, and he wasn't going to mess that up. And you don't have an affair with a cartel member's girlfriend if you enjoy breathing. Especially with the girlfriend of Alejandro Espinoza's brother. That's best left alone, he thought as he walked away from the glass. At least as long as he could resist her.

Santafe Suite
8 p.m.

WEST WOKE UP AND WAS SPLASHING WATER on his face over the bathroom sink. Looking in the cracked mirror, he said, "I need to get this taken care of quick so I can get to Lewisburg."

He wondered about taking off the Dominion Energy shirt and slacks but changed his mind. I need to look the part, he thought. Pulling the shirt out of his pants, he slid the 9mm into his right front belt and covered it with his shirt. He locked the door behind him and took the stairs to the street level below.

People were everywhere as he walked out the front door to the streets lit up with a yellow glow from the pole lights.

"*Me quieres?*" an older prostitute said to West as she walked up to him and shoved her large breast together with her hands as they spilled from her half-buttoned-up shirt.

"*No hablar espanol,*" West replied.

"You want me?" she asked in English.

"No. Going to Taya," West said as he continued to walk down the sidewalk. Welcome to Bogota, he thought.

REYNOLDS WAS SITTING AT THE BAR in the Tequendama lounge, nursing his first Aguardiente drink. Not bad, he thought as he took another sip and watched the lovely raven-haired woman in a flowing red gown sing as she leaned against the piano. Class act, Reynolds thought, looking around the room.

There were several people in the lounge. The men were all dressed in suits, and the women in attractive evening wear. He felt slightly conspicuous in his blue Dominion Energy slacks and white shirt but not enough to bother him. Part of the job, he thought and took another drink and made eye contact with the singer who smiled as she passionately sang the Bon Jovi song, "In These Arms."

"Hmmm," he said as he smiled back and nodded his head. "I bet *she* doesn't think I'm a pedophile," he whispered, still smiling and looking at the woman.

WEST WALKED INTO THE TAYA past the two big bouncers standing at the door. One of the bouncers smiled and smirked, looking at West's Dominion Energy shirt. West smiled back and thought, Yep, that's me, just another geek. The music was loud and the cigarette smoke thick. "Macarena" was being performed by singers and dancers on the stage, and most of the patrons were dancing. West slowly worked his way through the dancing crowd to the bar. Finally getting to a stool, he sat down and looked around. The club was dimly lit with an array of different colored lights, most with a blue hue. This is certainly a happening place, he thought.

Turning on his stool, he came face to face with the most beautiful eyes of a drop-dead gorgeous woman in a pink-flowered sundress.

"What can I get you?" she asked in English.

West couldn't speak and began to feel his left wrist pulse with his right-hand finger tips. "Hmmm," he finally said, frowning and gritting his teeth as he looked at the beauty.

"You all right?" she asked.

"I think my heart just stopped," he said, looking concerned at the woman while still frowning.

"Seriously?" she asked.

"Yes, I think it did. But I'm okay now," he said, smiling.

Tilting her head to the side, she gave the most beautiful smile he had ever seen, giggled, and said, "I'm glad I didn't kill you. Now what do you want to drink?"

Pausing again, West studied the woman's face and said, "A light beer, whatever you've got."

Lopez turned to walk away as West studied the woman. I think she's the most beautiful woman I've ever seen, he thought. She opened the cooler and glanced his way with a different look. A look of . . . he wasn't sure . . . of a professional, he thought. As he studied her, he thought, There's just something about her.

She returned with an Aguila Light, twisted off the cap, and set it on the bar in front of West, having changed back into the sweet young girl once more.

West could only utter, "What's your name?"

She smiled and said, "Sanita."

"Thank you, Sanita."

"What's yours?" she asked, looking intently.

The professional look appeared—almost—once more. It's there, just below the surface, he thought, but definitely there. "Nathan, Nathan West," he said, tapping the embroidered name on his shirt.

"Oh, I see," she said, flashing that beautiful smile.

"Nice to meet you, Sanita," he said as he extended his hand to hers.

Feeling the small soft hand in his own, West felt the hair stand up on the back of his neck. It was like he knew her. He fought the cold chill. It confused him.

"What brings you here?" the woman asked, looking at the Dominion Energy name and logo on his shirt.

"To fall in love," he blurted out while still holding her hand. He wasn't sure where the hell that came from, but he couldn't stop it. Letting loose of her hand, he shook his head, paused, closed his eyes, and bent his head down. "No, no, that's not it."

Sanita smiled, tilted her head, and giggled again, watching the man make a fool of himself.

Looking back up, West said, "Let me start over. I'm here to research natural gas supplies and see if Dominion can do a joint venture with Colombia. Yeah, that's it. That's why I'm here."

"You're funny," she said, turning and walking back down the bar.

"I wasn't trying to be," West replied, in a serious tone. As he watched her walk away, he took a big gulp of beer. Damn! he thought. She's so beautiful; it made me nervous to talk to her.

The men sat in the black Mercedes-Benz sedan across the street from the Taya. "You coming in?" Rafael Espinoza asked Alex Sanchez.

"No. I can't be seen with you. I may slip in later, but I want to sit here and watch who comes and goes out of the club."

"I would like to introduce you to Sanita."

"Who's that?"

"She works here and she's very lovely."

"No. I don't need to know your women, Rafael. My job is to protect you and Alejandro from the police. She'd be of no interest to me," Sanchez replied.

"We do appreciate your work, Alex. Thank you, I'll not be long," Rafael said as the driver opened the rear door and Rafael climbed out of the car. Getting back in the car behind the wheel, the bodyguard and driver, Jorge, said, "Alex, do you mind if I close my eyes? It's been a long week."

"No, I'll wake you if something happens," Sanchez replied as he stared at everyone that came and went.

WEST WAS NURSING HIS THIRD AGUILA LIGHT when he heard Sanita say, "Hi, Rafael," in a happy voice as she leaned across the bar to a man with dark hair and exchanged kisses on the cheek.

Well, shit, West thought as he took another sip. With the many people bellied up to the bar, he couldn't see the man well. What would be the odds? he thought, leaning back to try to get a better look at the man.

"I CAN'T STAY LONG," RAFAEL SAID. "But I wanted to stop in and say hi to you."

"Thank you. That's sweet of you. I don't get off until 2 a.m.," Sanita replied.

"I could say something to Carlos."

"No, please don't. I need this job, and that wouldn't be fair to the other girls."

"Okay, I may stop back later if I'm in the area. If not, I'll see you another time," Rafael said.

"I would like that," Sanita said, smiling.

"Bye, *carino*," Rafael said as he walked towards the exit.

"Bye, Rafael," Sanita said with a smile and thought, I've got your dick.

The man walked away as Sanita looked down at the floor and didn't move for a moment.

The professional's back, West thought, watching her stare blankly at the floor.

Sanita looked up and once again focused on the customers at the bar. Coming to West, she said, "You ready for another one?"

"Yes, one more, please," he said, turning to watch Rafael walk out the door as Sanita returned to the cooler. The man turned his head only slightly as he walked out of sight. Could be, West thought. But he still didn't get a good look.

Sanita returned with the beer and set it down on the bar.

"Your boyfriend?" West asked.

"Maybe. He just called me sweetheart for the first time," Sanita said, smiling.

"He's a handsome man. You would make a nice-looking couple," West replied.

"Thank you," she said as she walked away squinting her eyes.

That was an odd look, West thought.

"Here comes Rafael," Sanchez said to Jorge.

Jorge sat up in his seat, rubbed his eyes, and got out to open the rear door for his boss.

Getting in the back seat next to Sanchez, Rafael said, "She gets lovelier every time I see her."

"That's nice. How's she in bed?" Sanchez asked.

"I don't know, but I'm going to find out soon."

"Can we sit here a little longer? Sanchez asked. "I want to see who follows you out."

It was almost midnight when West finished his last beer. Laying down a ten-dollar bill, he asked Sanita, "Will this cover everything?"

"Yes. Do you want the change back?"

"No, keep it. I need to get going. First day of work tomorrow. Nice meeting you, Sanita."

"Thank you and you too, Nathan," she replied as West slid off the stool and headed back to Santafe Suite.

"WHO'S THE GRINGO?" SANCHEZ ASKED AS he watched West walk out Taya's door and down the sidewalk.

"I don't know, didn't see him inside," Rafael replied.

"Okay, I've seen enough for tonight," Sanchez said, still watching West as the car pulled out. Seeing West look back at the car, Sanchez thought, I'll remember you.

WEST COULD SEE THE DARK SEDAN out of the corner of his eye parked across the street. But the night and tinted windows prevented seeing inside the car. Glad I'm carrying a gun, he thought as he walked back towards his dingy hotel room. Hearing the Mercedes pull out, he glanced back.

CHAPTER 11

The Orphan

12:30 a.m., Friday, April 2, 1993

Reynolds was already in his room when West called. "Hello," Reynolds said.

"Jack, you do any good?"

"Maybe. There were many people in the lounge area. Some looked very shady, possibly cartel members. How'd you do?"

"Met a beautiful girl at the bar. Sanita was her name. She has a boyfriend by the name of Rafael, but couldn't get a good look at him. He could be an Espinoza," West said. "I just don't know yet; he never looked my way."

"Rafael is a common name here, so he's probably not," Reynolds said.

"Yes, I know. Hopefully, I see him again. I don't know about you, but I'm beat."

"Yes, I need to sleep too. I'll talk to you tomorrow," Reynolds said.

"Roger that," West said, hanging up and laying the phone on the night table.

Taking the 9mm out of his belt, he placed it on the table next to the phone. After undressing and laying the pants and shirt across the chair, he turned off the light and crawled into bed. I hope this thing doesn't have bed bugs, he thought, as he fell asleep in less than sixty seconds.

Taya
2 a.m.

SANITA WAS LEAVING THE TAYA when Carlos Rodriquez pulled up in his silver BMW. He couldn't resist her any longer; he just wouldn't let Rafael Espinoza know. "Let me give you a lift. I'm going that way," he said.

Looking at her boss, she knew if she got in that car what was going to happen. But she needed this cover job and his protection.

"Okay, if you don't mind," she replied, getting in the car with a smile.

"Not at all," he said. "Gives us time to get to know each other better."

A couple of other female employees saw Sanita get in the car as they whispered together.

Pulling out from the Taya, Rodriquez drove down the next block before he laid his hand on Sanita's leg and said, "I want you to know how much I appreciate you. You've turned out to be one of my best workers."

She knew that was bullshit as she placed her hand on his and said, "Thank you. I want to be a good employee," and slid his hand farther up under her dress to her inner thigh.

"That's good," he said. Glancing at Sanita, he moved his hand up to her panties, feeling her warm mound.

"Ahhh," she said as she spread her legs farther and pulled his hand harder into her wetness as she started to rhythmically move her hips.

"You're a hot bitch," Rodriquez said, trying to drive and move his fingers underneath her panties.

"I'm a slut, and I knew you wanted to have sex with me from the first moment I met you." She reached across and started rubbing his crotch and then unzipping his pants. "Find someplace to park," she said as she pulled his manhood out. Unfastening her seatbelt, she leaned across the center consul and began to suck him as he drove.

Quickly pulling in a dark alley, Rodriquez put the car in park and leaned his seat back to give this hot woman more room.

Sanita sucked and massaged the man's balls and manhood until he couldn't hold it any longer. With a loud grunt, he climaxed into Sanita's mouth as she continued to suck and squeeze his balls. She swallowed and licked up every bit until he stopped her.

"My God," he said, pulling her head up from his crotch. "That was incredible."

"Good," she said, returning to her seat and pulling up the end of her dress to wipe her mouth off. Leaning back, she stared straight ahead and said, "Now, I want a raise."

Rodriquez looked at Sanita, tried to catch his breath as he zipped his pants back up, and said, "You beautiful bitch." He paused and said, "All right."

Santafe Suite
5 a.m.

West tried to sleep longer but he couldn't. He never could, especially when he kept remembering his grandfather Ralph saying, "If you can't sleep, there's something you need to be doing."

As he sat up in bed, the five-foot-eleven, 190-pound man kicked the blanket down to his feet and did his morning routine of fifty crunches before getting up. Walking to the bathroom to relieve himself, he watched the yellow urine hit the water and thought, I wonder if she got home okay. Boy, what a beautiful woman. "Sanita," he slowly said. "That's so pretty."

West slid the blue plastic shower curtain out of the way, reached over, and turned on the water. He would give it a few minutes to get hot. As he walked back to the bed, he picked up his phone and called Reynolds.

"Hello," a sleepy voice said.

"You awake, pappy?"

"No. Why the hell don't you call at a decent hour?"

West chuckled and said, "If you could stop thinking about all the people you killed, you could probably fall asleep faster and wake up earlier."

"Yeah, well that's not happening. Call me back in an hour," Reynolds said, glancing at the clock, as he hung up.

Laughing, West laid the phone down and walked to the shower.

"Damn, this feels great," he said after he got in. The hot water ran over his back, ass, and legs. Nothing better than a hot shower, he thought. Planning his day, he would first find a place that served breakfast. I wonder what they eat around here?

After lathering up and rinsing off, West got out of the shower and dried off with one of the cheap, thin white hotel towels. He then wrapped it around his waist and tucked it in front to keep it up. Picking up his suitcase from the floor, he tossed it on the bed, opened it, and took his black leather shaving kit to the bathroom sink. After brushing his dark hair and then his teeth, he put on deodorant and after-shave over his stubble. That'll do, he thought, looking in the mirror.

He dropped the towel and walked back to the suitcase. From it he pulled out and put on a pair of boxers and socks, placed five pairs of folded Dominion Energy white shirts and dark-blue slacks in the dresser, but kept his black tactical clothes and shoes in the suitcase. Closing it, he placed it back in the closet and shut the door.

He then picked up the Dominion shirt off the back of the chair and smelled it. "Still good," he said and put it on and then the blue slacks, tightening the brown leather belt. Pulling on his dark brown dress shoes, he put one up on the chair at a time and tied the laces. As he walked to the bathroom mirror to see how he looked, he picked up his watch from the dresser and put it on—the dials showed 5:45.

"Hmmm, I'll give him a few more minutes to sleep," West said as he opened the door and walked down the stairs to the front desk.

"*Buenos dias,*" he said to the clerk.

"*Buenos dias,*" the half-awake man replied, lifting his head off the counter.

"My Spanish is poor. Can you speak English?" West asked.

"*Si, senor.* I speak English,"

"Great," West said. "Where can you get breakfast?"

"Breakfast?" the man asked.

"Yes, breakfast," West repeated. "Eat, coffee."

The man smiled and said, "Si, coffee, *arepas*," and motioned with his hands for West to follow him. Going into a small room next to the front desk, the man pointed to a hot plate with a small pot on it filled with water. Next to it was a jar of Nescafé instant coffee, paper cups, and three slices of well-crusted bread, cut in half.

"Breakfast?" West asked, looking at the man.

"Si, coffee and *arepas*."

"*Arepas?*" West asked.

"*Si, arepas*," the man said, pointing at the bread.

West forced a smile as the man began to walk away. "*Gracias.*"

The man smiled, nodded, and walked back to the front desk.

"My God," West said, nevertheless making a cup of instant coffee and picking up a half-slice of bread. Walking back to the room, he sipped on the coffee and ate the bread. Not bad, he thought. Inside the room, he once more called Reynolds.

"Don't be in a hurry to eat breakfast," West said.

"They don't serve much breakfast in Colombia," Reynolds replied.

"Jack, I'm from West by God Virginia. We eat big breakfasts there. You could've warned me, and I would have filled by suitcase with freeze-dried meat and fruit."

"Well, hillbilly, it must have skipped my mind. So I guess you won't need to be calling me at zero dark thirty anymore."

"I guess not," West said. "Do you want to meet with Lando Hernandez today?"

"Yes, I'll be over to pick you up with Luis at 9 a.m., so be ready."

"Roger that. I'll see you then."

In 1953, Lando Hernandez had been a three-year-old in a run-down Colombian orphanage when a rich American couple walked through the half-falling-down shantytown building outside of Bogota. The American woman was of Colombian heritage and couldn't have children. She convinced her wealthy husband that adopting a young Colombian child would be as close as they would ever get to having their own family. He finally agreed, as long as they adopted a boy who would, he hoped, follow in his footsteps and carry on with the automotive business that had taken him several years to build.

Fortunately for Lando, he was a smiling energetic child who grabbed a hold of one of the woman's legs as she studied the other nine children. Looking down, she took a deep breath and returned the smile to the charming little boy with jet-black hair. He had a pleasant face with the most precious smile and the whitest teeth she had ever seen in a child.

"Oh, darling, this is our son," she said, looking at her husband.

The man looked at the child for a few moments and said, "All right."

Lando was raised in Kansas City, Missouri. As a child, he spent most of his time in his father's Buick dealership when he wasn't in school. He learned all about business and especially selling cars. In high school, he excelled in sports and was a very good student. After high school, he began his studies at the University of Missouri at Kansas City. He did very well and graduated with a bachelor's degree in business administration.

But he had no interest in being involved in his father's dealership. This decision created a rift between him and his aging father. They rarely spoke now. Shortly after, his mother became ill with ovarian cancer and died within six months. Lando felt lost and believed the only family he had left on the face of the earth were somewhere in Colombia. So in 1972, at the age of twenty-two, he left America for his home country.

Lando ended up in Bogota, looking for work. He applied at many companies and with his BA degree received many offers. But none of the offers were as good as the one from Central Gas Investments. During his final interview, he explained that he knew nothing about natural gas but he was willing to learn. And learn he did. Lando started out in the billing department, and over the years, he advanced to the top. Now after twenty-one years with the company, he was the chief financial officer of Central Gas Investments.

It seemed Lando knew everyone in Bogota and most of Colombia, the good and the bad, from business executives and politicians to members of the drug cartel. And everyone liked him; he was one of the good guys for the Colombian society, providing cheap natural gas or propane to the families to heat their homes, make hot water, and cook their meals. Few men were as appreciated as he was.

This did not go unnoticed by the CIA. In 1991, under President George H. W. Bush, the CIA began an intelligence network in Colombia to track drug smuggling in his War on Drugs policy. Colombia had been a powder keg for almost fifty years, with rival factions killing thousands over politics, power, and drug money. Now the United States government wanted inside eyes and ears to help prevent those criminal elements from coming to America.

Lando Hernandez may have lived in Colombia, but he still felt an allegiance to his adopted country. After all, he would not have been in the position he now held without that fateful relocation to the United States as a child. So when he was approached by a special agent of the CIA, he agreed to provide information that he naturally came in possession of in his normal line of business. He didn't have to do anything other than make an occasional phone call to an encrypted number in Langley, Virginia. But he still took a tremendous risk—if it was ever found out that he was talking to the CIA, he and his entire family of wife, two sons, and a daughter would be horribly killed.

By 1993, Alejandro Espinoza was responsible for the murders of over three thousand people associated with the police, courts, rivals, and their families.

CHAPTER 12

Triangulation

9 a.m., Friday, April 2, 1993

"How many tons were shipped to the US last month?" Alejandro asked his older brother, Rafael, as they both sat in silk pajamas and sipped on the black coffee in the hidden home in Los Olivos on the outskirts of Medellin.

"Ten tons; we took in over 180 million dollars," Rafael replied, looking at his ledger.

"We are losing market because of our hiding," Alejandro said. "We used to make over three hundred million a month. Now we have to conduct business in the shadows."

"Yes, but we're still in business, and we can't possibly spend all the money we now have. And we're still alive. We have no choice, little brother."

"I still don't like it. We should have killed Gavotti and made an example out of him when we had the chance. Anyone that cooperates with the United States needs to die."

"There are some wars we cannot win, brother. And *Forbes* still has you listed as one of the world's richest billionaires."

"How much do we have?"

Looking at his sheets, Rafael said, "We have almost thirty billion dollars. Do you want to continue with the burial plans?"

"Yes, continue to keep one hundred million in cash, and bury the rest of it in the locations we selected. If anything happens to me, take what you can get and leave the country."

"Nothing is going to happen to you, and I won't need to do that. Alex will protect us both. I like and trust him. He knows what he's doing, and he's always on guard," Rafael replied.

"Mr. Hernandez, there are two gentlemen here from Dominion Energy to meet with you," the secretary at Central Gas Investments said into the telephone. . . . "Yes, sir. I'll bring them right in. Gentlemen, follow me please," the secretary said as she hung up the phone, got up from behind her desk, and led Reynolds and West to the next room.

The woman had her dark hair up in a bun and wore dark-rimmed glasses and a form-fitting, short, black sleeveless dress. Walking behind her, both men couldn't take their eyes off of her perfectly shaped ass, sensuously moving from side to side, and felt a huge letdown when she stopped and held the door open.

"Here you go, gentlemen," she said, smiling, knowing exactly what the men had been watching.

"Damn. Thank you," Reynolds said as he walked into the office.

West only smiled at the lady—still smiling—as she closed the door behind him.

"Welcome, gentlemen," Lando Hernandez said, meeting the men in the middle of the room and extending his hand to Reynolds.

"Hello, Mr. Hernandez," Reynolds replied, grasping his hand and shaking it. "I'm Jack Reynolds, and this is Nathan West."

"Sir," West said and nodded as he shook hands with Hernandez.

"Have a seat, men," Hernandez said, pointing to two chairs in front of his very large curved mahogany desk. Walking around the desk, he sat down in the brown, padded, leather-covered executive chair.

"Thank you for seeing us," Reynolds said. "I believe you know the reason we're here, and we appreciate your assistance. Dominion Energy feels we could have a lucrative arrangement in our joint natural gas venture. We're here to see if Central Gas Investments feels the same and how we can reach an agreement."

"Yes, I believe we may be able to do that," Hernandez replied, while placing one finger over his lips to signal quiet. Picking up the phone, he called the secretary's number. It rang only once before it was answered; Hernandez didn't hear her quickly walking away from his door to answer the phone.

"Lucia, could you go to the cafeteria and get us three cups of coffee, please? Thank you," Hernandez said and hung up. "She'll be gone a few minutes."

"Problems?" Reynolds asked.

"No. Sometimes I get the feeling she's listening to me. But you can never be too careful. And you two and I are in very grave danger while you are here. If any of this gets out, we're all dead men."

"Understood," Reynolds replied.

"May I call you Lando?" West asked.

"Yes, and you're Nathan?" Hernandez replied.

"Yes, thank you. Lando, where do you feel we need to concentrate our search?" West asked.

"The cartel's people are here every day. They roam the streets with impunity. The police will not touch them. They won't take the chance of having their families butchered."

"We understand that," Reynolds said. "Can you be more specific? I'm at the Tequendama. I realize Alejandro's family is there. Do you think he'll risk showing up?"

"Espinoza and the Medellin Cartel fear only one group and one man: Search Bloc run by General Marquez. If you know where Search Bloc is operating, that is the only place Espinoza will not be. He has more spies in Colombia than the entire Colombian army. The people love him. He has donated millions of dollars to open schools and hospitals in the poorest of neighborhoods. He's a saint here."

"How can we find out where General Marquez is operating without us contacting him directly?" West asked. "This is a black op. We're not communicating with anyone, including the DEA, Customs, or the Colombian National Army."

"That would be almost impossible," Hernandez said. "Without having someone on the inside of Search Bloc, you'll not know where they are. Espinoza will know, but you won't. I'm sure Espinoza has informants in Search Bloc. His tentacles reach far and wide. The only person he can't bribe is General Marquez."

"Why?" asked Reynolds

"Espinoza tried to kill the general with a car bomb. It didn't get him, but it killed his twenty-year-old daughter. Marquez will die trying to put Alejandro Espinoza in the dirt."

"Too bad we're not able to use Search Bloc's resources," West said.

"You're better off not associating with them. Alejandro would find out who you are and kill you both. Especially if he knew you were CIA."

"What do you recommend? Reynolds asked.

"Visit the clubs. Alejandro will not be there, but his brother Rafael loves the women and clubbing. He's a playboy. Marquez will not touch Rafael. He wants him free so they can follow him with hopes of finding Alejandro. If you can locate Rafael and get his travel pattern down, you have a chance. Other than that, gentlemen, you're wasting your time and endangering your lives. Colombia is like the Old West in America. If someone doesn't like you, they just kill you. Do not rely on any law enforcement here."

"We won't," West said.

Looking back and forth at West and Reynolds, Hernandez asked, "If you find Alejandro, whom are you turning him over to?"

"We're not; we're killing him," Reynolds replied.

There was a knock on the door.

"Come in," Hernandez said.

Lucia walked in with three cups of coffee on a large tray.

"Here you go, gentlemen," she said as she handed a cup to each man.

"Anything else, Mr. Hernandez?" she asked, standing there as the men stared.

"No, thank you, Lucia. That will be all."

"You're welcome," she said and turned to leave, shutting the door behind her.

All three men watched her leave.

"That is some woman," Reynolds said, swallowing.

"I have tolerated her for almost three years now. She can barely type, and her bookkeeping is not that great, but I can't force myself to fire her. Good luck, gentlemen," Hernandez said. "Your cover is solid here, but other than that, I can't help you."

SANITA WAS STILL IN BED, TRYING TO REST before going back out for what would be a very busy Friday night. She thought about what had occurred with Carlos. Running different scenarios through her head, she kept coming to the same conclusion: it had needed to be done. She was better off today than she was yesterday. Carlos valued here more than ever now, which she hoped, would benefit her cover in the future. As long as Rafael doesn't find out about the fling, I'm still good, she thought.

She needed to keep her eyes on the mission and handle all the other side distractions effectively. If she was able to do that, she felt confident Rafael would be wanting to bring her closer into his world. That's where she needed to be, in Rafael's bed, not Carlos's.

REYNOLDS AND WEST WALKED OUT OF CGI and got in the taxi waiting by the curb.

"Was there a pretty woman working in there?" Aguilar asked as he pulled out into Calle 19.

"Yes, a doll baby," Reynolds replied. "Have you seen her?"

"Yes, I've seen her before. So how did it go?" Aguilar asked, changing the subject.

"We've got our work cut out for us," West said. "Alejandro's basically a ghost hiding in plain sight."

"And we can't trust anybody but one man, and we can't talk to him," Reynolds added.

"So what's your plan?" Aguilar asked.

"I want to ask you a question," West said. "What happens to the cartel in the event of Alejandro's death? Does someone else step in, does the cartel fall apart, or what?"

"I've been here seven years," Aguilar said. "The way I look at that is Alejandro has not let anyone get close enough to him and or the operation to take over. His brother, Rafael, is an accountant. He doesn't have the murderous instincts that Alejandro has. Alejandro is a killer. There's a reporter that supposedly has gotten close to Alejandro, and I've given her rides. I've asked her what Alejandro was like. She said Jekyll and Hyde."

"So it would collapse?" West asked.

"Yes, it would, and the Cali Cartel is just waiting for that to happen. Cocaine is too big of a market. Somebody will take up the slack after Alejandro's dead."

"General, this is our latest tracking and triangulation equipment," Customs SAC Dale Wilson said, standing next to a table that held a portable receiver in Carlos Holquin School. "We got this from the CIA recently. With this on the ground and possibly in the air, we'll be able to track and triangulate a mobile phone's exact location. The problem will be to get there soon enough to catch the person using the phone. That's where your men come in. We need you to have several units stationed around the area we'll be working to respond in a moment's notice, or this will not be successful."

"What's the range and coverage?" the general asked.

"Miles, and 120 to 140 megahertz. But we must be very close to respond as quickly as possible. The triangulation works only as long as the phone is on, and hopefully it's not moving, at least not very far or very fast. If our receivers are on the ground, we are limited with obstructions from buildings and terrain. If we are lucky enough to have a receiver or two in the air, we'll be much better off."

General Marquez looked at Wilson and asked, "How long will we have to get a solid fix?"

"Twenty seconds, maybe thirty if we're lucky," Wilson replied.

Marquez looked back at the equipment, shook his head, and said, "Thirty seconds. What the hell are we to do with that?"

THAT EVENING THE GENERAL'S PHONE RANG. "Hello."

"I have your Taurus. I've been asked to go to Rio de Janeiro with Rafael this week," she said, before abruptly hanging up.

Placing the phone back in its cradle, the general thought, I pray it's not, but I fear it won't be long now; she's danger close. He shook his head with thoughts of his daughter and let out a big sigh.

CHAPTER 13

Romantic Get Away

8 a.m., Tuesday, April 13, 1993

Rafael had asked Carlos Rodriquez if Sanita could have a week off. Rodriquez wasn't about to say no to Espinoza, and Rafael whisked Sanita off to Rio de Janeiro in the cartel's private jet.

Before leaving, Rafael told Alex, "Come with me. You can meet Sanita, and you can bring Raya."

"I don't need to know your girlfriend, Rafael. The fewer number of people who know I work for you and Alejandro, the better. We are all safer that way, *mi amigo*."

"Ahhh, come on. I want your opinion of her."

Pausing, Sanchez looked at his boss and said, "Okay, if you like. I'll be there to pick you up on the way back. I can meet her then but only briefly, and do not tell her what I do."

"Wonderful," Rafael bellowed.

For the previous ten days, Rafael and Sanita had a very romantic time in Rio. She was wined and dined at the most expensive restaurants, and they stayed at the five-star Copacabana Palace, one of the world's most sought-after destinations for lovers. In the fantastically romantic ambiance, Sanita turned on her sexual charms.

She kept Alejandro exhausted in bed, and they embraced as if they had known each other for years. Sanita actually enjoyed Alejandro's advances and company. He is a gentlemen, she thought, not like his animal brother who will shoot a woman or child if it suits him.

On a mission, Sanita still kept her wall up, as only a woman can do. No matter how often she smiled, cooed, cuddled, or reached an orgasm, Alejandro was still a target. To her, this man was no different from the ones who had killed her sister. No amount of sex or money can sway a woman's heart when her sister paid for it with her life. She was locked on to the max, and she acted anything but. The only thing that bothered her that week was leaving her pistol in her room at the Tequendama; Rafael would surely have thought it odd if she was carrying a weapon. Other than that uncomfortable feeling, everything was working out perfectly.

"Do we really have to go back tonight?" Sanita pouted as she slid her tanned naked body under the sheet and back on top of Alejandro, straddling him. Moving her hips in a rhythmic motion, she ground her soft wet mound against his manhood as he threw off the sheet.

"If I stay here, you're going to kill me, my little rose." He smiled and glanced at the tattoo on her right ankle before he reached back and pulled her ass down on him even harder.

She arched her back as he leaned up and started kissing her breast.

"I'm falling in love with you," he said, sucking on one nipple and then the other as he gripped her rounded ass tighter and slapped it with his right hand.

"Mmmm," Sanita swooned as she reached back and guided his now hard manhood inside her.

For the past week and a half, West and Reynolds had become regulars at the several clubs and bars in their areas. They were becoming familiar with their new surroundings and local customs. The Colombian people were like any other people or culture. The vast majority were very nice and courteous souls who were trying to make the best of their own situations and living conditions.

The Colombians are very hard workers and love to party, sing, and dance. West thought his rock-and-roll music was loud as a teenager, but it paled in comparison to the music he was experiencing in the many clubs. These people knew how to have fun. Of course, no one past the age of fifty could hear worth a damn.

West had visited the Taya three times in the past week and never saw Sanita or the man called Rafael. He really needed to see Rafael again and get a clear look at the man's face.

"HELLO," MARQUEZ SAID, ANSWERING HIS PHONE.

"General, we have a location on a phone we think is Alejandro's," Customs SAC Dale Wilson said excitedly into the phone. We need to move now!"

"Where?" the general yelled back.

"Near the hospital. He's moving on Calle 80 and just passed Carrera 74, moving west."

The general picked up the radio mic in his other hand and said, "All units, all units. Target is moving west on Calle 80 near the hospital. All units respond to that area now!"

"Ahhh," Wilson said, on the phone. "We may have just lost the signal."

"What was said?" the general asked.

"Don't know who he was talking to, but he said Rafael was in Rio with his girlfriend, and it sounded like Alejandro."

"Roger," the general replied, knowing Sanita was in Rio de Janeiro with Rafael Espinoza.

"How long did we have the contact?" the general asked Wilson.

"Twelve seconds."

"Twelve seconds," the general repeated. "And we don't know what he's driving. How the hell will this ever work?"

"It's all we have, General. We're going to have to get lucky."

"I need more coverage. The twenty-man teams are too big and slow. I'm going to cut them down to five-man teams and locate them throughout the city. One vehicle per team with roving patrols. Maybe we'll get lucky that way."

"Yes, General. I think that would help. We need to be within a hundred meters after getting a location. Only then will we be able to respond quickly enough in this traffic to even have a chance."

The general nodded his head and said into the phone, "Yes, I'll give the orders."

LATER THAT DAY, WEST MET REYNOLDS AND AGUILAR at the Surtidora restaurant a couple of blocks from Santafe Suite for dinner.

"Needle in a haystack, fellas," West said to the men as they sat down in a corner booth.

"Yeah, I don't envy you two," Aguilar said from the other side. "This is practically impossible to do, wandering around and trying to find someone who has lived here all his life."

"Don't sell my partner short," Reynolds replied with a smile nudging West. "He has pulled some big pieces of shit out of his ass."

"Well, we'll see, Jack. But you're the bigger asshole," West said. "Seriously, have you identified anyone? I'm still batting zero."

"No, and I realize you'll run out of time soon," Reynolds said, looking at West. "We're into the middle of April now, so that gives us a little over three months to do something."

"Luis, any thoughts?" West asked.

"I received instructions from the director to assist General Marquez and Search Bloc. I gave some old triangulation equipment to Customs SAC Wilson. He'll get it to Marquez. I'll not go around their location at the old school. Too many cartel eyes watching that place."

"What type of equipment?" Reynolds asked.

"WWII type. They'll scan the radio waves from 120 to 140 megahertz and see if they can hear anything that sounds like cartel chatter. If something is heard, they can get a straight-line bearing. And if there are two or three units listening to the same conversation from different locations, they can get a pretty good triangulation on the signal."

"That's almost useless," Reynolds replied. "If the call is coming from a moving car, they will have seconds and that's all. Alejandro's not stupid; he's not going to sit still and talk on a phone for very long."

"Yeah, but Langley said deliver it, and Wilson was pleased."

"Are you getting regular intel from Wilson?" West asked.

"I am now. I can pass on anything that might be helpful," Aguilar said.

"All right. We need all the help we can get," West replied.

That evening the flight from Rio to Medellin was almost as romantic as the trip itself. Rafael and Sanita cuddled on the couch and kissed for almost three thousand miles. Rafael was head over heels at this point and had fallen deeply in love with Sanita's charms. He was thinking of a life with the young beauty and wondered how to extricate himself from the drug trade. He knew how dangerous his life was, and the last thing he wanted to do was bring Sanita into it.

Turning in his seat, Rico, the lead pilot, said to Rafael, "We land in ten minutes.".

"Thank you, Rico."

"I want us to get a place of our own. What do you think?" Rafael asked, looking at Sanita.

"What are you asking me?"

"I'm in love with you. I want you with me, but there are things about me you don't know and I don't want you to know."

"If I'm to be your woman, I need to know."

"Maybe soon, but not now. Would you be willing to move in with me if I got us a place away from everyone?"

"My darling, I just got out of a very horrible marriage. Can I have time to think about this?" Sanita replied, tilting her head and forcing a smile. No need to give in just yet, she thought. Keep him struggling.

"Yes, of course. I know this has been very quick. I have watched you sleep at night, and I know you are still running from something terrible."

Sanita looked at Rafael, and tears began to build in her eyes. Quickly wiping them, she looked out the jet's window and thought, I care too much for him, and I need to stop that now. But he is so sweet.

Rafael, seeing the tears, put his arms around Sanita, pulled her closer, and said, "It will be all right, *mi carino*."

She smiled and looked up.

He kissed her.

Rico saw the exchange and nudged the other pilot. "Rafael's in love," he whispered.

JORGE PULLED THE BLACK MERCEDES-BENZ 500E into the parking place next to a large silver metal-domed hangar at the Medellin International Airport.

"They should be landing any minute," Jorge said to Alex Sanchez as they both looked at the blue landing lights that trailed along the runway for a mile.

"I don't like being here. But Rafael is going to stay on my ass until I've met his new girlfriend."

"No harm in it, I guess," Jorge said.

Sanchez looked at Jorge and said, "Perhaps, but I don't like taking chances. And I really don't like being known by anyone. When people find out who you are, it can get you killed."

"Here comes a jet," Jorge said, watching the bright landing light of the aircraft break through the darkness and clouds and descend towards the runway.

"Remember, I'm just one of the hired help, a low-level nothing." Sanchez said.

"Yes, I got it."

"I'm not saying anything, and I'm not looking back at the woman or talking to Rafael. I'll get a good look at her after she gets off the plane, and I can tell Rafael how beautiful she is later," Sanchez added.

Jorge laughed and said, "Okay."

The Learjet landed, taxied up to the hangar, and then stopped. After a couple of minutes of letting the engines whine down, the left passenger door with steps began to extend and lower to the ground. Sanchez watched Rafael walk out the door and start down the stairs, followed by a woman. Its being dark, Sanchez leaned forward, squinted his eyes, and studied the woman as Rafael took her hand and led her towards the waiting sedan.

As Jorge was getting out of the car to open the back door, Sanchez hissed, “Shit,” under his breath and looked out his side window away from the couple.

CHAPTER 14

She's Customs

7:30 p.m., Wednesday, April 14, 1993

Jorge was standing next to the sedan with the back door and the trunk open as Rafael and the woman walked up to the sedan, followed by Rico who was carrying the woman's suitcase.

"You have a nice trip?" Jorge asked as he offered his hand to help the woman, who was now entering the back seat.

"Yes, lovely," she replied. "Thank you."

"Yes, amazing," Rafael said, smiling and getting in behind the woman.

"Wonderful," Jorge said as Rico put the suitcase in the trunk and shut the lid.

"Rafael, I'll fly the jet back to Bogota now," Rico said, as he turned to walk back towards the jet.

"Thank you, Rico," Rafael replied and then leaned over in the back seat to kiss Sanita and hold her hand.

"Wonderf—" Jorge stopped mid-word as he got back in the car and saw Sanchez holding his pistol on his lap. Repeatedly glancing at Sanchez, Jorge started the engine.

Sanchez would not look his way and then said, "Don't pull out."

"What?" Jorge asked.

"Rafael, did you have a great time?" Sanchez asked, still looking straight ahead so the woman in the back seat could not see his face.

Jorge continued to stare at him as he watched Sanchez move the pistol over to his left side with his right hand pointing it towards the back seat.

"Yes, I did. We had an amazing time," Rafael replied, squeezing Sanita's hand.

"Senorita, I'm sorry, but I didn't catch your name," Sanchez said.

"Hello, I'm Sanita."

"Sanita, that's a beautiful name for a very beautiful lady," Sanchez replied.

Rafael smiled and squeezed her hand even tighter hearing these words of praise coming from Sanchez. He knew he would find her beautiful too.

"What's your family name?" the man in the front seat asked.

Sanita kept looking at the back of the man's head and wondered who he was. "Perez," she said. "Do you know my family?"

"Sanita Perez, that's a very beautiful name. But it's not yours," Sanchez said as he turned in the seat and pointed the Glock at the woman. "Or maybe I should call you Mariana Garcia."

"Alex, what are you doing?" Rafael yelled.

"I'm sorry, Rafael, but this woman is not who she says she is."

"What do you mean?" Rafael asked, looking from Sanita to Sanchez.

"She was in Philadelphia when our group was arrested. Her name was Mariana Garcia then, and after the arrest, she disappeared. We never knew who the Customs undercover agent was."

"This can't be," Rafael said angrily.

"I'm sorry, Rafael, but it's true," Sanchez said.

"No, Alex. Put down your gun," Rafael pleaded.

"Rafael, as far as you know, have I ever seen this woman before?"

Rafael shook his head and said, "No."

"Then how do I know she has a tattoo of an upside-down red rose on her right ankle? I saw it on her in an apartment building in Philadelphia."

Rafael looked at Sanita and felt his heart break as she refused to glance his way. He let loose of her hand.

Glaring at Sanchez, Sanita knew she was dead, but she wouldn't let these bastards know her fear.

"Whom do you work for? Customs?" Sanchez asked.

"Go to hell."

"She's Customs," Sanchez said as Rafael backhanded her for the first time, causing blood from her lip to splatter onto the side window glass.

"You can go to hell too," she said, wiping the blood from her split lip and glaring at Rafael.

Sanchez reached across the seat and swiftly bashed her forehead with the Glock, causing a two-inch gash that showed skull and spurted blood. The blow knocked undercover US Customs Special Agent Angelina Lopez unconscious against the door. Pulling a flex-cuff out of his pocket, Sanchez handed it to Rafael and said, "I'm sorry. Put this on her wrist behind her back."

"I can't believe this," Rafael said as he grabbed her arms, pulled them behind her back, and tightened the nylon tie around her wrist.

"I'm sorry, Rafael," Sanchez repeated. "What do you want me to do with her?"

"Drive, Jorge," Rafael instructed. Still incredulous, he stared out the window, and then, looking back at Sanchez, he said, "The usual; take her to the ranch."

LATER THAT DAY, FORMER PRESIDENT GEORGE H. W. BUSH was scheduled to visit Kuwait and be honored for his victory in the Persian Gulf War. The day before, Kuwait Secret Service was alerted by the SVR to a car-bomb assassination attempt. The Kuwaitis found a massive car bomb near Bush's proposed travel route and arrested fourteen Iraqi IIS agents.

When President Crawford was notified by his chief of staff, he was livid. "That no-good piece of shit Hussein is still up to his tricks."

"Sir?" Chief of Staff Mack Lawrence asked, not understanding what the president meant.

"Mack, I'm going to make you privy to some top-secret information relayed to me by the CIA director. This is what the eyes-only meeting was about. I've known you a long time, and we've held closely guarded secrets before but none as important as what I'm about to tell you."

"Mr. President, you know my lips are sealed."

"Saddam Hussein was behind the World Trade Center bombing. He tried to include almost two thousand pounds of cyanide in the blast. It would have killed thousands and thousands, Mack. The three men that you brought in here a couple of weeks ago are a CIA team. They're the best they have. They stole the cyanide before it could be used. They saved countless lives, Mack.

"Hussein wants revenge for President Bush kicking his ass out of Kuwait. That's why he tried to kill him, and he's not done. He's now planning to build a nuclear bomb and use it on us or the Russians. The Russians have a double agent in Baghdad. He must be protected at all cost. He is the one that told us about the cyanide, and he's reporting on Hussein's nuclear program."

"My God," Lawrence said.

"Yes, Mack. Make inquiries to the Iraqi ambassador, and advise him that we are seriously looking into this assassination attempt. And if I get confirmation that Iraqi Intelligence is behind this, I'm doing something about it. But I won't jump too soon, so not to give the impression that I know anything about the World Trade Center cyanide and the fact that I'm already pissed. We need to continue to protect the SVR double agent and not even hint we know of him. You understand, Mack?"

"Yes, sir. I do."

"There's something else, Mack. I've sent that CIA team, called Team Thorn, to Colombia. They're there to find, capture, or kill Espinoza."

"I see, sir."

"To be absolutely truthful to you, Mack, I'm leaning towards kill, and they know it."

"Yes, sir. I figured that."

FOR THE REMAINDER OF THE WEEK, Reynolds and West did their normal routine of hanging out at the Hotel Tequendama bar or the Taya Night Club. Neither man was making any progress or developing any new leads.

"I wish Sanita would come back to work," West said to the man who was now tending the Taya bar.

"Who?" the bartender asked.

"A gal that works here, absolutely gorgeous."

"Oh, I know who you mean. She quit a few days ago. The owner said she moved back to Mexicali and she wouldn't be working here anymore."

"Well damn. She was a looker," West replied. "Mexicali, huh?"

"Si, that's what I was told."

West was just about ready to ask the man if he knew a Rafael, but decided that'd be plain stupid.

Rancho Blanca, Bogota
10 p.m., Saturday, April 17

"IF I EVER GET OUT OF THESE ROPES, I'm going to kill every last one of you bastards!" the naked Lopez screamed as she tried to force the broom handle that was tied to the foot of the bed out of her vagina. She lay splayed out with her arms and legs tied to the four corners of the bed. And this was the third day. Her vagina, wrist, and ankles were raw and bleeding from the broom handle and the coarse hemp rope digging into her flesh with every movement. Her forehead laceration was almost blood scabbed over, but you could still see a thin line of pearly white skull in the center of the gash. The seven men in the kitchen across the hall laughed and continued to drink the Aguardiente and play cards at the kitchen table.

"Juan, give her some more coke," one of the men said. "Shut her the hell up, and take her if you can. The bosses said to use her up and then dump the body. After that, the rest of these assholes can go back to Medellin where they live."

The men at the table laughed as Juan got up, picked up a plastic bag of cocaine and walked across the hall into the bedroom.

"I'm all spent, but here you go you little coke whore," he said as he got cocaine on his right index finger, grabbed her jaw with his left hand, and held her weakened head still while he shoved the white-covered finger up her left nostril and held it there until the cocaine was almost completely absorbed. Feeling her body go limp once more and watching her eyes roll back into her head, he pulled his finger out and rubbed it against her upper teeth gums until the finger was moist and clean. "That will hold you for a couple of hours, you little bitch," he said and walked back to the card game.

Medellin
7 a.m., Sunday, April 18

Former Navy SEAL and now lead CIA Special Agent in Bogota, Colombia, Luis Aguilar called Reynolds. "I need to see you and Nate ASAP. It's important," he said, holding the phone to his ear and looking at the tall slender man wearing the gray suit that was pacing back and forth in the hotel room.

"All right, pick me up. I'll call Nate and tell him we'll pick him up later," Reynolds said, wondering what the hell had happened.

"Roger that. I'll be there in a little over an hour," Aguilar said. Standing up to leave, he looked at the Customs Special Agent in Charge and said, "Dale, I'll let you know what they say."

The SAC looked forlorn and nodded his head. "Tell them I need their help in getting her back."

"I will," Aguilar replied.

Sixty-five minutes later, the yellow cab pulled up to Hotel Tequendama's curb, and the big man got in the back seat.

"What going on?" Reynolds asked.

Aguilar handed a large manila envelope over the seat to Reynolds and said, "We're missing an agent. Her picture's in the envelope." Then he turned the yellow cab towards Santafe Suite a couple of blocks away.

"Beautiful lady," Reynolds said after he pulled the picture out and looked at the Hispanic woman. "How long has she been missing?" he asked, sliding the picture back in the envelope.

"Last contact was on the second, so a week, maybe two. We don't know. She was to check in once a week with the general," Aguilar said as he made the turn on Carrera 16. Seeing a man leaning against the hotel in jeans and a black T-shirt, he pulled up to the curb.

West opened the rear door and jumped in the back seat of the cab next to Reynolds. "What's going on?" he asked, looking at Reynolds and Aguilar.

"We're missing an agent," Reynolds said, handing the envelope to West.

"How long?" West asked and took the envelope and slid the picture out.

"Week or more," Reynolds said.

"Oh my God," West groaned, staring at the photo and then looking at Reynolds.

"What?" Reynolds asked, looking intently at West.

"That's Sanita."

"Who?" Aguilar said from the front seat.

"Oh shit," Reynolds said, gritting his teeth.

"Who the hell is Sanita?" Aguilar asked again as he drove.

"Barmaid at the Taya Night Club. I met her a couple of weeks ago," West replied. "Who does she work for, and what's her real name?"

"Customs Service, Special Agent Angelina Lopez," Aguilar replied, pulling to the side of the road where he could see no one walking.

"Ahhhh, dammit," West growled. Touching the photo, he slid it back into the large manila envelope and dropped it into the front seat.

"What are you going to do?" Aguilar asked as he put the cab in park and turned in his seat to look at the men who now had looks of determination on their faces.

Reynolds stared at West who glared at the floor and took several deep breaths.

Looking up, West said, through clinched teeth, "I'm going to find her and kill the sons of bitches who took her."

"She's more than likely already dead," Aguilar said, frowning. "They'll rape, torture, and kill her in the most brutal ways. And besides, you have no idea who took her or where to look. Do you?"

Reynolds was still staring at West when West looked up and met his gaze.

"The hell I don't," he said. "Rafael Espinoza. Jack, there's been a change in plans."

Reynolds sat back in the seat, thought for a few moments, and said, "All right. Let's find her, kill the bastards, and get her home. We can bury the Espinozas later, and if we're real lucky, we can do it all at the same time."

"No man or woman left behind," West said, now looking intently at the former SEAL.

"Roger that," Aguilar replied nodding. "I'm all in."

"Yes, we leave no one behind, gentlemen," Jack Reynolds, former captain of the Green Berets instructed, looking keenly at the men.

CHAPTER 15

The Hunt Is On

8 a.m., Monday, April 19, 1993

"Is she still alive?" Rafael asked from a chair in the living room, rubbing his face with his hands and then brushing his long black hair back over his head.

"Yes," Sanchez replied as he leaned against the wall and sipped on the large white cup filled with black coffee.

"How could I've been so blind and stupid? I almost got us all killed."

"Brother, they're here hunting us as we speak," replied, Alejandro, leaning forward from the couch. "We can't trust anyone who we don't already know and have trusted in the past. Any newcomer must be avoided, or we'll all die."

Rafael sat back in his chair and put his bare feet up on the plush red velour ottoman in the hidden home in the middle-class barrio of Los Olivos, Medellin.

"I was in love with her, but knowing of her betrayal of me, us, wiped that away before Alex dragged her out of the car. I'll not make the same mistake again."

Looking at Sanchez, Rafael said, "Feed her to the dogs when the men are finished with her."

Sanchez nodded and took another sip of coffee.

Alejandro smiled.

"LUIS, I NEED A KNIFE, KA-BAR or British stiletto if you have one," West said on the phone from his room in the Santafe.

"I have a couple Mark IIIs. I can loan you one."

"That'll work. Sharpen it for me, I don't have a stone here."

"It'll already shave the hair on your arm."

"Excellent. When can you drop it off?"

"Be there in five mikes. I have one with me. I just dropped off a fare. See you on the curb."

"Roger that. Oh and bring some electrician's tape."

"You won't need it. Its sheath has elastic and Velcro for your ankle. I'm wearing it now."

"You're the man. See you on the street," West said and started out his door.

Walking down the stairs, he kept running through his mind what he was going to do next. One thing for certain, it was going to be bloody. Wading through the whores and drug dealers who now left him alone, he waited for the cab.

No need wasting energy, they thought. The man had already turned each one of them down a dozen times.

Seeing Aguilar's cab pull up to the curb, he got in the back seat, and it pulled back out. "Drive around town for a few minutes. I need to ask you some questions," West said.

"No problem. What's your plan?"

"I'm going to find the owner of the Taya and make it so uncomfortable for him that he tells me what I want. Then I'm cutting his throat. I need to do this as quietly as I can."

Aguilar looked in his rearview mirror at the determination on West's face and said, "You'll definitely need this then," and handed the SEAL knife he had taken off his ankle back over the seat to West.

Taking the knife out of the molded black plastic sheath with straps, West flicked his left thumb across the edge of the blade. "Yeah, it's sharp," he said. "Any news from Search Bloc?"

"No, but I keep getting vibes that nothing's working out for them yet. President Crawford has agreed to Wilson's request to allow a team from Delta Force to join with Marquez. They've already arrived."

"How many men?" West asked.

"Twelve, from the First Special Forces Operational Detachment. But something just isn't right?"

"What do you mean?"

"They're being hamstrung. It's like they want them there, but they're not using them to their advantage. They've separated them and put one Delta Team member with each team of General Marquez's men."

"Why that? I'm sure they're all excellent men, but bust up a team?"

"It's what the president said to do. It's not unusual for Special Forces team members to be sent into areas or groups to help train and fight. But you almost never hear of an entire team being separated to the man. At least it's very rare. It's almost as if the president doesn't want Marquez to catch Espinoza. It's like he's doing this for show."

West thought for a moment and said, "I know why the president's doing it."

"Why?"

"He's waiting on us to find and kill Alejandro. Another thing, how long do I have to find the agent?"

"Honestly, Nate, she's probably already dead. Did you know her before here? I sense you have an attachment to her."

"No, never met her before the Taya. But I'm former Customs, and she reminds me of someone I knew in San Fran, Special Agent Kit Wallace, a very special lady."

Aguilar nodded his head as he drove. "I understand."

"One last thing," West said. "Who's the owner of the Taya, where does he live, and what does he drive?"

THE BROOM HANDLE HAD BEEN UNTIED from the foot of the bed and pulled out of Angelina's bleeding and swollen vagina as the two men began to use the woman. This was day five, and she barely had the strength to attempt to spit at the men anymore. Her mouth was so dry and lips swollen and cracked that the spit sat on her bottom lip as a small patch of white-and-blood-tinged foam. "You piece of shit," she barely groaned.

"No, bitch. I'm in your shit," the man said as he pounded harder on the woman. Several minutes had gone by when he finally let loose with his ejaculate.

Angelina was looking into the corner and ignored the dirty filthy man with breath like a sewer.

"Ahhh, there you go bitch," he said as he stopped thrusting, lay down on the agent for a few moments, and slowly withdrew.

"Your turn," he said to his partner. He climbed off the bed and began to pull his dirty jeans back on.

The next man picked up a water bottle sitting on the wooden crate next to the bed and poured a small amount into the woman's mouth.

"Why you doing that?" Sewer Breath asked, zipping up his pants.

"I won't have sex with a corpse, and she's real damn close. A little water will keep her alive for another day or two. I kinda like the whore."

"Okay, whatever you want. But you know we can get a fresh one in here next week."

Angelina tried to swallow the water. The voices seemed so far away. Partially opening her swollen and bruised eyes, she could see her sister hovering over top of the bed next to the ceiling. She was beckoning with her arms, and her lips were moving saying, "Come with me, come with me."

"Danielle," Sanita croaked and tried to smile as the other man climbed on top and entered her bleeding cavity. Tears streamed down her face as she closed her eyes once more smelling the stench of the man. I'm ready Lord, she thought.

AGUILAR PULLED BACK UP TO THE CURB by the Santafe and said, "Good luck, brother."

"Thanks. I'll let you know what I find and give Jack a call when I get in the room," West said as he got out of the cab.

"How does it feel?" Aguilar asked.

"Feels tight. Thank you," West replied and shut the door.

Walking past the usual crowd, he took the stairs to room 302. After getting inside, he put his right leg up on the chair and pulled up the pant leg. The Mark III was securely held with the elastic straps and Velcro against his outside ankle and calf. Pulling the knife up out of its sheath, he felt the weight and balance of the killing tool. "I like it," West said and slid the blade back into the sheath and pulled his pant leg back down, concealing the knife.

Taking his phone out of his pocket, he sat down on the edge of the bed and called Reynolds.

"Hello," he answered.

"Jack, what're your plans for tonight?"

"I'm supporting you, whatever you want."

"All right. Can you be here at 12:30 a.m.? I'm going to the Taya tonight and find Carlos Rodriquez."

"Who's he?"

"The owner of the Taya. If Rafael Espinoza was a customer of his, he'll know that. I bet he's selling some of their coke too. He'll also know what happened to Angelina, especially if Espinoza found out she was an agent. He'll threaten Rodriquez to be more careful in whom he hires."

"All right, I'll be there. We can talk more then."

"Roger that. I'm taking a nap," West said, and the men hung up.

12:30 a.m., Santafe Suite

Reynolds knocked on room 302.

Looking through the peephole, West could see Reynolds and Aguilar standing in the hall. "What's the all-clear phrase?" West asked.

"Is a frog's ass watertight?" Reynolds replied.

West unlocked the door.

"I brought reinforcements," Reynolds said as he walked into the room and shook hands with West.

"Sounds good to me," West replied and then shook hands with Aguilar. "Thanks for coming."

"I need to make sure I get my blade back," Aguilar said. "What's with the frog's ass shit?"

"You remember that phrase. That's our all clear. Is a frog's ass watertight," Reynolds repeated. "It means yes because, of course, a frog's ass is watertight."

Aguilar chuckled. "Got it." He sat down at the small table with Reynolds.

"What's your plan?" Reynolds asked West.

"I'm going to the Taya and locate Rodriquez. I'll play it by ear, so if you don't hear from me tonight, don't send the calvary. I may need to hide myself somewhere and wait. If that happens, I'll not move until the time's right."

"Roger that," Reynolds said. "The hunt is on."

"Yes, it is," West replied. "I'll have my phone turned off so it won't do you any good to call. But keep yours on, and if it rings, don't say anything. Just listen for taps. I may be close to someone and will communicate with Morse code by taping on the mic."

"Damn, I feel like I'm back with the teams," Aguilar said.

CHAPTER 16

Invisible

12:45 a.m., Tuesday, April 20, 1993

West stood in the bathroom and pulled the black short-sleeve T-shirt down over the Model 39, 9mm shoved in his front waist belt slightly right of center.

"Jack, if I had a belly like yours, I wouldn't be able to do this."

"Kiss my ass, I still do it."

Pulling up his right pant leg, West pulled the SEAL fighting knife from the sheath and walked out of the bathroom. Flipping the knife in his right hand from its handle to the blade, West turned and threw the knife into the bathroom door frame, sticking it firmly into the wood. "Ten feet's about right. I needed to know," he said, looking at the men. He extracted the knife from the frame, pulled his pant leg back up, and replaced the knife in its sheath.

All three men looked at each other, and none said, a word.

Walking to his bed, West picked up a map of Medellin and, after folding it, put it in his back pocket.

"Think you're going to get lost?" Reynolds asked.

West smiled and said, "No, but someone's bloody stub may be on it before the night's over."

"You guys are serious shit," Aguilar said.

West walked to the door, turned as he opened it, and said, "There's some arepas in the fridge and coffee in the cupboard. Make yourselves at home."

"Good luck, Yeager," Reynolds said, getting up from the table and walking to the door.

"What?" West said, as he turned to face Reynolds.

"Chuck Yeager. He's from West Virginia too, isn't he?"

"Yes, he's a Lincoln-county boy."

"Well, he has big balls too. Would you prefer I call you Chuck?"

West smiled and said, "No. Yeager's fine. Thanks." He walked out the door. Reynolds shut it behind him, and West heard a loud metallic click as Reynolds locked the door from the inside.

1:00 a.m.

"Is she still alive?"

"Yes. Barely, but yes, she's alive," Rico said.

Rafael looked at the floor while holding the phone to his right ear and held his forehead with the other hand. "I want her fed, and give her something to drink. When she's able, let her take a shower."

"Yes, Rafael. But we're deciding on where to dump her body. I thought perhaps to throw her out of the Cessna over the jungle."

Rafael sat down in the chair next to the phone and continued to hold his forehead while resting his elbows on his legs. "Ahhhh, noooo," Rafael said while letting out a deep sigh. "I can't do this. I want her kept alive. Do you understand? I want her kept alive. Stop the coke and stop using her. Keep the men away from her."

"Yes, Rafael. I'll do whatever you say. I'll give her something as soon as I get off the phone," Rico replied, sitting in the kitchen of the house where some of the enforcers and the pilot lived.

"Okay, get started, and call me back in the morning. Let me know how she's doing. In a few days, I'll come over," Rafael said and hung up.

Hanging up the phone, Rico looked at the big man across the table and said, "Wilfredo, you can't take her no more. Rafael wants her alive. We need to give her some food and water."

"Why the change?" the big sewer-breath man asked.

"Rafael loves her. It was obvious on the jet."

RAFAEL LAID THE RECEIVER IN THE phone cradle and covered his face with his hands as he sat in the chair. "What have I become? What have I done? I can't do this anymore," he said. He got up and walked out of the home in the dark night and stood in the middle of the street, Carrera 79B, near the Estadio Girardot, the soccer stadium.

1:10 a.m., La Catedral Heights

GENERAL MARQUEZ, DALE WILSON, and Master Sergeant Tim Holloway, leader of the Delta Team, were looking out from the guard tower on the high ridge at La Catedral. Down in the valley, the city lights of Medellin were bright, and you could easily make out people on the sidewalks and cars in the streets.

"Being this elevated on the ridge, we can look down into the city. This is where the microwave repeater and the remote-controlled zoom camera need to go," Holloway said. "From here, we can send the signal from the camera to our base at the school with the microwave. We'll have real-time info on what the camera can pick out in the city and be able to visually follow a car down many of the streets. If we can get a fix on a phone and then visual confirmation on a car at the same location, we can nail the bastard even after he hangs up."

"We need to do something fast, or I fear my agent will be dead," Wilson said.

"She's already dead, Dale," the general said, wincing. "It's been many days, and we've lost all contact with her. The longer they keep her alive, the more they're at risk. They're not going to take that chance." The general shook his head, thinking of La Ninita.

"You're probably right, General, but I'm not stopping until I find a corpse. I know the president is sending additional CIA help. Hopefully we can find Lopez before it's too late." Turning to look at Holloway, Wilson said, "Let's get it done and fast."

"Yes, sir," Master Sergeant Holloway replied. "I'll have it operational by daylight."

1:15 a.m.

Wearing his black T-shirt, jeans, and Nikes, West waded through the whores and drug dealers the two blocks to the Taya. The night was sticky and the air close. He could feel the sweat forming on his chest as he walked on the crumbling sidewalk and kept glancing from side to side to see if he sensed any danger. None so far. He checked his six often with a glance.

Angelina Lopez, he thought. Beautiful name for the agent. He then thought of what they were doing to her right now. He knew she was being tortured and raped. Stay alive, Angelina. I will find you.

Walking up the stairs to the Taya entrance, West nodded to the bodyguard and said, "Good evening, El Hombre."

"Good evening, Mr. West," the big man said.

"Any good-looking women in here tonight?"

"Every night," the man said with a smile as he opened the door.

In the doorway, West stopped and said, "I bet the owner enjoys many of these ladies."

"Si, he watches them every night from his upstairs office," he said, nodding his head towards the dark glass on the second floor over the dance floor. "He gets his pick," the man said with a laugh.

"Good for him," West replied as he walked in. "Thank you, amigo."

"You're welcome, Mr. West."

West walked to the bar along the right wall and took the first stool on the end. "Good evening, Maceo," he said to the bartender who had replaced Sanita.

"Hi, Nate. Aquila Light?" he asked.

"Si, thank you," West replied as he looked around and glanced at the large dark-glass window on the second floor.

Maceo set down the bottle of beer with the yellow-and-blue label in front of West.

"*Gracias.*"

"*De nada.*"

"Maceo, what's behind the dark glass upstairs?"

"That's the boss's office. He keeps track of everything that goes on down here."

"He sees everyone that comes and goes?"

"Si. If he sees a customer that has caused trouble in the past, he calls down to Miguel and tells him to throw him or her out. But it's mostly men."

"Hmmm. Does he ever come down? I've not seen him I don't think."

"Very rarely. Short, stocky with a goatee. Big gold chain around his neck. You can't miss him."

Hmmm. No I don't think I've ever seen the man."

"Between me and you, he's *estupido.*"

"I don't know that word."

"He's a stupid asshole."

West chuckled and took another drink of Aquila Light. Good; that makes this easier, West thought.

1:20 a.m.

Angelina Lopez was lying on her right side for the first time in almost a week. There was no way she could stand; breathing was hard enough. Not having anything to eat and barely anything to drink for days had almost killed her. The cocaine and the blood loss had amplified her weakened state. Both of her eyes were now swelled shut but for two small slits where she could just make out a man sitting in a chair next to the bed holding a cup of chicken broth. She had a continuous headache from the healing gash in her forehead after being pistol whipped by Sanchez. Her insides felt like they had been ripped out. She wondered if she would ever be able to have children, that is, if she lived.

The man put a small amount of broth on the spoon he was holding and said, "Here, take a little more," as he put the spoon into her open mouth and tilted the spoon until the liquid lay in her cheek.

It took several tries, but she was finally able to swallow the tiny amount of nourishment. She felt extremely nervous, coming off of the high amount of cocaine that had been forced into her body. But at least she was hungry and tried to swallow as much of the broth as the man would give. She knew the side effects of the cocaine would be out of her system in a couple of days, and she needed to be strong when she tried to escape.

If I can get a gun, I'm killing every one of these sons of bitches, she thought. She wondered where Sewer Breath was. I'm going to castrate him first before I kill him. This man, she thought, looking through her matted and dingy black hair dangling over her face as he spooned in some more broth, I may let him live. She swallowed several times and closed her eyes.

Taya
1:50 a.m.

"Good night, Maceo," West said, laying down a twenty-dollar bill and sliding off the black-leather-covered stool.

"Good night, Nate," the bartender replied, "Thanks for the tip."

"*De nada*," West replied and walked out the door.

West circled the block once to get a good look at the area before slipping into the alley behind the night club. Being Monday night and into Tuesday morning, most people were not out partying. They had just exhausted themselves over the weekend and were trying to sober up to be ready for the rest of the week.

Walking in behind the Taya, West could see a silver BMW. "That's got to be his," West whispered. He studied the back of the building. There was an outside staircase that went to the second-floor landing. With the light shining over the upper-level door, West could see a door of steel grating that was swung open and rested against the wall. That's the last thing he'll lock, West thought.

Looking around and not seeing anyone, West climbed the stairs without a noise from his soft Nike running shoes. The concrete steps and upper landing were perfect for his silent approach. Getting to the light, he reached up and quickly unscrewed the hot bulb until it stopped glowing. West stepped back into the dark shadows, touched his 9mm, and became invisible.

CHAPTER 17

He Just Struggled a While

Bogota
2:30 a.m., Tuesday April 20

Carlos Rodriquez was counting the money in the cash register after everyone had left and he had locked the front door from the inside. Each day, he started with one hundred dollars in bills and coins in the cash box. After putting the extra money in the blue money bag, he closed the register and walked through the doorway behind the bar and up the old wooden stairs to his office. The stairs creaked with each step as they had for years from the overweight man. In the office, he tossed the blue bag into the open large, black floor safe next to his desk. Shutting the heavy door, he spun the dial to lock it.

West heard the stairs creaking in the dark quiet night as he stood in the shadows. He knew it wouldn't be long now as he pulled the pistol from his waist belt and readied it in his right hand, squeezing the wooden grips.

Rodriquez picked up a partially smoked cigar from his desk, put it in his mouth, and lit it from a skull lighter sitting there. Putting the lighter back down, he took a big drag of the tobacco, tilted his head back, and let the mellow smoke roll slowly out of his mouth saying, "These Tintos are better than Cubans." Taking another long drag, he picked up his car keys from the desk and walked to the door, leaving his desk lamp on.

"Damn porch light must be burnt out," he said as he opened the door and stepped out onto the landing in the dark. Rodriquez turned to lock the door and then felt the barrel of a gun being shoved up against the side of his head.

"If you don't do exactly as I say, I'm going to blow your head off. Do you understand?"

"Si."

"Walk back into your office."

"Si," he said and opened the door.

As he stepped into the room, West quickly bashed the man over the back of his head with the pistol, knocking him to the floor. West glanced at the unconscious man, shoved the pistol into his belt, and then turned and locked the door behind them. Looking back around the dimly lit room, he saw the black safe. That'll do, West thought.

West grabbed the man by his right arm and dragged him across the floor to the safe while he groaned but was still unable to move. West pulled a large black flex-cuff out from under his belt on the left side where he kept one stored. Rolling the man onto his stomach, West pulled the man's arms up behind his back, wrapped the flex-cuff around both wrists, and cinched it tight. West then pulled his second flex-cuff from under the right side of his belt and used it on the man's ankles, tying his feet tightly together.

Pulling off one of the man's shoes, West peeled down and removed one sock, shoving it into his right front pants pocket. He rolled the man over onto his back, grabbed him under his arms, and slid him up against the safe in a seated position.

"Big bastard, you need to lose some weight," West quietly said as he stood, looked at the man, and started repeatedly kicking his bare foot.

The man began to groan more and finally opened his eyes. "Who are you and what do you want?"

"I'm here to kill you unless you tell me exactly what I want. *Comprende?*"

"Si. I will tell you whatever you want. I need to leave soon. My wife will wonder why I haven't come home."

"That's bullshit, amigo. She'll just figure you're banging one of the girls that works for you."

The man stared at the gringo and asked, "What do you want?"

"I'll make this quick. Where's Sanita?"

"I don't know. She quit last week. I was told she went back to Mexico," he stammered.

West looked around the room and saw a black-and-red pillow with a matching folded blanket on a small flowery-print couch in the corner. "I'm going to ask you one more time, amigo. Where's Sanita?" he said as he walked to the couch, picked up the pillow, and returned to the hogtied man. "Tell me," West said as he dropped the pillow on the floor and pulled the sock out of his pocket.

"I'm telling you the truth. She went back to Mexi—ahhhh," he mumbled as West bent over, grabbed the man by the throat, and shoved the sock deeply into his mouth. Picking up the pillow, West placed it over Rodriquez's left knee, pulled out his 9mm, shoved the barrel hard into the pillow to muffle the blast, and pulled the trigger. The 9mm slug tore down through Rodriquez's knee joint, shattered the bone, and lodged in the floor underneath.

"Ahhhh!" he tried to scream.

"Does Rafael have her?" West asked, looking at the man and then picking up the pillow and putting it on the right knee.

"Ahhhh," he garbled while nodding his head yes, his eyes wide with terror and pain.

"Is she alive?"

"Ahhhh," he garbled again, raising his shoulders a couple of times and shaking his head no.

"Do you know if she's alive or dead?"

"Ahhhh," came out of his mouth as he again shook his head no.

"I'm going to take the sock out of your mouth, but if you scream, I'll cut your throat. Understand?"

"Ahhhh," the man said, nodding his head yes.

West pulled the sock out, dropped it on the man's lap, and asked, "Where are they keeping her?"

"I don't know for sure," Rodriquez gasped, heaving for breath and almost fainting from the pain.

"You pass out on me and I'm killing you."

"I'm . . . telling . . . the truth," he said, gasping. "Don't know . . . exactly . . . heard they take women . . . to enforcer's house . . . and rape them."

"Who are their enforcers?"

"Don't . . . know," he struggled to say. "No one. . . knows, b-but . . . pilot lives . . . with them."

"What's his name?"

"Rico. . . . I've met him . . . here."

"After Rafael took her, what did they say to you?"

"Alejandro . . . would kill me . . . if I hire someone . . . from outside."

"Where is their plane kept?"

The man winced in pain, gasped, and said, "Bogota Airport. . . . Picked up cocaine there."

"Where?"

"Northwest end near Bogota River. . . . Rico comes from . . . Bogota River Bridge Road. . . . Connects to Avenida Calle 24. . . . Gated entrance there, a guard," he said, trying to speak over the pain.

"Where's the hangar?"

"Past the guard shack . . . on the right. Big . . . dome shaped. On right side . . . of runway for private jets."

West slid the pistol back into his belt, stood up and found a pen on the desk next to the skull lighter. Kneeling back down he said, "Hold this in your teeth and make a mark," as he placed the pen in the man's mouth and him biting down.

Pulling the map of Bogota out of his back pocket, West opened it up and could see the airport emblem on the northwest side of Bogota. He held the map up to the man's face and said, "Touch the bridge."

Shoving the pen against the map, the man placed a single black dot on a road crossing the Bogota River.

West took the pen out of the man's mouth and dropped it to the side as he looked at the map. "You sure Rico crosses that bridge?" he asked, looking intently at the man's face.

"Yes . . . positive," Rodriquez replied, gasping. "Pain is terrible . . . going to throw up. . . . Help me . . . please?"

"Yeah," West said as he folded the map back up and placed it in his back pocket. Pulling up his pant leg, he slid the SEAL knife out with his right hand. Grabbing Rodriquez by his black hair with his left, he jerked his head forward.

"Whaaa?" Rodriquez said in disbelief. "Noo—" the man tried to yell, but the scream was cut short and became a gurgle.

The knife slashed across Rodriquez's throat until it hit bone. Blood gushed over the knife, West's right hand, and up his arm as the man struggled to take one more breath. West stood up to get away from the squirting blood as the red life dripped from the end of the blade. The man convulsed and tried to kick and thrash his bound arms and legs.

West walked to the couch and wiped the knife on the blanket as the kicking slowed. Bending over, he slid the blade back in its sheath and pulled the pant leg back down.

"What do you think Special Agent Angelina Lopez is feeling right now, you piece of shit?" West said, watching the man gurgle blood and stare at him until his pupils dilated and became fixed. The man's legs were still twitching when West locked the door behind him and headed to Santafe Suite. Rico is next, he thought.

Ten minutes later, he used his key to get in room 302. Both men were sitting at the small dinette table drinking coffee. Looking at West, neither man said anything as West walked into the bathroom to wash off.

In the mirror, he could see why nothing was said. He had dried blood all over his face where it had squirted thin lines. "Hmmm, didn't feel that. But I was busy," he said to the men as he picked up a white washcloth off the sink side rail and turned on the cold water. Getting it wet, he washed his face and arms.

Both men watched him.

"I got a good lead," West said.

"That's good," Reynolds said. "Have any problems?"

"No. None I couldn't take care of."

"Gentlemen, if this is how you work, I'm honored to be with you on this," Aguilar, the former Navy SEAL said, looking at West and then Reynolds.

West walked out of the bathroom and leaned against the wall. "Rafael Espinoza took her. She's at a house where the cartel's enforcers live. Their pilot also lives there. His name is Rico. I know where they keep their plane."

"Who gave you this information, the guy that bled all over you?" Reynolds asked.

"Yeah, the owner of Taya, Carlos Rodriquez."

"This is probably a stupid question, but is he able to cause us any problems?" Aguilar asked. "Because he's a heavy roller with Espinoza."

"No, we called in the dogs and pissed on the fire. It just took a little effort before the flames died out."

Reynolds looked at West and said, "That's a new one. But I understand what you're saying."

"I'm lost," Aguilar said, looking at West.

"No, the asshole's dead; he just struggled a while."

"Roger that."

"You mind if I keep your blade a while longer, Luis? I like it."

"Brother, it's yours now. She's now part of your fighting heart and legacy."

"Thank you," West said, rubbing at a blood spot on his right arm he'd missed. "I need to see Rico next."

CHAPTER 18

SHE MUST NOT DIE

3 a.m., Tuesday, April 20

"LUIS, I NEED YOUR HELP WITH SOMETHING," West said, still leaning against the wall and rubbing on the blood spot.

"Whatever, just say when," Aguilar replied.

"I need you to make a phone call for me to the Bogota Airport later tonight."

"What are you planning?" Reynolds asked.

"Years ago when I was stationed in Coos Bay, Oregon, there was a man by the name of Ray Hurst who was a drug smuggler. He had a small plane at the Gold Beach Airport that he used in his smuggling operation. Instead of kicking in his door to arrest him and possibly getting someone shot, I called him and said I was the airport and his plane had been broken into. He immediately left his home, and we arrested him on the highway to the airport without incident.

"Luis we're going to need two cars, one for me and one for Jack. When Jack and I get in position, I need you to call the airport and say Espinoza's hangar has been broken into. The airport will know whom to call, and they'll not take the chance of not calling Rico. Jack, we'll wait at the airport for Rico to come and check on his plane. We'll then follow him back to where he lives with the enforcers and hopefully Sanita."

"Angelina. I can get the cars in a couple of hours," Aguilar said. "And let's do this. Whenever you're out of the car, lock it and leave the key on top of the right rear tire in case someone else needs the car."

"Roger that," West replied, looking at Jack who nodded.

"Sounds like a plan," Reynolds said.

"Who wants some coffee?" West asked as he got a pot, filled it with water, put it on the stove, and pulled the instant coffee jar out of the cupboard.

Rancho Blanca
5 a.m.

"CAN YOU SIT UP?" RICO ASKED as he placed a pillow against the wall at the head of the bed.

"I need help," Lopez weakly replied, trying to get her arms in position to push herself up. But she could barely move her head, let alone lift her body.

Rico placed her arm over his shoulder, reached around the frail woman, and slid her up against the pillow.

"Why are you helping me?" she groaned weakly.

Looking at the women, he whispered, "My name is Rico. Rafael called earlier and ordered me to start taking care of you," as he pulled a sheet up over Lopez's naked and bruised body. "He couldn't live with himself. He loves you."

A tear began to run down her cheek as she began to weep. Looking up she said, "Thank you."

"I'm going to get you some soup and some clothes. I'll be right back."

Search Bloc Headquarters
5:15 a.m.

GENERAL MARQUEZ PACED BACK AND FORTH in front of the men

seated in the large converted classroom. "How many calls have we intercepted, Dale?"

"Seven," Customs SAC Wilson replied.

"Seven," Marquez yelled as he stopped and glared at the men. "Seven and we still have nothing. How soon will we get the CIA air support?" Marquez asked, now looking back at Wilson.

"I've been told soon, sir. I'm in close contact with the local agent, and he said it will not be long. They are expediting it due to our current situation," Wilson stated, without exposing the information on Lopez.

Marquez shook his head, closed his eyes, and silently breathed, "Ninita." Looking again at Wilson, he turned to face his men. "Master Sergeant Holloway."

"Yes, sir."

"I want you to set up two strike teams, six men each, three of my men and three Delta operators."

"Yes, sir."

"I want the city divided in half, north and south, with our location here the dividing line. Place one strike team one mile north and the other one mile south."

"Yes, sir."

"The remainder of our men will now be two-man teams to a car. We must get more coverage and faster response. That will give us thirty two-man surveillance cars. I want fifteen teams north and fifteen south."

"Yes, sir."

"Dale, we need those CIA planes as soon as we can get them, and make sure they have their own monitors. If we can get a triangulation with the planes and from the tower on La Catedral, we'll have a much better chance of having a surveillance team nearby. With the tower camera and from the air, we may get eyes on a car so we know what we're looking for."

"Yes, General, I'll do that," Wilson replied.

The general turned to his men and said, "Dismissed. Master Sergeant get on it."

"Yes, sir. We'll be in new operational status in one hour, sir."

General Marquez waited until the other men left the room. Turning to Wilson he asked, "Can I meet this CIA agent?"

"No, General. The agency won't allow that. But whatever you need, I'll get it for you."

"All right. Get me those damn planes as soon as you can."

The general stopped, softly said, "Ninita," again, and walked out of the room.

5:20 a.m.

After helping the woman pull on one of his large white T-shirts and a pair of his underwear, Rico pulled on the elastic and tied it into a knot so the underwear would not fall off the skinny waist. "Can you hold this?" he asked, handing a cup of soup to Lopez.

"Yes, I'll try," she said, taking the small white cup of yellow chicken broth with shaking hands.

Rico steadied the trembling fingers as she moved the bowl to her lips. "Not too fast; small sips," he said, looking concerned at the badly beaten face.

"Okay," she replied after she took a sip and lowered the bowl to set it on her lap.

"I'm having a doctor come over in a couple of hours. We need to get your head sewn up. It is still a very bad cut," he said, looking at a thin line of exposed skull and softly tilting his head as he grimaced in concern.

Nodding her head, Lopez replied, "Thank you," tears once more swelling up in her eyes as she tried to take another sip of broth.

Rico steadied her hands.

Yes, I will let him live, she thought.

6 a.m.

"Ricardo, it's Luis. Sorry it's so early, but I need a big favor. I need to rent two cars. No, it doesn't make any difference what they are. Yes, use the credit card on file. Oh and make sure the tanks are full and park them next to the building. Yes, of course, charge the extra fee. Thank you, I'll be over in thirty minutes to pick them up," Aguilar said as he hung up his cell phone. "You going to need anything else?" he asked, looking at West.

"No. After we pick up the cars, I'll park my car up the block from here so none of the dealers or hookers see me in it. Jack, I'll meet you one block north at midnight tonight. We'll go to the airport from there."

West took the Bogota map from his back pocket and laid it across the small table. "This is where we're going," he said, pointing at the airport. "Here, to the northwest is the Bogota River Bridge. Rodriquez made that pen mark. He said Rico comes from that direction. Jack, I want you parked on the other side of the bridge pointing away from it. I'll get as close to the hangar as I can and let you know when Rico shows up."

"Roger that," Reynolds replied.

"Luis, once we're in position, I'll let you know when to make the call to the airport. Rico will be heading that way in five minutes. How fast he gets there lets us know how far away the house is where they're keeping Sanita."

"Angelina," Aguilar replied.

"Yeah," West said. "Jack, you take the eyeball when he comes back across the bridge. Break off as soon as you need to, and I'll take the lead."

"Roger that. You're not wanting to hit the place tonight, are you?" Reynolds asked.

"No, let's find where it's at. I need to recon it to make sure we don't get Sanita killed."

"Angelina."

"Dammit, Luis," West said, frowning and looking at Aguilar. "Would you stop correcting me? I know her as Sanita; it's hard for me to call her anything else."

"Okay, I'll stop. My bad. They used to call me Louie when I was a kid, and I hated it."

West glanced at Reynolds who was starting to snicker.

"Yeah, well, you're a damn SEAL. A SEAL!" West repeated, still frowning and staring at Aguilar.

"Roger that, I won't do it again."

"What?" West said, looking at Reynolds who was still trying not to laugh.

Looking at Aguilar, Reynolds stopped laughing and said, "You have no idea what you just did. This crazy hillbilly will never forget you hate being called Louie."

"I swear I'll take that knife back," Aguilar said, looking keenly at West.

"Don't worry, we're good. I like your knife. All right?"

"Yeah, okay."

"Jesus, back to the mission, fellas," West said. Shaking his head, he continued, "After we find the house, I'll try to get as close as I can to see who and what's there. Once I lay eyes on it, we can then make a plan on hitting the place and getting Sani—ahhh . . . her out of there. Dammit, Louie, I can't even say her name now."

"What did you call me?"

"I said Luis. I said Luis. Right, Jack?" West said, looking at Reynolds.

Reynolds burst into laughter. "I told you," he said, in between laughs.

"I want my blade back," Aguilar demanded.

"Okay, my mistake. Won't happen again," West said, holding both hands up in front of him. "Seriously, I'm done."

"I'm a damn SEAL. Don't mess with me, or never close your eyes. I have another knife."

"Seriously, I'm done," West said, trying not to smile as Reynolds chuckled and Aguilar stared at both men.

"All right, can we go get the cars now? We good?" West asked.

"You bastards," Aguilar said as he got up and started out the door. "Get in the damn taxi."

Reynolds was still chuckling as West looked at him and raised his eyebrows and smiled as they followed the SEAL.

8 a.m.

"How long ago did this happen?" the elderly, gray-suited doctor shrieked, looking over his wire-rimmed spectacles at Rico.

"About a week."

"My God. What's her name?"

"Sanita."

Sitting on the side of the bed and looking at the woman, the doctor leaned over and asked, "Sanita, can you understand me?"

"Si."

"I need to numb your forehead with some medicine. I need to trim your cut and then sew it up."

"You can't just sew it?" Lopez asked in a weakened voice.

"No, my dear. It's been too long, and the edges of the skin have dried. If I don't trim the edges, it will never heal."

Lopez nodded her head yes.

"You're going to have a scar, but I'll do my best to make it small."

"Thank you," she whispered.

Rico walked into the next room and called a number on his phone.

"Hello."

"Rafael, the doctor is here now and sewing up her head."

"Is she doing better?"

"It's too early to tell. She's very weak but taking some broth slowly."

"What have I done? What have I done?" Rafael moaned.

"Rafael, you have saved her life now. She's a strong woman. She'll get better, I'll make sure of that."

"Get her well, Rico. She must not die. Do this for me, please."

"She'll get better, Rafael. I'll make sure she lives," Rico replied as he turned and watched the doctor inject lidocaine into the bruised and gashed forehead.

CHAPTER 19

RANCHO BLANCA

12:05 a.m., Wednesday, April 21, 1993

WEST WATCHED THE LIGHT-GRAY CHEVY MAZDA pull up. "Did you bring your shit just in case?" West asked, leaning against the dark-blue Renault a block north of Santafe Suite on Carrera 16.

"What the hell do you think?" Reynolds replied, getting out and shutting the car door.

"All right, let's get in place, and then I'll contact Luis to make the call. I did a drive-by a couple of hours ago. It's about five miles. We need to go up Calle 13 to 17 and get off on a gravel road that's west of the Bogota River. It circles up around the airport to the Bogota River Bridge Road. There's a guard shack on the bridge road, so we can't park there."

"Where we going?"

"We'll pass a flight observatory parking area on our right. I'll stop there. You go on up the road. On your right, you'll pass the River Bridge Road. Keep going another quarter-mile, and park at the fruit stand on the right."

"Roger that. Did you believe the Taya owner?"

"Everything matches the description Rodriquez gave before I cut his throat."

"Was he in any condition to lie?"

"No, I'd popped his knee. He was telling the truth."

"Okay, let's do it. I'll follow you," Reynolds said, getting back in the Mazda.

West got in the Renault and pulled out, heading south to Calle 13.

Fifteen minutes later, West pulled to the side of the road at the flight observatory where people can watch the jets land and take off from the Bogota International Airport. It was directly in line with runways 13R and 31L. Directly east, West could see a large domed hangar across the field.

Talking into the phone mic, West said, "The next road on your right is the River Bridge Road. Go a quarter-mile past that to the fruit stand."

"Roger that," Reynolds replied as he drove out of the gravel road dust and past where West was now parked in the dark. A few moments later, he said, "I see a big hangar over there. Can you see it?"

"Affirmative. I should be able to see if that's Espinoza's hangar by the car lights."

"Roger that. Passing the River Bridge Road now."

"Let me know when you're in position, and I'll call Luis," West said and waited.

A minute later, Reynolds said, "Ten twenty-three," indicating he was ready and on station.

"Roger that. It's twelve thirty. I'm calling Luis," West replied and then pushed 911 on his phone.

"Hello."

"Luis, it's West. We're in position. Make the call and give it your best Colombian accent."

"Roger that. They'll know English, so that's not a problem. I've got the airport security office number, and I'll put both phones on speaker. I'm using a different phone that I'm pitching after the call."

"Where're you at in case they can trace the call?"

"Nowhere important. I'm sitting in an alley. Here goes."

West listened to the call coming over the phone.

"Airport Security, Commander Alvarez speaking."

"Commander, I just received very good information that my cousin broke into a hangar at the airport trying to steal electronics from the planes."

"Who is this?"

"I can't say, Commander, but I saw a radio that had wires dangling from it, and it looked like it came out of a plane."

"Do you know what hangar?"

"Only that it was the big domed one on the north end," Aguilar said and then hung up. Stepping out of the taxi, Aguilar dropped the phone on the cobblestone street and then stomped it into several pieces. He got back in and, into the other phone mic, said, "How'd that sound?"

"Great. That commander is shitting his pants right now because he knows that's Espinoza's hangar, and he needs to make a call."

"Roger that. Let me know how it goes. I'll be standing by here," Aguilar replied.

"Ten-four. Thank you, Luis," West said, hung up, and then called Reynolds. "Jack, the call's been made. Let me know if you see anything."

"Roger that," Reynolds replied.

"WHAT WAS THAT ABOUT?" an airport security officer asked, sitting in the office at the Bogota Command Center.

"Get me Rico's number," Commander Alvarez said. "His hangar may have been broken into."

"You think this is legit?"

"I'm not taking any chances. We can meet him at the hangar when he gets here."

12:35 a.m.

IN THE LARGE BEDROOM AT THE MEDELLIN cartel property, Rancho Blanca, the phone rang next to Rico's bed.

"Hello," Rico said, answering the phone after he woke up.

"Rico, sorry to awaken you. This is Airport Security Commander

Alvarez. I just received a call that your hangar may have been broken into and some electronics stolen. What do you want me to do?"

Rubbing his face and sitting up in bed, Rico said, "I'll be over in a few minutes. Can you meet me at the hangar?"

"Yes, of course. I'll be there."

"Thank you. I'll be right over," Rico said and hung up.

"What happened?" Sewer Breath asked from his bed across the room.

"Hangar was broken into."

"You need me to go with you?"

"No, I'll meet security there."

"Okay, I'll check on the whore while you're gone."

Rico stopped and stared at the man. "Wilfredo, you touch her and I'll have you killed. Do you understand? Rafael said not to touch her."

"Yes, I was only joking," Sewer Breath replied.

Rico pulled on his clothes and said, "I'll be back in a few minutes, and you'd better still be in bed." Rico picked up his 9mm Glock from the nightstand, placed it in his waist belt, and walked out the door to his black Land Rover. "Piece of shit heathen," he said, getting in the car and pulling out to drive the mile to the airport.

12:40 a.m.

"Nate, a car just pulled out of a side road a couple hundred yards down the road, and it's coming towards me," Reynolds said into the phone.

"Roger that. Let's see where it goes. That would be damn close if it's him," West replied.

Reynolds paused and then said, "He just went past me, black Land Rover, one man in the car from what I could see."

"I can see headlights," West said and then paused. "I'll be dammed. He turned in the airport road. That must be him. Could you see where he came out of?"

"Yes, two hundred yards down on the left. I think it's the first road you'll come to."

"Okay, let me see if he goes to the hangar. He's at the guard shack now."

After a few moments, West said, "He's moving away from the guards. Hold on." He paused and then said, "I'll be a son of a bitch. That's him. He parked at the hangar."

"Roger that. Now what?"

"You stay there. I'm going to see what road he came out of. Moving," West replied, as he pulled out and headed towards Reynolds.

"Roger that." When he saw West pass him, Reynolds said, "Next road on your left."

"Roger that. I'm going to go up it a short ways. Watch for that Rover," West said as he turned the Renault left onto the unmarked gravel road.

"Roger that," Reynolds said, watching in his rearview mirror for headlights to come out of the bridge road going to the airport.

West drove to the end of the gravel road that went almost a half-mile. "Dead end, about a dozen side roads that look like they go to homes," West said into the phone. "Government building here on the end. Anything yet?"

"Negative, nothing yet, no headlights."

"Jack, I'm going to stay here at the end of the road at this government building. I need to see what driveway he turns into."

"Roger that. If he doesn't turn back down your road, I'll follow and let you know."

"Sounds good. Let me know when you see the Rover," West said.

12:42 a.m.

"GOOD EVENING, RICO," ALVAREZ SAID, extending his hand to the man after he got out of his Land Rover.

"Good morning, Commander. You see anything?"

"No. We checked around the hangar but couldn't find any doors broken into. They could have picked the lock. You'd still better check."

"Yes," Rico said and walked to the hangar side door and used his key to open it. Turning on the light switch next to the door, the hangar's bright, large overhead lights came on. He walked to the small white-and-blue Lear jet and up the jet steps to the cabin and cockpit, followed by the commander and the other security officer who accompanied him.

"Anything disturbed?" the commander asked, standing in the jet doorway.

"No, everything looks all right," Rico replied. "Who called?"

"Don't know. He wouldn't give his name."

"Okay, let me check the Cessna," Rico said. He waked to the 182 Skylane and opened the left door. "Hmmm, well, everything looks good. Must have been a prank call," Rico said, turning to the security officers.

"Yes, perhaps. We'll check the other hangars just to make sure," the commander said. "Sorry to get you out of bed, Rico, but I wasn't going to take the chance since it sounded like your hangar."

"That's not a problem, Commander. I'm glad nothing was taken. I sure as hell don't want to tell Alejandro someone stole from him. He's very sensitive that way, so thank you."

The commander nodded and said, "I'll let you know if I find another hangar broken into. And thank you for the money."

"Thank you, Commander. That monthly money is worth having someone here to keep a special watch on our hangar. Let's lock up and get out of here," Rico said.

12:50 a.m.

"How's your phone battery?" West asked Reynolds on the phone.

"Good. Yours?"

"Getting weak."

Reynolds paused and said, "Hey, I got headlights. After another pause, he said, "They're coming back this way. . . . Yes, the Rover just passed. . . . He's slowing to turn left. He's heading your way."

"Got 'em," West replied, watched the headlights drive towards him, and then said, "He's turning to his left. Can you see lights through the field on your left?"

Reynolds looked over at the tree-lined field. "Negative. Let me back up." He put the Mazda in reverse and backed onto the road. "Yes, I see lights. They're about a quarter-mile across this field. They just went out. Drive back this way so I can see your headlights on the road."

"Roger that," West replied. He turned his headlights on and drove back towards the main road.

"Yes, I see your headlights. He stopped about one hundred yards up the road you're passing now."

West stopped on the gravel road and looked up the side road the Land Rover had turned up. He could still see dust hovering over the road. "I see an outside light up there on the left. I bet that's where he stopped."

"Ten-four," Reynolds replied. "We got the bastards."

"Roger that." Staring at the light in the pitch black, West said, "Got you, you son of a bitch." He paused and then said, "I'm coming, Sanita," as he started to drive the Renault back towards Reynolds.

West pulled up beside the Mazda, and both men rolled down their windows.

"How about we get a couple hours of sleep and you pick me up at 5 a.m.?" West said.

"You going to watch it?"

"That's my plan. I want to watch it all day. You drop me off here before daylight, and I can walk over through the field. It looks like there's a fence row about a hundred yards from the house. I can hide there. Once we have an idea on how many targets we have, we can hit it tonight without all of us getting killed."

"Roger that."

"I'll be waiting outside the Santafe at five. Bring all your shit," West said and then turned the Renault towards Bogota.

Reynolds nodded and pulled out following the car.

CHAPTER 20

She Cried

1:15 a.m., Wednesday, April 21, 1993

West parked the Renault up the block from the hotel, placed the key on top of the right rear tire, and walked back. There was just a splattering of whores and dealers still awake on the sidewalk trying to make what little money they could. They gave West little notice as he got to the bottom of the stairs at the Santafe. He climbed the flights of stairs and, on the third floor, opened his door and glanced at the clock on the nightstand: 1:27 a.m.

"Hmmm," he said as he locked the door behind him and walked to the clock, setting the alarm for 4:45 a.m. "I need sleep," he said, as he lay down on the bed in his clothes and shoes. He pulled the blanket over his arms, closed his eyes, and was asleep by the time the clock showed 1:30.

Rancho Blanca
4 a.m.

The phone rang next to Rico's bed for the second time that night.

"Hello," Rico said, holding the phone to his ear.

"Rico, how is she?"

"Good, Rafael," Rico replied, sitting up in bed. "She's doing better."

"I can't sleep thinking about her. Is she well enough to travel?"

"She's still very weak. What are you wanting to do?"

"I'll be over in the morning with a couple of men. I'm bringing her back here to Medellin so my maid can take care of her."

"To your home with Alejandro?" Rico asked, concerned knowing what the younger brother would do.

"No, I have another home. And this is important, Rico. I need you to promise you'll not speak a world of this to Alejandro. If he finds out, it needs to come from me. I need you to give me your word."

"Whatever you want, Rafael. I give you my word because Alejandro will kill her."

"Perhaps. I'll hide her in a home a few blocks away. My maid is also a nurse. She'll be well cared for. Then maybe I'll be able to sleep if she's under my roof. I haven't been able to sleep in days."

"I know you love her, Rafael. And I know how hard this has been on you. I'll do whatever you need."

"Thank you, Rico. Get her ready to be moved by 10 a.m."

Santafe Suite
4:45 a.m.

The buzzer on the alarm clock startled West, causing him to quickly reach for his pistol. Rubbing his eyes, he laid the pistol back on the nightstand and looked at the ceiling. There was just enough streetlight glow through the windows where he could see the old pealing white paint.

"Let's kill some son of a bitch today," he said as he threw the blanket off and began his morning routine of fifty crunches. Finished, he got out of bed and walked to the bathroom to relieve himself. Looking in the mirror, he splashed water on his face and ran wet fingers through his dark hair. Before turning off the water, he leaned over and drank his fill from the spigot.

Walking back to the other side of the bed, West pulled the MP5 from under the mattress and laid it on the bed. From under the bed, he pulled out the black bag that contained the extra magazines and extra phone. He unzipped it, placed the machine gun inside, zipped it back up, and laid the bag on the end of the bed. At the small refrigerator, he took the last of the arepas and shoved it into his mouth. Chewing and then swallowing the hard bread, he picked the pistol up off the nightstand and slid it into his belt, saying, "Hang in there, Sanita," as he glanced at the clock and started towards the stairs carrying the black bag.

Outside, the sidewalk was vacant, no whores, pimps, or drug dealers. West leaned back into a shadow against the brick wall. It felt cool with the nighttime temperature in the low sixties. He didn't have long to wait. Headlights began to make their way towards the hotel, and he could make out the gray Mazda. West walked back out into the light and stood by the curb as the car slowed to a stop.

Neither man spoke as West got in the passenger side and laid the black bag on the floor between his legs.

As Reynolds drove the car back out, he asked, "You got this worked out?"

"Yeah," West replied. "You?"

"Yeah. I'll stay near the fruit stand as long as I can. I may have to move if it looks like someone is taking notice."

"That's what I thought you'd do."

"Other than that, I guess we're playing this by ear."

"Yeah, we still have no idea what we're up against," West replied.

Reynolds continued to drive west towards the airport and said, "You know what this reminds me of?"

"What?"

"When we were trying to decide when and where to do the pit maneuver on the cyanide van."

West chuckled and said, "I think that would have worked if I hadn't stolen it first."

"Yeah," Reynolds said. "Do you think she's still alive?"

West shook his head and said, "I pray she is. I know this. If I get the chance, I'm killing some asshole for some payback."

Reynolds nodded as he drove the car onto the gravel road towards the fruit stand. Passing the Bogota River Bridge Road, Reynolds asked, "Where do you want me to let you out?"

"Just before the fruit stand. It'll be daylight soon, but I'll have enough time to get in position."

Making a slight right-hand turn, Reynolds slowed the car and stopped in the road, turning off the car and headlights. "This good?" he asked.

West took the MP5 out of the black bag and stuck the extra magazines and phone in his pockets. "Yes, I'll get some exhaust black for my face and arms before you pull out."

"Roger that. I'll be waiting for your call. Even if I have to change locations, I'll never be more than a mile away."

"Sounds good. If I have to move fast, I may not get a chance to call. You may hear some shots, so keep your window down."

"Affirmative. If that happens, I'm coming in hot with hate, and I'll drive to that front porch."

West nodded and said, "Roger that." He got out of the car, hung the sling connected to the MP5 over his neck, and walked to the back of the car. Bending over, he placed two fingers in the tailpipe, twirled them around several times against the inside of the metal, and then rubbed the blackened fingers over his face, hands, and arms. He walked to the driver's window and asked, "How do I look?"

"Pretty good from what I can see in the dark. Your skin looks dull. I think you're good," Reynolds replied.

After shaking hands, West nodded and said, "I'll see you later."

West crossed the road to the fence that bordered the field, climbed over it, and watched Reynolds drive the Mazda down the road towards the fruit stand. Turning back to face the field, West could see a single light in the distance about two hundred yards away. Slowly making his way towards the light, he knew he would run into a fence before he got there. "I wish I had some moonlight," West softly said. With the almost pitch blackness, he couldn't see more than a few feet away, even as his eyes adjusted to the dark.

Reynolds pulled over at the fruit stand and slowly backed up in the parking lot to where he could just make out a light through the trees towards the house. Keeping his window down he thought, Let's do this, Yeager.

West continued to move towards the light, carefully placing his feet to make sure he didn't step in a hole and sprain an ankle. It was slow going, but after ten minutes, he could make out a fence in front of him. Touching the wire, West could feel the barbs as he moved to be behind a post. He lay down on his back on the ground and separated the grass to where he could see the light in the distance without moving his head.

"This'll do," West said and waited for daylight with the MP5 resting on his stomach. He closed his eyes and thought about Angelina Lopez. Those thoughts made him grip the machine gun tighter, and he let out a deep sigh. "Hang in there."

Rancho Blanca
8 a.m.

"Someone is coming to get you this morning. You'll be taken someplace where you'll be better cared for," Rico said.

"Who's coming for me?" Lopez asked softly, looking into Rico's eyes.

"Rafael."

Tears swelled up in her eyes as she asked, "Why?"

"You know why," Rico replied and slightly smiled, tilting his head.

Lopez began to sob as she closed her eyes and lowered her head. Looking up, she whispered, "Thank you."

Rico nodded and stood up from the bed.

8:30 a.m.

It had been daylight for two hours, and still no movement came from the house. There were two vehicles in the driveway, a black Land Rover that looked like the one that had traveled to the airport and an older beat-up, yellow pickup truck. These guys sure like their Rovers, West thought, as he crawled down the fence line to a spot where he had a better view of the front porch. Even though he couldn't see the front door, he could still see the porch and the walkway to the parked vehicles. Punching the call button, he put the phone to his ear.

"Hello."

"Jack, it's Nate. No movement here," he whispered.

"Roger that. No movement here either."

"Affirmative. I'll check in later," West replied. "The phone will be on vibrate."

"Roger that," Reynolds said and laid his phone on the seat.

West put the phone back in his front left jean pocket, lay back down to watch the house, and finger tapped the black shoulder stock of the MP5.

Outskirts of Bogota
9 a.m.

"Hello," Rico said, answering the phone at the ranch house.

"Rico, we are coming into Bogota now. We should be there in about thirty or forty minutes."

"Okay, Rafael. I told her you were coming to get her."

"What did she say?"

"She cried."

Tears swelled up in Rafael's eyes. Unable to speak with the lump in his throat, he hung up the phone and blinked his eyes several times, looking out the window of the Land Rover. After a few moments of composing himself, he said to the driver, "Hurry."

CHAPTER 21

A Guy Committed Suicide

9 a.m., Wednesday, April 21, 1993

"MR. PRESIDENT, CIA DIRECTOR WOLFE IS HERE to speak to you," Chief of Staff Lawrence said, standing in the doorway of the Oval Office. "He says it's urgent, sir."

President Crawford looked up from his morning intelligence report and said," Bring him in, Mack."

"Yes, sir," Lawrence replied and held the door open for Director Wolfe.

"Good morning, Mr. President. Thank you for seeing me," Wolfe said as he walked in.

"Take a seat, Roger. What's going on?" Crawford asked from behind the presidential desk.

Wolfe looked back at the door to make sure it had closed before speaking. "We're missing an agent in Colombia."

"One of the Thorn agents?" Crawford asked.

"No, sir. A Customs agent that was working with Colombian General Marquez to capture Espinoza."

Crawford sat back in his seat and said, "Damn. Well, when those guys sign up, they know it's a dangerous job."

"It's a female, Mr. President."

"Ahh shit," Crawford said. "You think she's dead?"

"We don't know, sir, but they'll torture, rape, and starve her to death if they don't cut her throat first. I don't know how long she can hold on."

"Oh my God. Those brutal bastards. How old is she?"

"She's a young agent, sir, twenty-four."

"Those bastards. What can we do?"

"Sir, I received a request from Customs Commissioner Williams to assist in finding her, which we think will lead us to Espinoza."

"All right. What does he want?"

"He wants aircraft to help track and triangulate phone calls from Espinoza. Customs SAC in Bogota, Dale Wilson, is working closely with General Marquez to do this. They're using some equipment we gave to Customs."

"How easy is it to track someone that way?"

"It's not, Mr. President. There's a very small window of opportunity, and you've got to be damn lucky to be close enough to the source before the line goes dead."

"I see. Go on."

"I have authorized two Cessna 210RGs to be flown to Colombia to assist Wilson and the general. If we can find Espinoza, we may have a chance in recovering the body."

"If she's dead."

"She's been missing for a week or more, Mr. President. If she's still alive, it would be a miracle."

"So there's a chance she's still alive?"

"I would have to say a very remote chance, sir."

"Hmmm," Crawford said as he looked down at his desk and folded his hands. "What's Thorn doing?"

"This is the good news. The CIA lead agent called me early this morning. Last night, West and Reynolds may have found where they are keeping her. We don't know yet. They need to check it out further before they raid the place, possibly tonight."

Crawford sat back in his chair and looked at the floor for several moments, letting out a long sigh. "Well that's good news. Roger, get her back," Crawford said, slowly nodding his head and now looking at Wolfe. "If we can kill some of the bastards in the process, let's do it."

"Yes, sir. Also with your permission, I'm going to get DEA involved with the aircraft. We're going to need the manpower, and they have some of the best pilots."

"Permission granted. But I want Thorn kept independent. Let's not water them down or get in their way."

"No, sir. I thought you would feel that way, and I have already given the order for them to stay away from the other personnel. The only person in Colombia that knows they're even there is CIA Officer Luis Aguilar."

"That's good, Roger. What's the agent's name that's missing?" the president asked.

"Customs Special Agent Angelina Lopez."

"Angelina," the president softly said and shook his head. "Get her back, Director."

"Yes, Mr. President."

Rancho Blanca
9:40 a.m.

Feeling the phone vibrate, West pulled it out of his pocket and said, "Hello."

"Nate, a black Land Rover is heading your direction fast," Reynolds said.

Lifting his head up so he could look down past his feet towards the gravel road, West could hear a vehicle and then was able to see the Rover. "Got it," West replied, hanging up the phone and placing it back in his pocket. He lay flat as he watched the black vehicle pull up to the house and three men get out. "Hmmm, is that Rafael? Dammit, I need binoculars this far away," West said as he watched the trio walk up to the porch and disappear into the home.

"Where is she?" Rafael asked Rico who met him at the door.

"Come with me," Rico said and led the men to the far bedroom passing Sewer Breath, standing in the kitchen doorway. Opening the door, Rico walked into the room, followed by Rafael and his two bodyguards. Lopez was asleep in a fetal position covered with a blanket. Rafael could see the bruised face and the multiple sutures across her forehead. He let out an audible gasp. "My God," he said.

Looking at the biggest bodyguard, Rafael motioned with his arms to pick her up and take her to the car.

The big man walked past Rafael to the side of the bed and pulled the blanket around the woman. Bending over, he slid his muscular arms underneath Lopez and easily picked her up.

Waking, Lopez looked at the man and then around the room. Seeing Rafael, she once more began to cry and closed her swollen and bruised eyes.

"Get her out of here," Rafael said and motioned as the two bodyguards headed for the car. He bent over and placed his hands on the foot of the bed. Taking several deep breaths, he said, "Thank you, Rico. I should've never let this happen."

"I understand. We live in a violent world, my friend. You did what Alejandro expected of you."

"Come and follow us. I want you there for a couple of days. She's comfortable with you, yes?"

"Yes, I believe so. She knows I was helping her."

"Thank you. Follow us," Rafael said as he straightened and walked out of the house.

Passing Sewer Breath, Rico said, "Wilfredo, I'll be gone for a couple of days," as he followed Rafael off the porch and then to his own Land Rover.

"I'll be here," the big ugly man said, now standing on the porch and watching the two vehicles leave.

WEST WATCHED AS TWO OF THE MEN came out of the house carrying a person wrapped in a blanket. But West couldn't see who it was. Possibly Lopez, he thought as the man carrying the person got in the back of the Rover. The other man got in the driver's seat. Lying there,

West watched the tall man walk down the steps and get in the front passenger seat of the Rover. I think that's Rafael, West thought.

Then West saw a shorter man come off the porch and get in the other Rover that possibly Rico had been driving. "Hmmm, so that's Rico?"

West could also see a large man standing on the porch, who then turned and walked back into the building as the two Rovers drove away.

"Shit," West said as he lay there for a moment and thought, watching the two Rovers quickly disappear down the road towards Reynolds.

Jumping to his feet, West vaulted across the fence and raced towards the house. Reaching in his pocket he pulled out the phone and hit the call button as he ran.

"Jack, Jack," West said, but there was no reply. Glancing down he saw the battery had died. "Dammit," West hissed as he shoved the phone back in his pocket and vaulted the next fence beside the house. Holding the MP5 in his right hand and shouldered with the sling still around his neck, he walked up the steps to the porch and opened the front door. Stepping inside, he swept the living room with his weapon and continued into the hall.

"Rico, what did you forget?" a man's voice asked, coming from the last room up the hall on the right.

Glancing into the first room on the right as he moved up the hallway, West could see several beds. Moving into the room's doorway where he heard the voice come from, a man was bent over at a refrigerator with his back towards West.

"You move, and I'm going to shoot you right up your ass," West said, crouching and pointing the weapon at the man. "Get your hands up where I can see them."

"Don't shoot," Sewer Breath said as he slowly raised his hands.

"Turn towards me," West demanded.

"Don't shoot," the man repeated, now gingerly turning around and looking at the man with the blackened face and arms holding a machine gun. "Who are you? You're making a very bad mistake."

"I'm the man who is going to cut you in half if you don't do exactly as I say, and I don't make mistakes." Looking at the pistol in the right side of the man's waist belt, West said, "With your left hand, pull that pistol out very slowly with two fingers and lay it on the table."

The man hesitated and stared at West.

Seeing the look on the man's face, West said, "I'm going to blow your guts all over this room if you don't move your left hand right now."

Sewer Breath blinked twice, licked his lips, and then started moving his left hand very slowly, removing the .45 auto from his waist belt, and laid it on the table next to the refrigerator.

"On your face," West said, motioning with his head towards the floor while pointing the MP5 at the man's chest.

"What do you want?" the man asked as he went to his knees and lay flat on the floor.

"Put your hands together behind your back and cross your legs," West said as he pulled a flex-cuff from under his belt. Flipping the MP5 onto his back, West knelt down and placed one knee on the back of the man's neck while pinning the man's arms to his back. Slipping the flex-cuff over both of the man's wrists, West clinched it up tight.

"Where did they take the girl?" West asked, getting up off the man, pulling a chair out from the table, and sitting down on it facing the prone man on the floor.

"What girl?" the man replied.

West pulled the SEAL knife from his right ankle sheath and stuck it in the floor beside the man's head so he could see it.

"I'm going to ask you one more time, and then I'm cutting your asshole out. Now where did they take the girl?"

"Medellin," the man replied, staring at the knife.

"What's her name?"

"Sanita."

"Who took her?"

"Rafael and his body guards,"

"Who was the short man that left last?"

"That's Rico," the man said.

"Where in Medellin?"

"I don't know."

West slid off the chair, pulled up the knife, pinned the man's head down with his left hand, and stuck the knife into the skull of his right temple.

"Ahhhh, I don't know," the man screamed kicking his feet. "I overheard Rico talking to Rafael. They are taking her to another home somewhere in Medellin but not to Alejandro's. He's not to know about it."

"What else do you know?" West asked, still pinning the man's head to the floor.

"I don't know anything. What do you mean?"

"How many times did you hurt the girl?"

"What do you mean?" the man gasped as the blood ran down over his face.

"How many times did you rape the girl?" West yelled. "Five, ten, how many?"

"I don't know, maybe five. Not many," the man said, trying to look at West. "They ordered us to rape her and then feed her to the dogs after she died."

"Who ordered it?"

"Rafael and Alejandro."

"Who stopped it?"

"Rico on orders from Rafael. Alejandro doesn't know about it."

"Okay," West said, as he got up off of Sewer Breath. "Get in this chair," he said, as he picked the chair up and sat it down on the other side of the man. Helping the man up off the floor, West guided him into the seat with his hands still tied behind his back and the knife sticking out of his head.

"Will you take that knife out of my head?" the man asked, looking at West still standing.

West picked up the man's .45 pistol off the table and said, "So you only violated her five times?"

"Yes. Will you take the knife out?"

"Sure," West said, and he pulled the knife out and laid it on the table, leaving an inch-wide gash in Sewer Breath's head. "Why the hell does your breath stink so bad?" West asked, looking at the man.

"My teeth are no good. Some are rotted."

"Okay, where in Medellin does Alejandro live?" West asked, cocking the .45 and pointing it at the man's head.

"I've never been to his place, but it's near the soccer stadium," Sewer Breath said as the blood trickled down the side of his head.

"What soccer stadium?"

"Giradot Estadio."

"Giradot Estadio," West repeated.

"Yes. I will answer any questions you have."

"I think that's all I need."

"What now?"

"It's time for me to leave. I need you to look towards that wall," West said, motioning to his right with the barrel of the .45.

"Why?"

"Just do it. I don't want you looking my way when I leave. You shouldn't have raped the girl."

"I won't next time," Sewer Breath said as he looked to the side.

"There won't be a next time," West said. He pulled the trigger on the .45 and sent a slug through the cut on Sewer Breath's head, blowing his brains into the sink as he convulsed out of the chair and onto the kitchen floor, his feet kicking the chair back against the wall.

Picking the knife up off the table, West reached down and cut the flex-cuff off the man's wrist and slid the knife back into his ankle sheath. After shoving the barrel of the .45 against the smoking hole in the man's head to smear it with blood, West put the pistol in the man's right hand and laid it beside the body. "It's a terrible thing when a man commits suicide."

West picked up the cut flex-cuff and walked out of the house, glancing in each room and at the stairway leading to the basement as he left. Reaching the porch, he could see Reynolds quickly pulling up to the house in the Mazda.

"I thought I heard a muffled shot," Reynolds said, getting out of the car with his MP5.

"Yeah, you did. A guy committed suicide. Let's get out of here," West said and got in the front passenger seat of the Mazda.

CHAPTER 22

FLETC, FLETC

10 a.m., Wednesday, April 21, 1993

"I tried to reach you when the two Rovers came back out," Reynolds said. "I wanted to follow them, but I wouldn't leave you. I drove to the end of the driveway to be closer."

"My battery died. I tried calling you as I went to the house. No time to pull out the reserve and use it."

"What did you learn?"

"That was Rafael who just left. He took Sanita to Medellin. Don't know where, but one of their houses is near the Girardot Estadio, the soccer stadium."

"So we're back to square one?"

"No, Rico went with them. He'll know exactly where she's at. I now need to get my hands on him, and I know where he lives."

"The dead man will look suspicious," Reynolds said.

"Yeah, but it looks legit. They just won't know why he did it," West said, looking at Reynolds. "And Rico still needs to be near the airport. He's not leaving this area. They'll just clean the body up."

Reynolds nodded.

"I need sleep," West said.

"Yes, me too. Let's rest up and get back together tonight with Luis and make some more plans."

"Sounds good," West said, looking out the window. "Dammit, we were close, Jack. We may not have gotten her today, but we now know she's still alive."

"Yeah, Roger that."

Thinking for a few minutes, West asked, "Hey, Jack, what would Luis do if we told him about the soccer stadium?"

Reynolds looked at West and said, "He's obligated to pass that information on."

"What would Marquez do with that information, Jack? We know she's alive now. I don't want to get her killed," West said, looking at Reynolds.

Reynolds thought as he drove the rest of the way back to Bogota. As he pulled the Mazda next to the curb at the Santafe Suite, he asked West, "How does eight sound tonight?"

"That'll work. What do you think about the stadium information?"

Reynolds was quiet for a moment and then said, "For the time being, we need to keep that to ourselves. I agree, Marquez will go in with guns blazing. He'll have a smaller area to monitor, and he'll shift all his men and resources there. If we want the best chance to get her out alive, we need to keep our mouths shut. We can tell what we know after she's safe."

"Thanks, Jack. See you and Luis at eight," West replied. He got out of the car with the black bag and headed towards the stairway.

Safe House, Carrera 78, #29, Medellin

A little more than two blocks from Alejandro and Rafael's home on Carrera 79B, the black Land Rover pulled up to an older two-story, tan, stucco home with bars on the windows and doors. It was one of many safe houses the brothers owned but rarely used. This was also the only one in walking distance of the main residence and could be used in an emergency if they had to flee their home.

After traveling over an hour from Bogota, Rafael said to the driver, "Pull into the garage," as he pushed on the electronic door control lying on the dash.

The bodyguard pulled the Rover down into the basement parking area and turned the vehicle off as Rafael pushed the garage door control to close the door behind them.

Rafael looked at the large man in the back seat still holding the sleeping woman and motioned with his hands for him to carry the woman upstairs.

"Felipe, Maria will show you what bedroom to use," Rafael said, speaking to the driver.

"Si, sir."

Lopez had not spoken a word the entire trip and pretended to be sleeping, but she'd heard everything that had been said, and it hadn't been much. All she knew was she was somewhere in Medellin. She opened her eyes and looked at Rafael as the man carried her out of the car and up the steps to the main floor. Rafael met her gaze, but neither spoke.

"Bring her in here," Maria, the elderly maid, said and motioned to the big man as she walked into the bedroom on the right at the beginning of the hall. The sheet and blanket had been turned down on the clean bed.

"Be gentle with her," Maria said, as the man laid Lopez down on the bed.

"He will," Felipe said.

Lopez could see Rafael standing in the doorway as Maria covered her up.

Turning, the maid said, "Shoo, shoo, everyone out. We need privacy now," as she waved her hand for the men to leave the room. Closing the door, she returned to the bed and sat down next to Lopez. "My name is Maria. I am a nurse. I'll be taking care of you. Do you understand?"

"Si, thank you."

The maid nodded. "You must listen very carefully. If you try to escape, you will not get very far and Alejandro will have you killed. No matter what Rafael says, Alejandro will kill you. Do you understand?"

"Si."

"I'll not leave this house. I'll always be here to protect you," Maria said as she softly moved the matted black hair out of Lopez's bruised and scarred face.

"Thank you," Lopez said as she held the woman's hands.

"I'm going to make you some soup and bread. Have you been able to bathe?"

"No, I'm too weak to stand."

"All right, we'll do that first. I'll bathe you here in bed, and when you're strong enough, you can bathe yourself in the tub or shower. I have a toilet chair I'll put beside your bed. If you dirty the sheets, don't worry; I will wash them."

"Thank you," Lopez said. Tears began to stream down her face. "Thank you."

Medellin Airport
6 p.m.

The yellow cab pulled up to the curb next to the heavy-set man with thinning gray hair and mustache, dressed in a dark suit and sunglasses, and holding a suitcase.

"Who's your mother?" the cabbie asked the man through the open passenger-side window.

"Roger."

"Throw your suitcase on the back seat and get in the front."

The man opened up the back door of the car, threw in his suitcase, and got in the front seat.

"I'm Luis Aguilar with the agency," he said, reaching over to shake the man's hand.

"Julio Piniella, DEA," he replied, shaking hands with Aguilar.

"Welcome to Bogota."

"Thanks. It's a shithole."

"Yes, and a dangerous one. I need to introduce you to Customs

SAC Dale Wilson. He'll introduce you to General Marquez of Search Bloc. I'm not to meet the general, so I can't be at that meeting."

"Why not?"

"Compartmentalization, my friend. I'm not to be known by any foreign nationals here. Too much money floating around for bribes, and we've had some people come up missing in the past. So it's precautionary."

"So what does that make me?" Piniella asked.

"Expendable, so be on your toes."

"Who knows I'm in country?"

"It's only supposed to be me, Wilson, and the general. But this is Colombia, and secrets are rare."

Piniella nodded his head and said, "That's normal for shitholes."

"You're to be the liaison between the DEA pilots and Search Bloc. I'll pass whatever you need back up the chain of command. You can go through your own agency if you wish, but I can get things done quicker than they can."

"That's what I was told. If I need anything, I'll be contacting you."

"Good. Open the glove box. Take the Sig .45, phone, charger, and room key; 911 goes straight to me."

"Thanks," Piniella said. He opened the glove box, took out the .45, and slid the receiver back slightly.

"One's in the tube," Aguilar said.

"Yeah," Piniella replied, sliding the pistol into the small of his back underneath the coat. Next, he retrieved room key 723 and the black Nokia phone, sliding those into his inside coat pocket. "When do I meet Wilson?" he asked.

"Right now. We're going to the Hotel Nutibara. He's going to meet us there. You're in room 723. Wilson's meeting us in 721. Are you aware of the missing Customs agent?"

"Yes, I was briefed before leaving."

"Okay. Wilson is taking it pretty hard, so don't be surprised with his appearance."

Carrera 78
6:30 p.m.

"Do you feel better after your nap?" Maria asked, sitting down on the edge of the bed.

"Si, I do," Lopez said, rolling over to face the woman. "Thank you so much for washing my body. It had been a long time."

"You're welcome, my dear. I want you to eat some more soup and bread. We need to get you strong again."

"Si, but can you answer some questions for me first?"

"My dear, it all depends on what you ask."

"Do you know who I am?"

"No, I've not been told. Rafael only said he wanted a young girl cared for. That's all he told me."

"I trust you, mama. I want you to know who I am."

"All right," the elderly lady said, patting her hand.

"My name is Angelina Lopez and I work for the US government. My being here may be putting you in danger. I know my government is looking for me. I don't want to see you hurt."

"The older lady smiled and said, "No one wants to hurt an old lady, my dear. I'll be fine."

"If anything ever happens, I want you to raise your hands and say FLETC,"

"FLETC?"

"Si, FLETC. But don't let anyone know I told you this. If something happens, say it over and over again and keep your hands up."

"FLETC, FLETC?" the lady said softly.

"Si, do that, but scream it if someone comes."

"What is FLETC?" Maria asked, looking confused.

"It's where the US government trains their agents. They will not shoot you if you say that."

"Oh, okay. Let me get you some more soup. FLETC, FLETC," she whispered as she left the room.

Santafe Suite
6:45 p.m.

WEST COULDN'T SLEEP ANY LONGER. Getting up, he glanced out the window at the street below. It had already gotten dark, and he could see the normal lineup of street workers. Walking into the bathroom, he turned the shower on to get the water hot and dropped his underwear. As he waited, he held onto the sink and looked into the mirror. He appeared tired.

Taking a deep breath and letting it out, he said, "Sanita, you'll be my last official act. But I'll get you home before I leave this hellhole. I promise."

He climbed in the shower. The hot water felt great as it streamed over West's head and face. After washing, he turned off the water and climbed out. "I feel better," he said, brushing his hair, thinking he had an hour before Jack and Luis would arrive.

CHAPTER 23

Screaming Eagle

6:45 p.m., Wednesday, April 21, 1993

As Aguilar knocked on the door to room 721, Piniella stood in his adjoining hotel room and heard the door unlock. It opened, and Piniella saw a man shaking hands with the CIA operative.

"Hi, Dale," Aguilar said. "I can't stay long."

"Okay, come on in," Wilson said as he opened the door wider.

"Dale, this is Special Agent Julio Piniella of the DEA," Aguilar said, walking into the room. "Julio, this is Customs SAC Dale Wilson."

"Glad to meet you, Julio," Wilson said, extending his hand.

"Likewise, sir," Piniella said, looking at the man wearing wrinkled slacks and a stained white wife-beater T-shirt. He appeared to be worn out and unshaven for at least a week.

"Sir, I'm here to help. I understand we're missing an agent."

"Yes, we are. Please have a seat," Wilson said as he sat down on the edge of the bed and the men took chairs.

"Luis, when are the aircraft arriving?" Wilson asked.

"They're arriving this Sunday, the twenty-fifth."

"That's great news. We need to located these assholes and get Angelina back."

"Do we know if she's alive?" Piniella asked.

"No," Wilson said. He lowered his head and shook it. "No, we do not."

"Hmmm," Piniella said.

"Dale, do you need anything right now?" Luis asked, getting to his feet. "I've got a meeting in an hour, and I was told it was an important one, so I have to go."

"No, just get me those damn planes."

"All right, I need to run. I have to get to Bogota. You men decide on how you're wanting to move forward and just let me know what you and the general decide. I'll back you in every way I can. Nice meeting you, Julio," Aguilar said, shaking hands with both men.

"Likewise," Piniella replied.

"See you in few days, Dale. Get some sleep. You look like shit."

"I'll try," Wilson said.

Aguilar opened the door to the hallway, shut it behind him, and headed towards the stairs.

"HELLO," REYNOLDS SAID, ANSWERING HIS PHONE.

"Jack, I'm running a little late," Aguilar said as he got in the taxi. "I'm leaving Medellin now. Be there shortly after eight."

"No problem. I'll let Nate know. And we got some great news, but I can't say over the phone."

"Wonderful. I need some. I'll hurry," Aguilar said and hung up.

Reynolds laid the phone down and looked around the room. "I've got time for a drink before I call Nate," he said as he got up and looked in his walk-in closet. "I don't need to be Dominion tonight," he remarked as he slid the white long-sleeve shirts and blue slacks over in the closet to get to his black T-shirt and jeans on a hanger. After putting those on, he slid the phone and wallet into his pants, the Beretta into his waist belt, and pulled the shirt down over the pistol.

This'll be fine for a quick drink, he thought as he headed for the lounge on the first floor. Maybe there'll be some pretty women there tonight. Getting downstairs and walking in the dimly lit room with scented candles burning on each table, he thought he had won the lottery: three beautiful women were sitting at the bar laughing. All three presented professionally applied makeup, beautiful long black hair, low-cut, expensive sundresses, and high heels on long seductive legs. Damn, he thought, my lucky night. He took a stool at the bar several seats down from the group.

"*Buenas noches*," he said, smiling at the women who were now looking at him.

"*Buenas noches*," they all replied, smiling and whispering to each other.

I bet *they* don't think I'm a pedophile, he thought smiling and nodding back to the ladies. "Nathan, you can kiss my ass," he said softly.

"What would you like to drink, sir?" the young handsome waiter wearing a black suit, white shirt, and thin long black tie asked in English.

"Light draft beer, whatever you have on tap."

"Aguila Light, okay?"

"Yes, that's fine," Reynolds replied, glancing back up at the ladies who were now speaking softly among themselves. Hmmm, don't think they are working girls, or one of them would have approached me by now, he thought as the waiter placed the glass of beer down on the bar. "Thanks, I'll run a tab for my room."

"That won't be necessary, sir. The lady on the end of the bar has paid for your drinks tonight."

"Which one?"

"The one farthest away, the lady in the yellow flower dress."

Leaning back to see the woman better, Reynolds said, "*Gracias, senorita*."

"You're welcome," the woman replied in perfect English. Sliding off her barstool, she walked to Reynolds and asked, "May I sit with you?"

"Be my pleasure," Reynolds replied, looking at the stunning beauty as she sat down on the stool next to him. "Your English is perfect. Where'd you learn that?"

"I grew up in Miami. I'm only here on business."

"Oh, I'm here on business too," Reynolds replied.

"Really? My name is Raya," she said, extending her hand.

"I'm Jack. I live in Virginia and work in the gas field," he said, as he shook the small hand. "What do you do, if I may ask?"

"Yes, you can. I do consulting work for an attorney group here."

"Oh, so you're an attorney?"

"No," Raya said, smiling, "I'm more of an organizing clerk."

"Well, you're the most beautiful clerk I've ever seen," Reynolds said.

"Thank you. Sometimes one's looks can cause problems for a woman."

"Yes, I'm sure. But I see you're married, so that should keep most of the assholes at bay."

Raya laughed and said, "I think that ring is a magnet for some."

Looking back towards the door, she whispered with a put-on smile, "And here comes the biggest asshole."

Reynolds turned on his seat to see a group of five men walk into the lounge as Raya slid off the stool to meet the first man.

"Hi, honey," she said, leaning up on her toes to kiss the check of the man sharply dressed in a very expensive suit and now glaring at Reynolds who had turned back to the bar.

"What are you doing down here? You're supposed to be upstairs," he said, gripping her left arm tightly and bending his face down to hers.

"We were just taking a break. No harm, Alex."

"Raya, get back upstairs and take those whores with you now," he said, glaring at her and motioning with his thumb to the other two women who quickly got off their stools and walked out of the lounge behind Raya.

Alex Sanchez watched his wife and the two prostitutes leave the room. "Ahhh," he groaned as he sat on a stool halfway down the bar from Reynolds. The other four well-dressed men began to sit down on the other side of Sanchez as Reynolds glanced their way just in time to see the jacket on the second man move back far enough to expose a pistol in a shoulder holster.

"I apologize, amigo, for the interruption," Sanchez said to Reynolds.

"No problem, friend. None of my business," Reynolds replied as he noticed the waiter didn't bother to ask the men what they wanted to drink but pulled a two-thousand-dollar bottle of Dictador Wixarika rum from the shelf behind the bar and started pouring the men drinks. Cartel for sure, Reynolds thought.

"Thank you, amigo. Please, don't take offense, but with your clothing, do you work construction?"

Reynolds turned slightly to face the man. "Close. I work for a natural gas company in the States. I'm here to look into a joint venture with Central Gas."

"I see. Natural gas is very important here," Sanchez said, forcing a smile as he glanced at the tattoo on Reynolds right forearm. Taking a drink of the rum Sanchez tapped the man next to him with his knee, who tapped the next, who tapped the next.

"So, amigo, what are you doing here at the Tequendama? It's more upper-class than what you're probably accustomed to."

Reynolds sat his beer down and turned to completely face the man. "I'm sorry. I didn't catch your name."

"My name is Alex Sanchez," he said, getting up off the stool and walking towards Reynolds, followed by the other four men. "And if you reach for your gun," he continued as he approached Reynolds, "you may kill me, but you'll not get all of us and you'll certainly die."

The other four men now had their pistols pointed at Reynolds and walked to get behind him.

"Fuck," Reynolds said. He picked up his beer and took a long drink as the waiter also pointed a pistol at Reynolds's head.

"Put your hands flat on the bar," Sanchez ordered and waited until Reynolds set the beer down and complied.

Reaching into the front of Reynolds's pants, Sanchez lifted the shirt and pulled out the 9mm Beretta.

"Nice weapon, but the Israeli Mossad didn't care for them. The grips were too small. But I always heard that the US Army Green Berets and Rangers loved them," Sanchez said, glancing at the tattoo of the 101st Airborne Screaming Eagles on Reynolds's right forearm."

"I'll get it back," Reynolds calmly said.

Sanchez shoved the Beretta into the back of his belt under his suit coat. "Stand up and keep your hands on the bar," Sanchez demanded.

Sliding off the stool, Reynolds stood as Sanchez started searching his pockets. He pulled the wallet from the back right pocket, opened it, and glanced at the Virginia driver's license. "Jack Reynolds, nice to meet you," Sanchez said, as he closed the wallet and put it in his coat pocket. Searching further, Sanchez pulled the Nokia phone from his left front pants pocket. "I wonder whose numbers you have on this," Sanchez said, staring at the big man who didn't respond.

"Unless you want to die tonight, this is how this is going to work," Sanchez said. "We're going to walk out of here, and you're getting in the back of a black Mercedes parked outside. Go now."

Picking up the glass of beer, Reynolds drank the rest of it and set the glass back down on the bar as he turned to face the men.

Sanchez motioned with his head to one of the men who started out first with Reynolds close behind as the other men, pointing their guns at Reynolds's back, followed him out of the hotel and onto the sidewalk.

"Get in the back," Sanchez said.

One of the men opened the rear door of the Mercedes as the first man went to the other side of the car and got in the backseat, pointing his gun at Reynolds as he got in.

Another man got in after Reynolds and shut the rear door.

Turning, Sanchez said, to one of the men, "Thiago, you stay here. Go back upstairs, but don't tell anyone what happened. I'm taking him to the ranch."

"Si, sir," the man said and turned to go back into the hotel.

Getting in the front passenger seat, Sanchez said, to the driver, "Go to Blanca."

"Where are you taking me?" Reynolds asked with his two seatmates pointing their pistols at his chest.

Sanchez turned in the seat to face Reynolds. "Just a little drive out into the country. We call it the ranch. It's near the airport, so the sounds of the jet engines will drown out any screams you might have, that is, if we time it right."

"I work for the gas company, asshole."

"We'll see. Give me your hands," Sanchez said as he took a pair of handcuffs out of his pocket.

Reynolds leaned forward and extended his arms. Sanchez quickly slapped the cuffs on both wrists and tightened them.

"When I'm done, I'll know everything about you," the Israeli Mossad–trained Medellin Cartel intelligence officer said and turned to face the front of the car.

CHAPTER 24

Jack's Missing

8 p.m., Wednesday, April 21, 1993

I'll be damned, Reynolds thought as the car pulled into the house he had been to just hours before near the Bogota Airport.

"Get him to the basement, and strip him," Sanchez ordered.

The two men in the back seat held Reynolds's arms and led him into the house.

"I want those clothes burned. I want no trace of him here after we get rid of the body," Sanchez said to the driver.

"Si, sir."

Walking in behind the men and down the stairs to the basement, Sanchez watched as Reynolds was stripped and then placed in a high-backed metal torture chair.

"Tie him tight," Sanchez said. He took the handcuffs off Reynolds's hands and watched the big man strain against the rope that had been placed around his neck and was pulling him tightly back against the chair. His ankles had already been shackled to the legs of the chair as his arms were now being held down and strapped to the metal arms.

Picking up a clear plastic jug, Sanchez showed it to Reynolds and said, "This is sulfuric acid. If I put one drop of it on the head of your dick, you will never have sex again, amigo."

"Well, that's no good," Reynolds said, struggling to speak against the rope around his neck. "I still like to play."

"I'm afraid, my friend, your play time is over unless you tell me who you are and why you were at the Tequendama."

"My name is Jack Reynolds, and I work for Dominion Gas Company out of Virginia, USA."

"I doubt that, my friend," Sanchez said, setting down the jug of acid and taking one of Reynolds's hands in his own. "No, you do not work in the gas fields. Your hands have no calluses. And you're not office personnel either. No Green Beret would ever sit in an office. So whom do you work for, Jack Reynolds?"

Before Reynolds spoke, the black Nokia phone in Sanchez's pocket began to vibrate. "Gag him now," Sanchez ordered. He took out the phone and looked at the incoming number as it vibrated while a large cloth gag was tied across Reynolds's mouth. "Well this is interesting. Nine-one-one is calling you, amigo," Sanchez said, showing Reynolds the number displayed. "And Colombia doesn't have a 911 service, but they do at Langley."

The phone vibrated several times and stopped.

"Don't worry. They'll call back in a minute or so," Sanchez said. "But I'm not answering it and getting pinged. So no one is going to know where you're at, ever."

"Ahhggghhh," Reynolds groaned as he tried to speak through the gag.

"Take the gag out," Sanchez instructed. "I want to hear what he has to say."

The gag was untied and pulled out of Reynolds's mouth. He spit onto the floor, looked at Sanchez, and said, "Don't be so sure."

Smiling, Sanchez said, "Gag him and let's leave him for a while so he can think about what he wants to tell us."

Turning to climb the steps, Sanchez looked back at Reynolds and said, "I'll be back, amigo."

"Taa yur fukenn tiiim," Reynolds groaned as the gag was placed back in his mouth and he heard his phone start to vibrate again.

"You see," Sanchez yelled, standing on the stairs, holding the phone up so Reynolds could see it. "They're looking for you."

AGUILAR HAD CALLED REYNOLDS TWICE WITH no answer. Now he slowly drove around Hotel Tequendama, ignoring a woman who waved for a taxi. Parking the car in the reserved spot for taxis and before getting out, he checked his Sig Sauer pistol for a live round in the chamber, placed it in the small of his back, and pulled his shirt down. Opening the glove box, he took out the extra key for room 217. After getting out of the cab, the former SEAL stood by the car for several moments to check around. His situational awareness was hitting on all cylinders.

"Where are you, Jack?" he whispered as he walked to the front entrance of the hotel and went inside. After climbing the stairs to the second floor, he stood by the door of room 217 and listened. Hearing nothing, he used his key, opened the door, and pulled his pistol before entering. "Jack," Aguilar said as he began sweeping the rooms with his pistol ready and his finger on the trigger. "Jack," he repeated as he went into the bathroom. Nothing looked like it was disturbed, and in the bedroom, he found the black bag underneath the bed containing the extra phone and MP5 mag. Checking under the mattress, he found the MP5 and placed it in the black bag.

"Dammit," he said, pulling his phone out of his pocket and hitting the second call button.

"HELLO," WEST SAID, ANSWERING HIS PHONE.

"Nate, I can't find Jack," Aguilar said.

"What?"

"I was running a little late and called Jack's phone as I came into town about eight. No answer. I called back. Same thing. I'm here in his hotel room now. He's gone, but his black bag and MP5 are here."

"Dammit. Did you check downstairs?"

"I will on my way out, but I don't have a good feeling about this. Watch your six. I'm heading your way now."

"Dammit. Roger that," West said, hanging up and pulling his MP5 out from under the mattress where he had placed it. Checking the weapon, he clicked the safety to F for *feuerstoss*, meaning full auto.

"Where the hell are you, Jack?" West said as he sat down in the chair facing the door.

Rancho Blanca

Sanchez walked up the stairs and was met by one of his bodyguards.

"I found Wilfredo. He's dead."

"Where?"

"In the kitchen," the man said and walked back through the house followed by Sanchez. Turning the corner into the kitchen, the man stood to the side to allow Sanchez in.

Seeing the body, he knelt down to get a closer look at the dead man and the pistol. "Why would he kill himself?" Sanchez asked, turning to look at the bodyguard.

"I don't know, but he was crazy and always complained about his teeth hurting."

"Hmmm," Sanchez said, as he examined the wound closely. It had powder burns on his hair and flesh, so the pistol was very close to the head when fired, he thought. Looking at the end of the pistol, he could see dried blood on the barrel. "Hmmm," Sanchez said again as he got up. "Get him out of here, and clean this place up."

"Where do you want me to take the body?"

"Drive out into the countryside and dump him somewhere. Just get him the hell out of here. He's already starting to stink."

Feeling Reynold's phone start vibrating again, Sanchez looked at the display as it showed a local number.

"Word's out," Sanchez said, looking at his watch. "Ten minutes."

Aguilar arrived at the Santafe Suite and quickly climbed the stairs after looking around. Standing to the side of room 302's door so he wouldn't get shot, he lightly tapped on the door and said, "The frog's ass is watertight."

West opened the door and let the SEAL into the room and then locked it. "Nothing?" West asked.

"No, not a sign," Aguilar said.

"I called his phone too a few minutes ago, and no answer. I think we need to assume Jack and the phone are in cartel hands," West replied.

"Yes, I agree."

"Are the calls made from these phones monitored by Langley?" West asked.

"Yes, if the phone was answered, we could get a location."

Shaking his head, West said, "They'll know that and not answer that phone, and they'll know we're looking for Jack if we call it anymore."

"Yes, I agree. They probably already know we're looking after three calls."

"Yes, damn," West said.

"And you're not going to like this, but I'll need to call this in," Aguilar said. "They may want to scrub this mission and get you back to the States before we lose any more people."

"You can't do that."

"Give me a good reason not to and I'll consider it."

"If they ship me back, Jack and Sanita are as good as dead. I have an in."

"They're probably both dead anyway. And what's your in?"

"That's why we needed to meet with you tonight. Sanita is alive. I saw her at ten this morning, I saw her."

"Where?"

"After you made the phone call, we followed a black Rover and a man back to a house about a mile from the airport. It was Rico. This morning before daylight, I went back in to watch the place; Jack stayed on the road in his car. At ten this morning, Rafael showed up, and they carried Sanita out of the house, put her in Rafael's car, and left. Rico followed them."

"How do you know this?" Aguilar asked.

"I hit the house as soon as the cars pulled out and caught one of the bodyguards in the kitchen. He told me Rico left in the second car and was going to assist in getting Sanita healthy again."

"Did the man in the house know where they were going?"

"No."

What happened to the man in the house?"

"He shot himself, or so it will appear," West said. "Rico will be back at that house in the next few days. That's where he lives because he's the pilot and he needs to be near Espinoza's aircraft. He'll know where Sanita and Jack are being kept."

Aguilar studied West, nodded, and said, "Yes, that seems logical."

"You need to trust me, Luis. I'll find them both. I have a long history of being able to do this. But I need your help to do it."

Aguilar sat back in his chair and drummed his fingers on the table. "If asked, I could say things are progressing with Team Thorn. And this wouldn't interfere with me assisting Wilson and the others."

"Who told you Team Thorn?" West asked.

"That's what they call you guys at Langley."

"I need to bring one more guy into this. What he has to say may help you in making this decision. All right?"

"Yes," Aguilar replied.

West picked up his phone and called a number on St. Simons Island, Georgia.

CHAPTER 25

Pure Manhunter

8 p.m., Wednesday, April 21, 1993

"Hello," a female voice said, answering the phone.

"Melinda, it's Nathan."

"Hi, Nathan. How are you doing?" Melinda Hicks Hayden asked.

"I'm good. Is Buddy handy?"

"Yes, just a moment. I'll get him."

West could hear Mrs. Hayden yell, "Honey, Nathan's on the phone."

"Nathan West?" Buddy Hayden yelled back up the steps from the downstairs garage.

"Yes."

"Okay, I'll get it down here," Hayden yelled as he picked up the garage phone.

"Got it, honey," Hayden said after he picked up the receiver.

"Okay, honey," she said to her husband and then, "Take care Nathan," as she hung up.

"Why the call?" Hayden asked.

"Jack's missing."

"Jack Reynolds is missing?" Hayden asked, astounded.

"Yes, it's been about an hour now," West said. "I'm putting you on speaker. Luis Aguilar, the agency lead is here with me. I need him to hear your comments.

"Okay. Hello, Luis. This is former CIA Senior Supervisor Buddy Hayden."

"Hello, Buddy. I've heard of you. You're a legend to the people in the field."

"Yeah, well legends are all past tense. Give me the details on this," Hayden instructed.

"We don't have much at this point," West began. "Luis was to pick Jack up and bring him to my hotel. We can't find him now. He was taken from the Tequendama."

"Dammit, the cartel must have him."

"Yes, that's what we think too."

"What's your plan?" Hayden asked.

"For right now, I need you to do damage control. This can't get back to Wolfe, or they'll decide to pull me out of here. If they do that, Jack and the missing Customs agent are dead."

"Nathan, there's not a man alive that I have more faith in finding them than you. This is what you were born to do. I've never known a more pure manhunter than you are. Luis, are you hearing this?" Hayden asked.

"Yes, sir. I hear you."

"Luis, I've been in your shoes, and I know what the agency would want you to do. But you need to look at the man there with you, listen to what he says, stay out of his way, and give him anything that he needs. There's no one that has his instincts."

"Yes, sir. I understand and I'm prepared to do that."

"Excellent. Nate, where you starting?" Hayden asked.

"I've got an in. I know where the pilot lives, and he knows where the Customs agent is. He should also know where Jack is being kept."

"If they're still alive," Hayden said.

"I can't say for Jack, Buddy, but I saw the girl this morning at 10 a.m."

"Where?"

"At the pilot's home. Rafael was moving her, and Rico, the pilot, went with them. When he returns home, we're having a chat."

"You saw Rafael?"

"Yes."

"All right, well, we both know Jack has been tortured before and lived. I wouldn't count him out anytime soon," Hayden said. "That bastard is almost indestructible."

"Yes, Jack's tough," West agreed.

"Find them, Nathan. You know Jack is expecting you to bust through that door at any moment. Find them."

"I will, Buddy. I wanted to give you a heads-up so you can keep them off my ass. This may take some time to sort out."

"Will do. I'll contact Gales and let him know. He'll agree with us, and he can take it a step further if we need to."

"Buddy, is my phone number displayed for you?"

"Yes, it is. I've got it."

"Okay, I've got work to do. I'll let you know something as soon as I know," West said.

"Thanks, Nathan, Godspeed. Good bye."

"Talk later, Buddy. Bye," West said and hung up the Nokia. Looking at Aguilar, West asked, "Satisfied?"

"Yes. You tell me what you need and I'll support whatever."

"Thank you."

Carrera 78
9 a.m., Thursday, April 22

"Rafael is pulling in," Maria said to Rico as she looked out the front window and then walked back to the kitchen where Rico continued to sip on his coffee.

Sounds of the garage door opening in the basement and the vehicle pulling in penetrated the kitchen. Then car doors opened and shut as footsteps sounded coming up the creaking stairs.

Opening the door into the living room, Rafael walked in and continued into the kitchen, looking at Rico and Maria. "How is she?" he asked

"She's doing some better," Maria replied. "But it will be slow."

Rico nodded his head before taking another sip of coffee.

"Do you want some coffee, Rafael?" Rico asked.

"I'll get it," Rafael replied, paused, and then asked, "Will she speak to me?"

"I don't believe she wants to speak to you just yet," Maria said. "Perhaps in a few more days."

Rafael nodded and walked to the counter. Turning he said, "Rico, I want you to stay here a week or so. I need a man in this house that I trust," Rafael said as he poured himself a cup of black coffee from the pot on the stove.

"Yes, Rafael, that's no problem for me."

"Do we need to do anything for the jet?" Rafael asked, sipping on the hot black liquid.

"The annual is coming up, but I'll take care of that. Everything else is fine at the hangar. We did have a false alarm a few nights ago, but everything was good."

"What false alarm?" Rafael asked, turning to look at the pilot.

"Airport Security Commander Alvarez called me the other night and said someone had possibly broken into the hangar. But I went over and nothing was disturbed. We think it was a prank call."

"All right. You stay here until I say you can go back to the ranch."

"Yes, Rafael."

"There are some other things going on there right now, so being here is probably better anyway."

"Yes, Rafael," Rico said and thought, What other things?

DEA Special Agent Julio Piniella woke up in room 723 at the Nutibara Hotel. He had needed that sleep after traveling the day before.

What a shit show, he thought, thinking about the discussion with SAC Wilson the night before and into the early morning hours. Piniella was an experienced agent and understood the pressures Wilson was under in losing one of his agents. He knew the same tragedy when he was stationed in Guadalajara, Mexico, a few years before when Kiki Salazar, a fellow DEA agent and close friend was kidnapped and killed in the most brutal of ways in 1985. That killing still haunted Piniella. "Damn shit show," he said, thinking of how distraught Wilson was. "Alejandro needs to be killed, that will put an end to a lot of this."

After getting out of bed, taking a hot shower, and getting dressed, he knocked on room 721's door before he opened the unlocked adjoining door. "Good morning, Dale," Piniella said, looking at the worn-out man sitting at his desk writing.

"Good morning, Julio. Be with you in just a minute," Wilson replied, finishing up on his daily journal for the day before. Closing the book, he turned to Piniella and said, "This morning, I'll introduce you to General Marquez. He's a straight shooter and a hard charger. He can be trusted, and he hates Alejandro Espinoza."

"Yes, I understand Alejandro was responsible for killing the general's daughter."

"Yes, he blew her up in a car bomb. We were only able to recover small pieces of that young lady's body, pieces the general buried. He cried for weeks."

Piniella nodded, "There's no greater hate."

"No. Let me get a hot shower, and I'll be ready in a few minutes."

"Sir, may I suggest you shave as well?"

Wilson looked at the agent and rubbed his face with his right hand. After letting out a deep breath, he said, "Yes, it's time."

Carlos Holquin School,
Search Bloc Headquarters, Medellin
11:30 a.m.

"GENERAL, THIS IS DEA SPECIAL AGENT JULIO PINIELLA," Wilson said, standing in General Marquez's office.

Marquez got up from behind his desk and shook hands with the large man. "Firm grip, I like that in a soldier," Marquez said.

"Thank you, sir."

"Have a seat, both of you," Marquez said as he shut his office door.

"How long have you been with the DEA?"

"Twelve years, sir. Prior to that I was a deputy sheriff for almost ten years. I've been around, so whatever you need, I should be able to make it happen."

"Good. The CIA aircraft will be here Sunday with DEA pilots. Is that correct?" Marquez asked.

"Yes, sir. Originally, they were going to be agency pilots, but they turned that over to us. So I'll be the lead on directing the aircraft. How do you want to do this?"

"I have the Delta Team that's here embedded with my troops. We have two strike teams north and south of here, and we have thirty two-man mobile units that can respond quickly when we intercept a transmission from the cartel. We have a telescopic camera and relay equipment on a tower at La Catedral on the mountain. Delta sat that up. What we're missing are eyes in the sky. You're here to provide that."

"Yes, sir. We can do that starting next week. How many hits have you had?"

"Dale, what are we up to now?"

"We're past twenty," Wilson said, looking at Piniella. "But we haven't been able to get there soon enough to lay eyes on any target vehicle. I know we have driven past them multiple times, but there are thousands of vehicles out there at all hours."

"I see," Piniella said. "General, do you have quarters here where I can stay? I want to be here until this is over. And just to be clear, General, I am not here to capture Espinoza. I'm here to make sure he's put in the dirt."

General Marquez smiled and said, "I'll make quarters for you, and you'll have a maid that will be available night or day. She'll cook, clean, and do whatever you want. Let me know when you're ready to move in."

"Thank you, General. I brought my luggage with me. I won't be leaving."

CHAPTER 26

It's a Waiting Game

12:05 a.m., Saturday, May 1, 1993

It had been a long week, and West was feeling exhausted. Daily surveillance of the house near the Bogota International Airport showed several people coming and going in a black Mercedes, but Rico in his Land Rover was not one of them. Every day, from 5 a.m. to midnight, West had been lying in the tall grass next to the fence row.

Aguilar would drop West off at 5 a.m. and then pick him back up after midnight. The rest of the day, he would assist SAC Wilson and DEA Agent Piniella. The CIA aircraft piloted by DEA agents had been flying for days, but there were no hits from anywhere. It was like the Medellin cartel had disappeared.

Now on his back, West pulled out his phone and turned it on. He wasn't going to be without battery again when he needed it. If there was any trouble, Luis was to drive to the fruit stand and blow the car horn. It would be easily heard from West's position, but that had not been necessary so far. "Moving," West said in the phone after hitting 911 and hearing it answered.

"Roger that," Aguilar said as he sat along the road in the blue Renault. The taxi would only draw attention and had been left near the Santafe Suite.

Crossing the final fence next to the road, West got in the passenger side of the Renault, and Aguilar pulled out.

"Anything?" Aguilar asked.

"No, Rico hasn't shown yet. I've seen a black Mercedes come and go, but Rico's not in it. There are usually two or three men in the Mercedes, and the front passenger appears to be the one in charge and giving orders. I thought I could hear someone scream a time or two, but my hearing sucks. Too many gunshots close to the ears, and I may only be hearing my tinnitus."

"I'm the same way; my hearing is gone. So what's next?" Aguilar asked.

"I have no what's next. Have you ever hunted a mature whitetail buck, Luis?"

"No, I grew up in Philadelphia. The only thing I ever hunted was pussy."

"Well, that's close. Mature whitetail bucks are pretty much totally nocturnal animals almost all year."

Aguilar drove back towards Bogota and said, "So basically you're screwed if you can't see them during the daylight."

"Yep, except during the time of the year that they're chasing pussy. It's called the rut, usually around the first two weeks in November, around my birth date. They get with it and try to breed as many does as they can. Nature at its finest, and that pussy gets them killed."

"What are you getting at?"

"A West Virginia bowhunter will sit in a tree stand for hours, days, weeks, and months just to get a glimpse of a mature buck. The probability of seeing just one mature buck is very slim during the entire season of three months. You'll see a ton of young bucks, but a mature wall hanger, they're very rare. And when you do see one, it'll only be for a few seconds. That's your window of opportunity, seconds, not minutes, and he's gone."

"And?" Aguilar asked.

"You learn to wait and be patient. Get me back here at five in the morning," West said, as he laid his head back on the seat and closed his eyes. "It's a waiting game, Luis."

Rancho Blanca
1 p.m.

It had been a longer week for Jack Reynolds. The daily shock treatments were taking their toll. He hadn't eaten any solid food since the day he had been captured. When not in the metal chair, he was lying on the cold concrete floor naked and chained by his left ankle shackled to a concreted eyebolt in the floor. He could move only in a circle around the eyebolt. His urine, what was generated, would trickle into the drain he now lay on. He hadn't had a bowel movement in over a week. Nothing in, nothing out. They did give him some water daily, but he had already lost enough weight to where he was seeing abdominal muscles and his ribs. Reynolds lay on the floor exhausted. Hearing someone coming down the stairs, he looked up.

"How are you doing today, amigo?" Sanchez asked.

Reynolds was barely able to reply, "Fuck you."

"Get him in the chair," Sanchez said to the two men with him.

Taking Reynolds by the arms, the men picked him up and sat him in the cold steel chair and fastened his legs and arms tightly.

"Okay, amigo, whom do you work for today? Yesterday, it was still Dominion Gas," Sanchez said and laughed.

Reynolds raised his head slightly and hissed, "Fuck you."

Sanchez nodded at one of the men who climbed onto a stationary bike that was attached to a high voltage generator.

"One last chance, amigo. Whom do you work for?" Sanchez asked, walking over to the wall where a throw switch was located.

"Fuck you, you son of a bitch."

"Okay, gag him and let's go for one minute today. You won't die, but you'll wish you could," Sanchez said and nodded to the man on the bike who started pedaling rapidly. Sanchez waited until the gag was tied around Reynolds head and then moved the switch down to make contact as the heavy wires that went from the generator to the steel chair began to get warm. Reynolds screamed through the thick cloth gag that had been placed over his face and mouth as his body convulsed with every muscle going into spasms. Before going unconscious, Jack Reynolds roared one more primordial scream.

West rolled onto his side, tilted his head towards the house and cupped his ears with his hands. He lay perfectly quiet and held his breath so the sound of his breathing wouldn't interfere with his hearing. Squinting his eyes closed, he listened for several seconds, and then he heard it again.

"There's somebody in that house screaming," he said. "I'm sure of it now," and rolled onto his back. He felt it was a man's scream. Could it be Jack? he thought. But he still couldn't move, even if it was Reynolds. If he hit the house now, it would perhaps save the person screaming, but it would doom Sanita, even if West lived in the process. Once that place was raided, it would be written off by everyone, including Rico. And he didn't know if it was Jack or not. West couldn't take that chance. One thing he was absolutely sure of; Jack would want him to wait. No matter what, Jack would want West to wait.

Carrera 78
7 p.m.

"Tomorrow, you can return to the ranch," Rafael said. "I'll send two of my men here, and they can watch her."

"I can stay longer if you want me to," Rico said.

"No, it won't be necessary. She's getting well enough to try to escape, and I don't want you in that position. If she tries to escape, they'll be better able to handle that."

"What are you saying, Rafael?"

"I told Alejandro that she's here," Rafael said. "He's my brother, and we have no secrets. Alejandro will only tolerate her being kept alive if she stays in this house. If she tries to leave, we'll have no choice. Alejandro wants Alex here if she tries to escape."

"I understand, Rafael. I'll leave when the men arrive tomorrow." Rico said and glanced at Maria who was now standing in the kitchen doorway. They both knew Sanchez would find an excuse to kill Sanita.

"GOOD EVENING. GALES RESIDENCE," a female voice said.

"Good evening. This is Buddy Hayden. Is Director Gales in?"

"One moment, please," the lady said, and then Hayden could hear muffled voices.

"Buddy?" former CIA Director Robert Gales said.

"Yes, sir. I'm here at FLETC. Can you call me on your STU at my number here?"

"Yes, I'll call you right back," Gales said and then hung up.

Less than a minute later, Hayden's STU at FLETC started beeping. "Hello, Director, three, two, one," Hayden said as they turned their STU keys to encrypt the call.

"What's going on, Buddy?"

"Jack Reynolds is missing, and we're presuming he's been kidnapped by the cartel."

"When did this happen?"

"Last week, but I wanted to wait and see if this would be resolved one way or another before I brought you into this."

"What do we know?" Gales asked.

"He was taken from the Tequendama hotel. Other than that, we know very little. West has a possible lead, but it has not panned out as of late last night when I spoke to him."

"How can I help? Do you need me to send this on up?" Gales asked.

"No sir, and that's why I'm calling. West doesn't want to be interfered with, and if this gets out, Wolfe may want to pull him out to prevent anymore missing personnel."

"Yes, and that's exactly what he will do. I would probably do the same thing with these circumstances."

"Sir, we can't let that happen. We must leave West in play."

"Can he pull this off, Buddy?"

"I believe he can, sir. And frankly, he's probably the only man I know that can."

"All right. What's the lead you mentioned?" Gales asked.

"West knows of a man in the cartel that knows where the missing Customs agent is located."

"Yes, I was told about her. But is she even still alive?

"Yes, we believe so, sir. West saw her last week when they were moving her from one location to another. He now knows the name of the cartel member who knows where she is being kept, and West knows where that cartel member lives. West is waiting for the cartel member to return to his home. West will make him talk when he does, one way or another. West also believes this man will know where Jack is being held if he's still alive. So it's been a waiting game."

"I see," Gales said.

"There's one more piece of information, sir. And it may be relevant."

"What is it?"

"West said, he could hear a man scream in the house he's watching."

"Dear God," Gales said.

CHAPTER 27

Alex Sanchez

8 a.m., Sunday, May 2, 1993

"Good morning, Angelina," Rico said, carrying a bowl of warm oatmeal and toast into the bedroom.

Sitting up in bed by herself, Lopez said, "Good morning, Rico. Maria told you my real name?"

"Si, she did. We both care for you and want you healthy."

"Thank you. You both have been wonderful to me," Lopez said with a small smile.

Rico smiled back and sat the bowl holding the toast on the stand next to the bed.

"I need to talk to you. I'm leaving this morning. Rafael wants me to return to Bogota and continue my work there."

"As their pilot?"

"Si."

"I remember you flying Rafael and me."

"Si."

"I will miss you, Rico. You have been so kind."

"Thank you. I need you to listen to me carefully. Rafael is sending two men to take my place. He has told Alejandro that you are here, and Alejandro has demanded some changes if you are to be kept alive."

Lopez looked intently at Rico and asked, "What changes and who are the men?"

"One of the men is the man who hit you, Alex Sanchez. The other is one of Sanchez's men."

"What changes?" Lopez asked, her hopes dying.

"Maria will not be allowed to be here long. And they have orders to kill you if you try to escape. You must not give them any reason to hurt you, or they will," Rico said forcefully. "Do you understand?"

"Si," Lopez replied, as her heart sank. After pausing, she said, "I have faith in God that I will be rescued. I know they're looking for me, and they will find me eventually."

"Perhaps," Rico replied.

"Please listen to me, Rico. It will happen. And when it does, you and Maria are in danger. I told Maria this, and I'm now telling you."

"What?"

"When they come, the only chance you have of not being shot is to immediately raise your hands and say 'FLETC, FLETC.'"

"Si, Maria told me that," Rico replied.

"You must do it, Rico. Being a man, you will be automatically killed when they come."

"All right, I'll do that. But I'm sorry, it may never happen."

Lopez looked at Rico, took him by the hand, and said, "Yes, it will."

Rancho Blanca
9 a.m.

"You get a break today, amigo. It's Sunday, and we don't torture American agents on the blessed day," Sanchez said, sitting on the stairs and looking at Reynolds lying on the floor.

Reynolds could barely raise his head to look at the man. He was too weak to speak, but he thought, Fuck you.

"Also, we will feed you today. So it is a blessed day, amigo. I'll be back tomorrow. To be honest, I've never seen anyone last two weeks with this treatment, so you need to be giving it some serious thought on when you want this to stop. Of course, we will shoot you when you tell me what I want, but at least it will be over. So think about it, amigo." Sanchez said as he stood and walked up the stairs.

"Mateo come with me," Sanchez said when he got to the living room. "Felipe, you and Bruno stay here. Feed the American something and give him more water. I need to go babysit the bitch for Alejandro. I'll be back tomorrow."

"Si, sir," Felipe replied and turned to the largest of the men, his younger brother, Bruno, and signed to indicate for him to stay there at that house.

"Ahhhh," the deaf mute replied and nodded as Sanchez and Mateo left.

"Hmmm," West said as he watched two men leave in the Mercedes. "That leaves two there with no car."

So, far that day there had been no screams coming from the house. West hoped Jack was there and at the same time wished he wasn't. Rolling onto his back, he remembered Reynolds telling him three months earlier in Jersey City when they were trying to stop a van full of cyanide to "Hang tight, Nate. We need to let this play out; hang tight."

West took a deep breath and said, "I'm hanging tight, Jack. You do the same. I'll find you and Sanita," as he glanced back towards the house.

"Come on, Rico," he said, as he closed his eyes and whispered a prayer. "Lord, I need some help."

Carrera 78
10:30 a.m.

Mateo pulled the Mercedes into the downstairs garage and followed Sanchez up the stairs.

"Where is she?" Sanchez demanded from Rico who was standing in the kitchen.

"Bedroom on the right in the hall. Maria is bathing her now."

"I don't care," Sanchez said, and he turned, walked into the hall, and kicked the door open.

Maria was startled and jumped back from the tray of warm water and soap that was next to the naked Lopez who sat on the toilet chair. Lowering the washcloth from her left armpit, she glared at Sanchez who stood in the doorway.

"You're mine now, bitch. Just give me a reason, and I'll joyfully cut your throat," he said. "Maria, when you're done, get out. Orders from Rafael," he added and turned and walked back to the kitchen.

Maria closed the door to the bedroom, sat down on the bed facing Lopez while she put her arm around the young lady. Lopez lowered her head and placed it on the woman's chest as tears began to form. Stifling her emotions, she sat up straight, looked at Maria and said, "He will not break me."

In the kitchen, Sanchez was getting a cup of coffee and said, "Rico, you're free to go. We'll take over now,"

"Si, Alex. Can I speak freely?"

"No, keep your damn mouth shut," Sanchez said as he whirled around and glared at the man. "Collect your things and get back to the ranch."

"Si, sir."

Rancho Blanca
1 p.m.

West was lying in the tall grass half asleep when he heard a car coming down the main road past the fruit stand. Listening intently, he said, "I think it turned in." He raised his head to look past his feet and above the grass. Coming down the road was a black Land Rover. West let out a huge sigh as he watched it turn into the house driveway. Peering through the grass, West watched Rico get out of the vehicle and start into the house. Looking back down past his feet to the road, West figured he could run and beat the Rover before it got past him and to the main road if it pulled back out from the house.

"I hope you're staying, asshole," West said, but holding the MP5, he prepared to dash to the road if Rico got back in the Rover. He lay there and watched the house. One hour went by, then two, then four. He's not leaving, West thought.

Pulling the phone out of his pocket, he turned it on, hit 911 and placed it to his ear.

"Hello."

"Luis, what's your twenty?"

"Medellin. What's going on?"

"Target is home. Looks like he's staying. We hit it tonight zero dark thirty."

"Roger that. Where do you want to meet."

"I'm staying here in case he tries to leave. I need you to drive to the end of their driveway tonight at 0100. I'll meet you there."

"How many're in the house?"

"Two who appear to be bodyguards and Rico. He's less of a threat than they are."

"Roger that. I'll bring hate and meet you there."

"Affirmative. I'll turn my phone back on at 2300."

"Roger that."

West turned the phone off and slid it back into his pocket.

Carrera 78
6 p.m.

"I'M LEAVING THE DOORS UNLOCKED, so please, run for it," Sanchez said, standing in the doorway of the bedroom. "I would like nothing better than to chase you down the street and cut your throat in front of everyone on the block."

"What made you such a piece of shit, Alex?" Lopez asked. "I bet your mother doesn't even claim you, and from what I hear, she's a whore."

"I see you're getting your strength back," Sanchez said and smirked. "Well, just remember this: you're the scarred whore now and you always will be. You'll never be able to scrub your ass enough to get off what we left there, and you'll never forget what we did to you. And from what I was told, you climaxed on every man that had you. So who's really the whore, you little bitch?"

"I'll watch you die," Lopez said, glaring back at the man as he smirked again and left the room, shutting the door behind him. "I'll watch you die, you son of a bitch," she screamed at the closed door.

Rancho Blanca
11:00 p.m.

"Hello," Aguilar said, answering his phone.

"I'm back on. Any changes?" West asked.

"Negative. I'll be there at 0100. You good?"

"Affirmative, I'm ready. I think they have gone to bed. Looks like a single light is still on in the living room, and I no longer can hear the TV."

"Roger that. I'll see you in three hours."

"Hey, do you have a master key?" West asked.

"Ten-four. I'm bringing my breacher with me."

"Roger that," West replied and hung up.

Rancho Blanca
12:30 a.m., Monday, May 3

West stood up for the first time in nineteen hours. His jeans and black T-shirt were damp from lying in the grass all day. Rising up to his tiptoes, he moved both legs back and forth to get his circulation pumping. Sliding the MP5 sling around his neck, he let the weapon lie on his back as he slowly began to cross the barbed wire fence by pushing the top wire down and stepping over it. Once on the other side of the fence, he lowered his right shoulder and let the weapon swing back to his chest where he held the hand grip tightly with his right hand, thumbed the safety off, and placed his finger on the trigger. Walking across the field, he angled towards the end of the driveway where it connected with the gravel road. When he reached that fence, he slid the weapon to his back once again and pushed down on the top wire to step over.

After crossing, he slid the weapon back to his chest once more and stood in the driveway. Looking back at the house and the black Land Rover, he could hear no noise coming from the house.

Twenty-five minutes later, West could hear a vehicle. Looking back to the main road, he saw headlights that suddenly went out as Aguilar turned the Renault down the side road and towards West. Slowly pulling up to the end of the driveway one hundred yards from the house, Aguilar turned the car off.

In the night, he could see a figure walking towards the car. Aguilar slowly got out and quietly closed the driver's door. "Any problems?" he softly asked West.

"Negative, no one's up from what I can see or hear," West whispered.

Aguilar opened up the back door and picked up a sawed-off 12-gauge pump shotgun from the seat. "My breacher," Aguilar whispered.

West nodded and could see a holster holding his Sig Sauer 9mm on his right hip. "This is the layout of the house: living room inside front door, hallway is straight ahead, first door on left goes to stairwell leading to basement, second door on left is bathroom; at the end of the hall on the left is a small bedroom with one bed. First hallway door on the right is a large bedroom with four beds. I think that's where the muscle will be sleeping. Door at end of hallway on right is the kitchen."

"First door on the right," Luis repeated.

"Affirmative, that's where I think the threat will come from too. There's a light on in the living room. That'll give us enough light to see down the hallway. You blow the door lock, and I'm kicking it in. The door swings to the right, so I'm going left," West said.

"Roger that. Stay tight," Aguilar said, and both men fist bumped.

West nodded, "Always."

CHAPTER 28

You Were at the Airport

1 a.m., Monday, May 3, 1993

"Quiet, shhh," Rico whispered, holding a finger to his lips. "Here's some warm meat broth," he said, helping Reynolds to sit up and then handing him the small cup.

With shaking hands, the weakened man drank the broth under the single light bulb in the ceiling.

"Thank you," he could barely say. "The key's hanging on the wall. Turn me loose."

"I'm sorry, I can't," Rico said. "They'd kill me. But I'll help you as much as I can."

BOOOM! There was a very loud noise as the front door lock was blown into the living room by the 12-gauge slug and West kicked the door open.

"What was that? Rico said, jumping up and standing against the wall.

Reynolds smiled and said, "A shotgun. Don't go up there."

West quickly entered the room and cleared to the left as Luis came in behind him clearing to the right. Each man stopped and crouched on his side of the room, both pointing their weapons down the hall. The first door on the right burst open, and a man jumped into the hallway, pointing a pistol back towards the front door as he fired two shots that missed both men and went through the open door.

At the same moment, West's MP5 sent a short automatic burst of 9mm slugs into the man's chest as Aguilar's 12-gauge slug ripped through the man's throat, taking a four-inch piece of spine out the back of his neck and dropping him to the floor.

"Ahhhh," a man screamed as he appeared from the bedroom holding a machete over his head. The man saw flashes coming from both sides of the room, but the loud BRRRRRP from the MP5 and the BOOOM from the 12-gauge were sounds he never heard as he crumbled to the floor beside his brother.

"Down here," West heard someone call from the basement.

Motioning to Aguilar, West first pointed two fingers at him, next pointed spread fingers at his own eyes, and then shook them back at the basement door.

Aguilar nodded and pointed the shotgun at the basement door as West stepped over the bodies and continued down the hall. After quickly clearing all the rooms, West returned to Aguilar next to the door that went to the basement. Aguilar reached up to the doorknob and looked at West who nodded. Aguilar slung the door open as West pointed the MP5 down the steps.

"Identify yourself," West yelled down the stairs.

"Is a frog's ass watertight?" was the weakened answer that came back up the stairs.

"Jack!" West said as he hurried down the stairs pointing the MP5 into the basement.

"Don't shoot him," Reynolds said as West came down the stairs and pointed the weapon at the man now standing against the rock wall with his arms in the air.

"FLETC, FLETC, FLETC, FLETC," he yelled.

"Cover him, Luis," West said when he got to the bottom of the stairs with Aguilar behind him.

"Roger that," the SEAL answered, pointing the shotgun at Rico.

"What the hell took you so long?" Reynolds weakly asked, trying to sit up.

Kneeling beside Reynolds, West said, "I was told once to hang tight, and I did, even when I heard you screaming."

"Well, get me the hell out of here."

"Can you walk?" West asked.

"Get me on my feet and I can run. The key is hanging on the hook behind the stairs," Reynolds said.

Walking back behind the stairs, West retrieved the key and returned to Reynolds. Unlocking the shackle, he threw the key in the corner and took the chain off from around Reynolds's ankle. "Hold on a minute," West said to Reynolds.

Standing, West walked over to the man against the wall. "What's your name?"

"Rico," the man stammered, still holding his arms up as high as he could.

"Who told you to say FLETC?"

"Angelina Lopez. I was helping her the same I was helping this man," he said, nodding his head towards Reynolds.

West turned to Reynolds and asked, "Is that true?"

"Yes, he brought me broth. That's why he was down here when you came in."

West turned to Rico and said, "If I let you live, you must answer a few questions for me."

"Whatever you want."

"Where are they keeping Angelina?"

"In Medellin at house 29 on Carrera 78."

"How many men are there?"

"Two men, they're bodyguards."

"Tell me about them."

"The one in charge is Alex Sanchez. He's Alejandro's security man. The other man, Mateo, works for Sanchez."

"Does Sanchez drive a Mercedes?"

"Yes, he has a driver, but yes, he has a black Mercedes."

"Has it been here?"

"It sure the hell has," Reynolds replied. "He's the asshole who has been running the 110 volts up my ass."

West glanced at the generator attached to the stationary bike.

"Where is Alejandro's home?" West asked.

"I don't know, but it's close to where they're keeping Angelina. I've never been to their home. I only fly their jet, and they keep me here most of the time."

"What is Alejandro's phone number?"

"I don't know. Alejandro changes phones almost daily."

"How do you contact them?"

"I call Rafael. That is the only number I have."

"What is it?"

"I don't know. I can't think right now. It's on my phone upstairs in the bedroom."

"Go get it and write the number down on a piece of paper. Luis, go with him."

"Roger that," Aguilar said as he followed Rico up the stairs.

Turning to Reynolds, West said, "I'll get you out of here in just a minute, Jack."

Reynolds nodded as he lay back on the concrete floor.

Hurrying back down the steps, Rico handed a piece of paper to West.

"This is it?" West asked.

"Yes," Rico said.

"It is. I confirmed it," Aguilar said.

West shoved the piece of paper into this pants pocket and said, "If I let you live, how are you going to explain this to Alejandro and Rafael?" West asked.

"I don't know. They will torture me if they think I know something. Maybe it's best if you kill me too. I can't be tortured; I'm a weak man. I'll tell them I told you where Angelina is. I want her rescued."

West looked at Rico and then turned to look at Reynolds, who shrugged his shoulders.

"Close your eyes," West said, and he started pulling the trigger of the MP5 pointed at the man's head. Suddenly, he let the finger pressure off the trigger and looked at Rico who was squinting his eyes tightly shut and grimacing. "Do you ever work late at night on the aircraft at the hangar?"

Rico opened his eyes wide and said, "Si, all the time. Sometimes, I'll sleep in the bed on the jet."

"You were at the hangar tonight, get the hell out of here," West said, as he moved out of the man's way. "Now, Rico! Move your ass!" West yelled, as the man started running up the stairs and out to his Land Rover.

"Let's get you out of here, Jack," West said as he and Aguilar picked Reynolds up by his arms and helped him up the stairs and out of the house. Reaching the car, they laid him on the back seat of the Renault.

"Turn on that damn heater," Reynolds said. "I'm freezing."

"My jacket's on the back seat. Cover up with it," Aguilar said, as he got in the car and started it.

West ran to the other side and jumped in the front passenger seat, turned the heater on high, and said, "The hotels are blown. Where can we go?"

"You're going to my safe house outside Medellin," Aguilar said as he turned the car around, and the men headed back towards the main road.

West nodded and turned in the seat to look at Reynolds who was shivering as he pulled the light coat around him.

"Good to have you back, Jack," West said.

"I knew you would come and get me," Reynolds replied, nodding his head and trying to get warm.

Bogota River Bridge Guard Station
1:22 a.m.

"Rico, why are you here so late?" the young guard asked after coming out of the guard shack and standing next to the gate.

"Couldn't sleep. I might as well work on the jet electronics. The annual is coming due soon, and there's a lot of work that I need to do," Rico replied. "Those damn worries are keeping me awake."

"Wish I had your talents and didn't have to stay out here all night, being a guard."

"Well, you're young yet. Come by the hangar when you get off, and I can show you some things. I didn't get my pilot license until I was about your age."

"I would really like that, Rico."

"You're never too old to learn. Stop by. I bet you would find flying as enjoyable as I do."

"Thank you, I will," the young guard replied with a smile as he opened the gate for the Land Rover.

"Oh my God," Rico said as he drove to the hangar.

St. Simons Island, Georgia
1:45 a.m.

"HELLO," A SLEEPY VOICE SAID, ANSWERING the phone.

"Buddy, I've got Jack," West said.

"Goddamn," Hayden yelled and jolted up in bed, startling his wife with the yell. "How is he?"

"He's weak but good. You can't kill this old bastard."

"Can I talk to him?"

"Sure," West replied and handed the phone to Reynolds in the back seat.

"Hey," Reynolds said weakly into the phone.

"I just wanted to hear your voice, you son of a bitch," Hayden said.

"Yeah," Reynolds replied. "Good to hear yours too, Buddy."

"You been shot or anything?"

"No, just fried with 110 up my ass."

"Well, they say that's good for arthritis."

"I hate to bust your bubble, but I hurt all over."

"All right, where you going?"

"Luis is taking us to an agency safe house outside Medellin."

"Roger that. Did you kill the asshole that was cooking you?"

"No, Nate and Luis got a couple cartel men that were keeping me there. The cooker wasn't present, but we know where he's at, and he's with Lopez."

"Hell, that's great. Rest up, Jack. Give the phone back to Nathan."

"Will do," Reynolds replied and handed the phone back to West.

"Yeah?" West said into the phone.

"That was a great job, Nathan. I'll let former Director Gales know we got Jack back."

"I couldn't have done it without Luis's help. I'll contact you later when we get settled at our new location."

"Roger that. Good bye," Hayden said, hung up, and lay back down on the bed.

Melinda put her arm over Hayden and quietly asked, "Nathan found Jack?"

"Yeah, that son of a bitch did it."

Melinda smiled and said, "I told you he was something."

CHAPTER 29

Leg Cramps

3 a.m., Monday, May 3, 1993

Aguilar drove almost an hour northwest on Route 56 to La Ceja, a small, low-income community ten miles southeast of Medellin. West and Reynolds slept the entire way.

"Wake up," Aguilar said as he hit the garage door opener.

West sat up and Reynolds continued to sleep.

"Where are we?" West asked.

"Home, La Ceja."

West watched the natural-colored, wooded garage door open on the gray-stucco, two-story home with green wooden trim. Looking to the right, West could see the apartment was in one large building and the second residence in from the end. On the left side, there were five or six apartments joined until you got to the end of the building.

"How're the neighbors?" West asked.

"So far, not a problem."

"How long have you been here?"

"Seven years. I've had people come and go, and so far, nothing out of anyone."

West nodded his head as Aguilar pulled into the garage and lowered the garage door behind them with the remote control.

Getting out of the car, West went to the driver's side and opened the back door.

"Jack, wake up. We're at the safe house." West said.

Reynolds barely responded with a "Hmmm" and continued to lie covered with the coat in a fetal position on the back seat.

Reaching in the car, West got a hold of Reynolds's left arm and pulled him up to a seated position. Reynolds screamed "Fuck you," as he opened his eyes and jerked his head back. When he saw he was face to face with West, Reynolds let out a deep sigh, relaxed, and placed his hand on West's shoulder. "Damn, Nate, I thought this was a dream."

"No, it's over, Jack. You're home."

Reynolds nodded as he staggered getting out of the car. West shut the door and with Aguilar's help got Reynolds up the stairs to the living quarters.

"I've got three bedrooms," Aguilar said. "They're small, but they'll do. Let's put Jack in the one on the left. The bathroom is just across the hall from him."

"All right," West said.

The two supported Reynolds as he made his way out of the living room and into the bedroom, collapsing onto the bed.

West pulled the blanket out from underneath Reynolds and covered him up as the weakened man went immediately back to sleep. West stood and looked at him. "He's lost a lot of weight, and I'm sure his electrolytes are way the hell off," West said. "You got sugar and salt?"

"Yes, in the kitchen," Aguilar replied.

Turning, West followed Aguilar back to the kitchen that was connected to the living room. In the refrigerator, West saw twelve-ounce bottles of Coke. Can I have one?" he asked.

"You can have anything you want. Glasses are in the cupboard."

"Thanks." West got a large glass off a shelf and poured the entire Coke into the glass. "I'll drink that. I'll make Jack the electrolytes and carbs in the bottle. He can't have any caffeine." West found the salt container and the sugar. Pouring a half-teaspoon of salt into the plastic bottle, he followed that with four large tablespoons of sugar.

"Do you have any multivitamins?" West asked, as he picked up the glass of Coke and drank it all.

"Yes, I have Centrum," Aguilar replied.

"I'll need them. Can you get the bottle?" West asked.

Aguilar walked into the bathroom and returned with the white plastic bottle containing the light-orange vitamins.

Taking two vitamins out of the bottle, West wrapped them in a paper towel and crushed them on the sink with the glass that had held the Coke. Carefully, he poured the powdered vitamins into the Coke bottle. Next, he ran warm water into the bottle from the sink, almost filling the bottle. Then he replaced the cap and shook it several times until the vitamins, salt, and sugar were dissolved.

"I'll let him sleep a little and then I'll start making him drink one of these every hour until he can stand on his own and piss. We need to get his kidneys hydrated and functioning again, or they're going to shut down and Jack's screwed."

"Where did you learn this?" Luis asked.

"I'm from a family of doctors, and I grew up raising abandoned colts and calves. If you don't get them hydrated and the electrolytes in balance, they die from acute kidney failure, and they can die fast. My dad and that farm were good teachers."

"Sounds good," Luis said. "Let's get some sleep." He started walking back to the hall. "My room is on the left; yours is on the right," he said and pointed to the right as he entered his room and closed the door.

West looked into the living room at the couch. He could see Jack's door from there. "That's where I'll be," he said. He walked to the couch and lay down.

"God dammit!" Reynolds screamed.

West didn't know how long he'd been asleep. Jumping up off the couch, West raced to Reynolds's room and switched on the light. "What?" West yelled.

"Straighten out my legs. Both legs are cramping," he screamed.

West jerked the blanket off the naked man and grabbed both legs by the ankles and started lifting them up off the bed.

"Ahhhh," Reynolds screamed as he clutched the sheet covering the bed with both hands. "Higher," he yelled.

Aguilar bust into the room with his Sig Sauer in hand. "What's going on?"

"Muscle spasms. Grab the right ankle," West said, as he put both hands on the left and shoved it towards the ceiling. Aguilar laid the pistol down on the bed and started lifting the right leg.

Finally the strong muscle spasms began letting up as the back of the legs were being stretched out.

"Better?" West asked, looking at the now pale Reynolds and holding his legs up for a few more seconds.

"Yes. Damn, that hurt."

"Jack, I need you to stand up," West said. "We're going to flip your legs to the floor, and you need to get up in one fluid motion, or those cramps are coming back. You understand?"

"Yes."

"Okay, three, two, one," West counted backwards as he and Aguilar shoved Reynolds feet off the bed and jerked him up by his arms.

Once Reynolds was standing, West said, "Luis, hold him. I'm getting the salt and that bottle I made."

"Roger that," Aguilar replied.

West walked into the kitchen and got the Coke bottle from the counter and started shaking it. He also picked up the blue salt container and walked back to the bedroom. "How do you feel?" he asked.

"Very weak. Not sure how much longer I can stand," Reynolds replied.

"Move your legs to increase circulation and stick out your tongue," West said. "I'm going to pour some salt on your tongue. When I tell you, close your mouth and move the salt around with your tongue."

"What does that do?" Reynolds asked, as he tried to walk in place.

"It's going to make your cramps go away," West said. "Stick your tongue out."

Reynolds shoved his dry tongue out through his cracked lips as West poured a small hump of salt on it.

"Okay, close your mouth and move that salt around."

"How does that work?" Aguilar asked.

"Letting the salt be absorbed by the mouth gets it straight to the blood stream. It will turn those cramps off in about one minute. Jack, your electrolytes are messed up, and you're severely dehydrated. We have to get your fluid level back up. Your tongue looks like a piece of beef jerky." West began to shake the Coke bottle again and stopped to look at the sediments. "Okay, you need to drink all of this if you want to stay out of the hospital."

Reynolds put the bottle to his lips and started drinking. After getting half of the bottle down, he said, "This is sweet and salty."

"Yes, it's better than having to drink you own piss, but it's not quite as good as an IV line."

"I'm not going to any hospital," Reynolds said.

"No, you're not. Where do you think Sanchez is going to look?" West said.

Reynolds nodded and drank the rest of the bottle and said, "I need to sit down," as he slowly lowered himself to the bed while holding onto Aguilar's and West's arms.

"Any cramps?" West asked.

"No."

"Okay, lie down and we'll raise your legs," West instructed taking the bottle from Reynolds.

Reynolds lay back on the pillow as the men placed his legs up on the bed. Aguilar then pulled the blanket back over the top of him.

"Better?" West asked.

"Yeah, damn that hurt. Thanks, fellas."

"No problem. You scared the shit out of me," Aguilar said, picking up his pistol.

"When was the last time you pissed?" West asked, glancing at his watch. It was 5:30 a.m.

"A couple of days ago."

"Days," West repeated, shaking his head. "Okay, you're drinking one of these bottles every hour until you start pissing."

"Roger that," Reynolds said and closed his eyes.

Search Bloc Headquarters, Medellin
7 a.m.

"GOOD MORNING, AGENT PINIELLA."

"Good morning, General," Piniella replied.

"What are you looking at?" the general asked, seeing Piniella leaning over a large map of Medellin in the Operations Room of Search Bloc.

"General, I'm fine-tuning our air search. We haven't picked up anything in over a week. I'm going to lay out grids for the aircraft to concentrate over. Flying in a circle is not working."

"You're going to concentrate the search patterns?"

"Yes, sir. If you're trying to catch a rat, you must concentrate on one hole. If you try to cover the entire house, you'll never catch the damn thing."

The general smiled. "Glad to have you on board, Julio."

"Yes, sir. I'll find him for you. We need only one little break, and if you wait long enough, it always happens."

CHAPTER 30

Promise Me

8 a.m., Monday, May 3, 1993

"Stick your tongue out," West said, leaning over Reynolds lying in bed.

Reynolds moved his tongue out past his lips. It glistened.

"Yay," West said. "We're getting some fluid in you. You need to piss yet?"

"No, not yet. But I'm beginning to feel something down there."

"That's a good sign, Jack. This will be your fourth bottle," West said as he handed the Coke bottle of water, salt, and sugar to the man. "Drink up."

West helped Reynolds sit up in bed as he put the bottle to his lips and started drinking. He downed it all in one try.

"I'm starting to feel better," he said, wiping his mouth with the back of his hand and handing the bottle back to West. West helped Reynolds lie back down.

Looking at Aguilar who was standing beside the bed, West asked, "Do you have potatoes, Velveeta cheese, chicken bouillon cubes, thyme, and a ham?"

"No, but there's a store not far from here," Aguilar answered. "What are you going to make?"

"The best fattening, delicious potato soup you've ever had if you can get those for me and if you have a big pot."

"Yes, I can, and yes, I do."

"Good, we need to put some weight on this skinny asshole," West said, looking at Reynolds who tried to smile.

"I'll be back in thirty mikes," Aguilar said and started down the stairs to get in his car.

Hearing the car pull out of the garage and the door close, Reynolds got to his elbows on the bed and said, "Listen to me. You don't go for Angelina until I'm healthy enough to go. I want payback with Sanchez. I'm going to kill that son of a bitch."

"Jack, it may take a week or so before you're ready for a mission."

"If they were going to kill her, they would've already done it. We have time. They're keeping her alive because Rafael's in love with her. I heard the men talk. Promise me you'll wait."

"You old bastard, you know I wouldn't do anything that you didn't want. Yes, I promise. But that presents a problem with Luis. He now knows that Carrera 78 is near Alejandro's home, and we have Rafael's phone number. He's obligated to pass that to General Marquez."

"Hmmm, let's talk to Luis, brother to brother. I think he'll let it slide until we can at least rescue Angelina and kill Sanchez. And I'm going to be there."

West nodded and said, "All right, I'll let you start that conversation."

"Okay, help me to the bathroom. I think I can piss."

"And we need to get some clothes on your scraggly ass and get you a shower. You smell like roadkill."

"Let's start with me pissing. Now help me up, dammit."

Rancho Blanca
8 a.m.

"Rafael, I just got home from the airport and something bad has happened here," Rico yelled excitedly on the phone.

"What happened?"

"Felipe and Bruno are dead, and the American is gone!"

"How were they killed?"

"Looks like they were shot, I think. The door was open when I got here, and they were lying in the hallway. It's terrible, Rafael. I can't stay here; it's not safe. What if they come back?" Rico yelled.

"Rico is there anything there to connect that place to us?"

"I don't think so, but maybe."

Rafael thought for a moment and asked, "Do you have gasoline there?"

"No, but I have kerosene for the heater."

Rafael thought again, paused, and said, "Rico, burn the house. Open the valves on the gas cook stove in the kitchen and burn that place now. Then come back here to Medellin where Sanita is being kept."

"Sanchez doesn't want me there," Rico replied.

"I'll take care of Alex. You burn that house and leave."

"Si, Rafael," Rico said and hung up the phone in the bedroom. I sure hope he believed me, he thought as he hurriedly pulled his large brown suitcase from under the bed, opened it, and began throwing all his clothes in it. Packing it full, he closed it, walked to the front porch, and threw the suitcase into the yard.

Returning into the house, he went to the basement and picked up the large plastic container of kerosene and carried it up the stairs. In the kitchen, he turned the valves open on the gas cook stove and picked up the red-and-white box of wooden matches used to light the burners and put it in his pocket. Taking the cap off of the kerosene jug, he began to pour the fuel on the floor as he backed up into the hallway where he poured more over the dead men.

"Sorry, Felipe; sorry, Bruno."

Continuing, he poured the flammable liquid into the living room where he doused the couch and chair until the container was empty, dropping the container on the floor. Rico walked back to the front door, pulled the box of matches out, lit one, and tossed it onto the couch.

"WOOOOOF." The fuel instantly caught fire, and black smoke began filling the room. As the couch burnt, Rico backed up onto the porch and watched the fire travel where he had spilled the fuel on the floor, over the dead men's bodies, and down the hallway towards the kitchen. Slamming the door shut, he walked into the yard, picked up his suitcase, walked to the Land Rover, and threw it on the back seat. Getting in the driver's seat, he hurriedly pulled out to the end of the driveway and looked back just in time to see the house explode when the natural gas from the cook stove ignited.

"Sorry, Felipe; sorry, Bruno," he said again and gunned the engine, heading towards Medellin.

CIA safe house
Noon

Aguilar had returned from the store and West had been cooking for an hour.

"Almost done, Jack," West said, from the kitchen.

"It does smell good," Aguilar said, standing next to the stove and watching West stir the thick soup in the large aluminum pot. "I can't believe you melted the entire block of Velveeta cheese in that."

"That's what makes it so good, that with the chicken broth, thyme, and cut-up ham," West said. "The potatoes are an afterthought. This shit will grow hair on a rock. Get some bowls out."

"Jack, you ready for a little bit?" West asked loudly.

"Yes, I'm hungry," Reynolds replied.

Taking a bowl from Aguilar, West put a dipper full in, picked up a spoon, and walked to the bedroom. "Here, it's still hot, so don't get in a hurry with it."

Reynolds took the bowl with the spoon sticking out and smelled it. "Smells like heaven," he said.

"It came from almost heaven."

"What?"

"You know the words in John Denver's song, "Take Me Home, Country Roads"—almost heaven, West Virginia."

"Oh," Reynolds said and chuckled as he took a small amount on the spoon and blew on it before putting it in his mouth.

"You're getting stronger; I can tell," West said.

"Yes, and I think this is the best soup I've ever tasted," Reynolds said, looking at West.

"Yeah, it's good shit. Should get you back on your feet in no time."

Walking into the doorway, Aguilar said, "This is delicious."

"Thanks. Think I'll get me a bowl too," West replied and walked to the kitchen.

"Luis, I need to ask you a favor, actually four," Reynolds said, setting the spoon in the bowl and looking at the SEAL.

"Sure. What is it?" Aguilar replied and took another spoonful of the soup.

"I need you to give me a few days to get back on my feet before you and Nate hit the house where the agent is."

"That's no problem."

"Well this might be. I also need you to not share with anyone the location, the fact that the location may be close to Alejandro's home, or Rafael's phone number with anyone."

"Why you asking that?"

"If Search Bloc knows where to narrow their monitoring, they'll be on to the Espinozas quick and that may get Angelina killed if they hit that house, which they will. Most military units don't give a shit about friendly fire in those situations. They'll go in blazing."

Aguilar stopped eating and took a deep breath and looked at Reynolds as West walked back into the room eating out of a full bowl of potato soup.

"Three, let me take Sanchez. I'm going to kill that son of a bitch, and I'm going to kill him slow."

"Hmmm," Aguilar said, looking at the floor for a few moments and then at West and said, "Get him another bowl. We need to get him on his feet ASAP," Aguilar said. "And what's the final request?"

"Can you please go to the Tequendama and get my damn clothes?"

"Yeah, I'll stop at the Santafe and get yours too, Nate," Aguilar said. "I have keys for both rooms."

"Thank you," Reynolds said and started eating again.

West walked to Reynolds and exchanged bowls saying, "Keep your spoon. Eat up, pappy. This team's a go." Turning to Aguilar, West said, "Thank you for everything."

"We're all brothers here. I'll drive to Bogota this afternoon and get your things."

"Do you need me to go with you?" West asked.

"No, I'll leave the Renault and key near the Santafe and get my taxi. We may still need the rentals later to get Sanita."

"Angelina," West corrected and frowned, looking at Aguilar.

Aguilar stopped and glared at West.

"Okay," West said, "let's just decide on what we're going to call her. Okay?"

Reynolds began to choke.

Aguilar said, "You bastard, don't go there."

"Luis, you pick the name," West said, holding his hands out as Reynolds spit his soup back out into the bowl.

"Let's use Sanita, you asshole," Aguilar said, looking at West and then back at Reynolds who had his eyes squinted tightly closed, trying not to hear what was being said.

"That's fine with me, Luis. It's Sanita. That's easier for me to remember anyway," West said, trying not to smile.

"You bastard," Aguilar said. "Okay, I can contact Ricardo later, and he can pick up the rentals when we think we won't need them anymore."

Reynolds opened his eyes, blinked several times, and tried to breathe normally as he looked at the bowl of soup, refusing to make eye contact with either of the two men. "Fellas, I can't laugh right now. Give me a break."

CHAPTER 31

Help Is Coming

7 p.m., Monday, May 3, 1993

ALEX SANCHEZ HAD BEEN IN BUCARAMANGA all day settling a dispute between two suppliers because the packing had not been properly secured. On his way there, he received a phone call from Rafael and was told about Felipe and Bruno and that he told Rico to go to Carrera 78. Felipe and Bruno had been with Sanchez for years, and he seethed over their deaths. But he was also upset over Reynolds escaping. He had Reynolds to the breaking point. Sanchez knew it wouldn't have been much longer before he would have started talking. They all do, no matter how tough.

But what was most concerning was who killed them and how did they know Reynolds was there? It was obviously a professional hit. CIA, DEA, Search Bloc, who? And even with the house being burnt, did they track Rico to the new location? Sanchez was pissed, and it was getting late in the evening. He needed to get started on the two-hour trip back to Medellin. He hadn't planned to be there all day anyway, but Alejandro had sent him to make sure the problem was fixed, telling him to be patient with the farmers. He was very tired of listening to the two men arguing over whose fault it was the packaging had failed on one of the recent shipments and the cocaine had gotten wet.

Finally Sanchez had enough. Standing, he looked at the younger man and said, "Do you know what to do next time?"

"Si, Alex. This old bastard made a mistake."

"I think so too," Sanchez said and pulled out the newly acquired Beretta and shot the old man in the forehead, knocking him backwards out of his chair.

"No more mistakes," Sanchez said, shaking the pistol at the younger man.

"Si, Alex."

Sanchez got back in his Mercedes and headed back to Medellin. Two hours later, he pulled the car into the basement garage on Carrera 78. Getting upstairs, he saw Rico sleeping on the couch. Pulling the Beretta out of the back of his belt, he walked up to Rico and shoved the black barrel roughly against his cheek, pinning his head to the cushion.

Rico awakened terrified, his wide eyes staring at Sanchez.

"Those were two of my best men. Why weren't you killed too?"

"I wasn't there, Alex. I had been at the airport working on the jet's annual inspection that is due soon."

"Open your mouth," Sanchez demanded.

Rico slowly opened his mouth as Sanchez slid the barrel off the cheek and into his mouth.

"Bite the barrel," Sanchez ordered.

Rico slowly started showing his teeth as he bit down on the pistol.

Sanchez flipped the safety up with an audible click.

Rico closed his eyes tightly and groaned loudly, "Ahhhh."

"I don't believe you, and if I find out you lied, I'm going to blow your head off." Sanchez jerked the pistol out of Rico's mouth, chipping a tooth with the front site.

Rico sat up on the couch and said, "You crazy bastard, you chipped my tooth," as he held his mouth with his hands.

"Be thankful I didn't blow all your teeth out the back of your head," Sanchez said and walked to Lopez's room kicking the door open.

"I'm back, you little bitch," Sanchez said, pointing the pistol at her head as she lay covered up.

Lopez, awakened by the yelling, glared back at the man but kept her mouth shut.

10 a.m., Tuesday, May 4

"WHERE YOU GOING?" RAFAEL ASKED ALEJANDRO as he started out the door.

"I need to call Juan. Haven't talked to him in a few days," Alejandro replied, speaking about his sixteen-year-old son who was being kept with his mother, Victoria, at the Hotel Tequendama in Bogota. "Limon is driving me around town. I'll make a quick call and throw the phone away."

"Have you forgotten what we were told by the police? They're trying to track us by the phone calls, especially calls to your family," Rafael said.

"Yes, I know, brother. But I need to talk to my son."

Search Bloc Headquarters
10:15 a.m.

THE PHONE ON DEA AGENT JULIO PINIELLA'S DESK began to ring. "Hello," Piniella said after picking it up.

"Julio, it's Steve. We have a call going to the Tequendama, and it sounds like Alejandro."

"Do you have a location where it's coming from?" Piniella asked excitedly.

"Hold on. Yes, it's coming from highway 62 traveling west. The target just pasted Avenida 80."

Piniella slammed his free hand down on the radio button and yelled, "All units, all units, go to highway 62. We have a target traveling west past Avenida 80." Talking back into the phone, Piniella asked, "Do you have eyes on the vehicle?"

"Negative, there are a hundred cars on that stretch of road."

"Get lower," Piniella yelled. "Get me a description."

"Roger that. Going to five hundred feet," Steve Masters replied, DEA pilot of CIA Aircraft 1. Shoving the nose of the Cessna 210 down, he throttled back slightly and shoved the flap switch down to full, feeling the aircraft slow.

"I was always told to never fly low and slow," the Delta sergeant said, sitting in the right seat as he studied the monitor and listened to the voices they were tracking.

"Yeah, that usually kills careless pilots and everyone on board. Give me a target," Masters yelled, watching his air speed indicator and making sure the 210 didn't stall out at such a slow speed and low altitude.

"All right, you fly; I'll look," the sergeant yelled. "It's straight ahead, five hundred meters, four hundred, three hundred, two hundred, one hundred. We're over top of him now," the sergeant yelled looking out his side window at the multiple cars on the highway. "I don't know," he said. "There're too many. Wait. Circle back. There's a tan car getting off suddenly."

Masters shoved the throttle all the way in making the 210's engine roar as he began the low altitude bank to the right.

Ten seconds before, Limon yelled at Alejandro in the back seat and pointed up towards the roof of the tan Mercedes. "Plane!" he yelled, hearing it get close with his window down.

"I need to go, Juan," Alejandro said to his son. "Do what your mother tells you to do. I love you. Good bye," he said and hung up the phone.

"Get off at the next exit and get underneath the overpass," Alejandro directed.

Driving off Highway 62 onto Calle 62, Limon steered the car underneath the overpass, pulled over, and turned the car off. Alejandro rolled down his windows so he could hear the aircraft too. It seemed to go away, and then the sound got very loud again as the plane came back above them and continued flying east.

Alejandro threw the phone out the window into the grass and said, "Take me home."

Turning in the seat, Limon looked at Alejandro and said, "Si, Alejandro, but please lie down until we get there."

Alejandro nodded and lay down on the back seat as Limon started the Mercedes and pulled out to drive down Calle 62.

"I DON'T SEE THE CAR. IT must have gotten off the highway," the sergeant in the aircraft said.

"What did it look like?" Masters asked as he began to pull the yoke back to climb.

"A tan four-door. Couldn't make out the model."

"You hearing this, Julio?" Masters asked, pushing the flap switch back up as the 210 picked up speed.

"Yes, hold on," Piniella replied. Hitting the radio button once more, he yelled, "All units, concentrate in the Calle 62 area ASAP. Look for a tan car, a tan car!"

THE DELTA OPERATOR SITTING IN THE passenger seat of the Search Bloc scout vehicle pulled the charging handle back on his M4 automatic assault rifle and racked a live round into the chamber as the Colombian military officer driving the car slowed in traffic on Calle 62. Looking at every passing car going in the opposite direction. They both knew what Alejandro Espinoza looked like and they looked closely at everyone.

"There's a tan car coming at us, third car back," the officer said.

"Roll down your window now!" the Delta operator instructed, clicking the safety off on the weapon.

The officer rolled the window down and held his head back as the operator leaned over in his seat across the driver and pointed the M4 out the driver's window as the tan car approached. His finger was firmly on the trigger to send a short burst of 5.56 into the driver's head if it was Espinoza. Looking sternly at the driver of the tan car as it passed, the operator took his finger off the trigger, pulled the barrel back into the car, and pointed it at the floor as he returned to his seat. "That's not him," he said.

The Search Bloc officer let out a loud sigh and looked at the operator. "You were really going to shoot?" he asked.

The Delta operator coldly looked at the officer with an expressionless face and sat back in his seat. Picking up the radio mic, he said, "Negative contact, negative contact."

"Dammit!" Piniella yelled looking at General Marquez.

Marquez turned and started to return to his office as he said, "Close Agent Piniella, close. Keep it up."

"Dammit," Piniella repeated. "I'll check the footage from the La Catedral camera and see if we got anything."

Carrera 78
Noon

"How are you feeling? Rico asked the woman as she sat up in bed.

"Much better," Lopez replied.

"Here, I brought you a sandwich for lunch and some milk," Rico said, handing the sandwich to Lopez and setting the glass of milk on the stand.

"Thank you," she said and took a bite.

Examining her forehead, Rico said, "We need to take those stitches out. They've been in long enough. I'll get a pair of scissors and tweezers. I'll be right back."

Rico got up and met Sanchez standing in the doorway.

"What are you doing?"

"I gave her some lunch, and I'm going to take the stitches out of her head."

"You don't do anything unless I say so."

"Get out of the way, Alex. You're not my boss, and if you don't like it, talk to Rafael."

"Rafael's weak. We should have killed her long ago."

Rico stopped to face Sanchez. "If she doesn't try to escape, you are to do nothing. Now get out of my way."

Sanchez turned and walked back to the living room, pulled the Beretta out of his belt, and laid it on the coffee table in front of the couch.

Rico went into the bathroom and got a small pair of scissors and tweezers from his overnight kit. Returning to the bedroom, he shut the door and said to Lopez, "Lay your head back and don't move so I don't hurt you."

Lopez did as instructed as Rico removed the dozen stitches, dropping each one into the toilet chair opening.

"I think it healed well," Rico said as he examined the healed laceration.

"Thank you," Lopez said with a smile.

"We need to get you into a shower. Do you feel strong enough?"

"Yes, I can stand well now. I've been walking here in the room."

"Good, we need to get you cleaned up, and I'll get you some better clothes to wear."

"Why?"

Rico leaned very close to Lopez and whispered, "Because help is coming," and placed a finger over his lips. "Shhh, you must be ready."

CHAPTER 32

Soulless Bastard

5:30 a.m., Saturday, May 8, 1993

West woke hearing someone banging around in the kitchen and running water. After glancing at his watch, he got up, pulled on his jeans, and walked down the hall. "Good morning," he said, seeing Reynolds standing there in a pair of Dominion Energy slacks.

"Good morning, Nate," Reynolds replied, pouring water into the top of the Bunn coffee maker.

"How do you feel?"

"I'm getting stronger. Not there yet, but getting better."

"Your color looks good. You're not so pale now," West said, looking at Reynolds and leaning over and resting his elbows on the counter.

"Yeah, that bastard took it out of me. To tell you the truth, I don't know how much more I could've taken," Reynolds said as he placed the decanter underneath the coffee funnel and watched the dark liquid start to run into the pot.

"Well you told me once that everyone breaks sooner or later. We're all human," West said.

"Hmmm," Reynolds said, shaking his head and then said, "Yeah. Do you want a cup?"

"Sure," West said, getting two cups out of the cupboard and placing one next to Reynolds on the counter.

"I've been thinking," Reynolds said as he waited a few more moments while the pot got half full.

"Yeah, what about?" West asked, holding a cup out.

Reynolds picked up the decanter and poured the cup full. "If we can get Angelina, you need to take her back to the States. She'll need someone to go with her, and you already know her."

"I would think Customs would send her with someone from their shop," West said, taking a sip of the hot coffee.

"Nate, you listen to me. I almost bought the farm," Reynolds said, as he poured his cup full, sat the decanter back on the heating plate, and turned to face West. "You have a new career waiting on you. You've got promise to be a great doctor. You've taken enough chances, and you're going to take a few more before this is over. If we're lucky enough to get her back and we're still alive, I want you on that jet with her."

"If I go, what're you going to do?"

"I'll stay behind and finish the mission. Everyone knows you're already obligated, and you've got to leave soon anyway. No one would think anything of you going back. So I want you to leave. If you get killed, I'll never be able to live with that."

"Well, we've got plenty of time to talk about it."

"Maybe, maybe not. What's the name of the medical school you'll be attending?"

"West Virginia School of Osteopathic Medicine. It's in Lewisburg, West Virginia."

"Do you have a contact there?"

"No, not really. I don't know anyone there. But my father knows the dean of the school."

What's his name?"

"Stoogey."

"Like the Three Stooges?"

"No, Stoogey with a Y, but that's a good way to remember it. I've never met him, but he knows my family."

"All right. After you get back, if we're that lucky, that'll be our point of contact."

"Roger that."

"If someone comes to you and gives you our pass phrase, you'll know we're getting ready to drop the hammer on Espinoza. At that point, watch the news."

"You just make sure you get your ass back to Maine, Jack. I'm not going to be here to watch over you."

Reynolds stared at West, took a sip of the hot brew, and said, "You're never gonna let me live that down, are you?"

"Nope, I rescued Jack Reynolds's ass."

"Yes, you did."

Carrera 78
8 a.m.

"What are you doing out of your room?" Sanchez asked as he blocked Lopez in the hallway.

"I'm going to take a shower."

"No, you're not. Get back in your room," Sanchez yelled.

"Alex," Rico said, walking into the hallway, "Rafael told me to let her take a shower. Do I need to call Rafael for you?"

Sanchez looked at Rico and said, "If she goes any farther than that bathroom, I'm killing both of you," and he walked back to the kitchen.

Rico looked at Lopez who was holding the shirt and pants he had gotten for her, nodded towards the bathroom, and said, "Go," as he returned to the living room and sat down in a chair.

Sanchez walked into the living room with a cup of coffee and asked Rico, "What time did you go to the airport?"

"When?"

"You know what I'm talking about. The night Felipe and Bruno were killed."

"Late that night. Why?"

"What time?"

"I don't know, midnight or something. I couldn't sleep. If I don't get the annual done, the jet is grounded, and we won't be allowed to fly out of the airport. Why?"

"Because I don't trust you. I think you know something, or you would've been dead too."

"And what would I have to know, Alex? I'll show you what saved me," he said. Out of his shirt, he pulled the small silver crucifix that he kept around his neck on a chain. "This is what saved me," he yelled. "The body of Christ."

"That piece of junk metal won't save you from me," Sanchez said as he began to walk back towards the kitchen. "One twenty-two a.m.," he said over his shoulder.

"What, you soulless bastard?" Rico yelled.

"One twenty-two a.m. was the time you passed the guard station," Sanchez said and turned to stare at Rico.

Search Bloc Headquarters
6 p.m.

"GENERAL, TAKE A LOOK AT THIS," Piniella said, sitting at his desk and looking through a magnifying glass at a picture.

"What is it?"

"I couldn't make out anything on the La Catedral camera footage last week, so I sent it to the DEA lab to see if they could enhance the images. This is what they sent back. I just got them from the courier. Tell me what you see. I've circled a vehicle with a pen," Piniella said, sliding the picture to Marquez and handing him the magnifying glass.

Holding the handle and looking through the glass, the general leaned over the desk and raised and lowered the magnifying glass until he stopped moving his hand and stood very still.

"That's a Mercedes. That's a tan Mercedes," the general said, looking back at Piniella and handing the magnifying glass back to him.

"I've checked my Espinoza files, General. I see no mention of a tan Mercedes. But that's the car the Delta sergeant described, a tan four-door. And I agree, it's a Mercedes. But I have no link for it to Espinoza."

The general straightened up and slowly said, "I do," as he looked away.

"What?" the DEA agent asked, looking at the general.

The general shook his head and softly said, "Ninita."

"What little girl, General?" Piniella asked.

The general sat down in the chair next to Piniella's desk, let out a long sigh, tilted his head, and looked at the floor.

Piniella turned to face the man. "General?"

Tears began to stream down the general's face as he looked up sniffing, "When my daughter was killed, the person who planted the car bomb that shredded her beautiful body was seen getting in a tan Mercedes when he drove away. It was Alejandro Espinoza," he said, wiping the tears from his face with his rough hands.

Piniella couldn't speak and only nodded.

"That's why he must die," the general said as he got up to leave the room.

CIA safe house
7 p.m.

"What do you think, Jack, a few more days? Aguilar asked as the three men sat around the table eating the pan-fried steaks and baked potatoes that West had cooked.

"Yes, a week at the most. I can tell I'm not there yet, and I would only be a liability at this point," Reynolds replied. "I don't have much reserve, and I probably wouldn't be able to run fifty yards."

"You just keep eating," West said. "I can see you gaining weight, but you're not back to yourself yet. I would agree, a week, Luis. A week of being starved and tortured will take it out of you for a while."

"I just want you guys to know that I'm starting to feel the heat from above," Aguilar said. "Wolfe and the president are wanting to know why it's taking so long to get something moving."

"I understand," Reynolds said. "But just keep stalling them for a few more days; then we can bust this loose."

"We'll have a much better chance of success if there're three of us rather than two," West said. "There will be at least two if not three guns in that house and possibly others."

"Yes, I agree," Aguilar said. "I'll keep stalling as long as we need to make sure Jack is healthy."

"If we're successful, can we bring Sanita here until we can make arrangements to get her out of the country?" West asked.

"Yes, that's not a problem. We can hide here as long as it takes. They won't find us here," Aguilar said.

Hotel Tequendama
10 p.m.

"THIAGO, WHAT DID YOU FIND OUT?" Sanchez asked, standing at the end of the hall on the fourteenth floor.

"None of the hospitals have seen the American. But a few days ago, a maid saw a cabbie go into the room where the Dominion Energy clothes were hanging. He came back out carrying a suitcase. Later she checked, and all the clothes were gone."

"Did she recognize the cabbie?"

"Yes, he's the black man that often delivers and picks passengers up here."

"Does she have a name?"

"Yes, she thinks it's Luis."

CHAPTER 33

Central Gas

9 a.m., Monday, May 10, 1993

"Mr. Hernandez, a Mr. Sanchez is here to see you."

"Did I have an appointment this morning, Lucia?"

"No, sir. He didn't have one, but he says it's urgent."

"Okay, give me a minute to clean my desk and then show him in."

"Yes, sir," she said, and she closed the door.

Hernandez stopped reading his reports on the new pipeline construction and placed them in his top drawer as Lucia knocked on the door and then opened it.

"Mr. Hernandez, this is Mr. Sanchez," Lucia said. She swung the door open fully and stepped aside, allowing Sanchez to walk in. After closing the door, Lucia hurriedly returned to her desk where she pulled her CIA-issued Glock 19 from her purse and placed it in her top drawer. That's Alex Sanchez, she thought, remembering his picture. He's the one the CIA learned was being trained by the Mossad. But then they lost track of him. So he works for the cartel. That explains it.

"Come in, Mr. Sanchez," Hernandez said, getting to his feet and shaking hands with the man across the desk. "Please have a seat. What can I help you with?"

Sanchez looked back to make sure the door had been fully closed and sat down.

"Mr. Hernandez, I understand that we may have a mutual acquaintance, a Mr. Jack Reynolds," Sanchez said. He watched Lando Hernandez wince.

"I don't recall that name."

Sanchez looked at the family portrait hanging on the wall behind Hernandez. "Mr. Hernandez, I work for some very powerful people. People that you know of. People that can be very ruthless if necessary. I'll ask you again, do you know Jack Reynolds?"

Hernandez took a deep breath and said, "Yes, but I'm not free to discuss business dealings with individuals unless they are listed in the contract. I'm sure you understand that."

"Of course, I do, but Alejandro Espinoza doesn't care about your contracts or your family. If they all burned in your home tonight, he would still sleep soundly."

"My God, what are you saying?"

"You tell me about Jack Reynolds, or your entire family will not be alive this time tomorrow."

Sanchez stayed for another ten minutes. When he walked out, Lucia said, "Have a nice day, Mr. Sanchez."

"I just did, thank you," he replied and walked out of the office.

Lucia pulled the Glock out of her desk, got up, and locked the front office door. Walking back into Hernandez's personal office, she closed the door and said, "We need to talk."

Hernandez took his hands away from his face, looked up, and saw the pistol in her hand. "What are you doing with a gun, Lucia?"

"My name is not Lucia. It's Brenda Timms, and I'm a CIA agent," Timms replied. "Did you tell Alex Sanchez that Jack Reynolds was CIA? You must tell me the truth. You and your family's lives depend on it."

"Yes, I had no choice. He said he was going to burn my family."

"He's still going to burn your family. You are a liability to them now. They will not let any of you live. Where are your children?"

"They're home with my wife."

"Call her now. Tell her something came up and you need to leave town for a few days and you want to take them with you. Tell her to pack the suitcases now, and you'll be right over to pick them up." Then pulling a phone out of her pocket, she dialed 911.

"Hello."

"Luis, I need emergency transport. Hernandez has been burnt by Alex Sanchez, who was the ghost that trained with the Mossad. He works for the Medellin cartel, and Sanchez now knows Reynolds is an agency man."

"Where you at?"

"Central Gas. Shake a leg."

"Roger that. Stay there. I'll be there in an hour," Aguilar said and hung up.

Looking at Reynolds and West, Aguilar said, "That was one of our agents. Hernandez has been burnt, and Sanchez knows you're CIA, Jack. I have to do an emergency extract. We'll pick his family up and get them on an aircraft and out of the country today."

"You need me to go with you?" West asked.

"No, stay here. This place may be burnt too, so eyes up. And we have no way of knowing," Aguilar said. He headed down the stairs to the taxi.

Timms hung up her Nokia phone, looked at the bewildered Hernandez, and said, "Call now!"

West and Reynolds both walked to their rooms and took their MP5s out of the black bags and racked live rounds into the chambers.

"The only way to get to us is up those stairs," West said. A screwdriver and hammer are in a drawer in the kitchen. Let's pop the doors off the bedrooms and use them to make shields here in the living room and kitchen. We'll have them in a crossfire."

"Sounds good," Reynolds said. "I'll take the kitchen so I can sit on a stool behind the counter. You have the corner of the living room behind the couch."

"Roger that. I'll get the doors," West said, as he walked in to the kitchen with the MP5 hanging around his neck to get the tools.

Bogota
10 a.m.

AGUILAR PULLED THE YELLOW TAXI UP to the main office building at Central Gas. Sig Sauer in hand, he raced to the door and pounded on it. Timms appeared, followed by Hernandez. Unlocking the door, Timms grabbed Hernandez by his arm and hurried him to the waiting car.

"What about my truck?" Hernandez asked.

"It probably already has a bomb in it," Timms said. She pushed Hernandez into the back seat of the taxi and followed him in, shutting the door behind them.

"Drive," she said to Aguilar, who jumped behind the wheel and spun the tires on the taxi as he pulled out.

"I need to get my family in West Lake," Hernandez said.

"Yes, Lando, we know where you live," Aguilar said. "I'll be there in ten minutes. Brenda, do you have the flight taken care of?"

"Yes, I got him and his family on LAS flight 217 to Miami. It boards at 1100," she replied.

"Perfect," Aguilar said. "And the pick up?"

"Agents will be in Miami to take the Hernandezes to a safe house."

Aguilar nodded.

"Thank you," Hernandez said looking at the woman who, for the previous three years, he thought was nothing more than a sexy bimbo.

Reading his thoughts, Timms said, "I'm not just a pretty face and nice ass."

Spreading her legs, she pulled her skirt up and placed the Glock in a thigh holster next to her panties. "I don't want to frighten the kids," she said and pulled the skirt back down.

"I've missed you, baby," Aguilar said, looking in the rearview mirror at his beautiful girlfriend and partner.

"Missed you too, honey," Timms replied. "After this, we need to catch up," she said and winked at the cabbie.

"You're on," Aguilar replied with a big smile as he raced the taxi to the West Lake community.

Carrera 79B, Medellin
11 a.m.

Sanchez was sitting in the living room with Alejandro, Rafael, and Limon. "Jack Reynolds, the man I had at the ranch and who escaped, is CIA."

"How'd you learn this?" Alejandro asked.

"Lando Hernandez, manager at Central Gas. He's been feeding the CIA information for several years."

"How did you get him to tell you this?" Rafael asked.

"I told him I would burn his family alive in his home if he didn't talk."

"How did they find the ranch?" Alejandro asked.

"They followed someone there or we have a rat," Sanchez said. I don't trust Rico. I think he knows more than he's telling. It doesn't make sense that he just happened to go to the hangar the night Felipe and Bruno were killed and Reynolds was rescued. I don't believe in coincidence."

"We've known Rico all our lives; he's family," Rafael said. "I don't think he would talk, or we'd have been killed years ago."

"That's true," Alejandro agreed. "What do you think we should do, Alex?"

"You asked me to keep you safe," Sanchez replied. "To be safe, we kill Rico, the girl, and Hernandez tonight."

"No," Rafael said. "Alejandro, let me talk to Rico. He'll tell me the truth, and the girl's not to be touched."

"Brother," Alejandro said looking at Rafael, "you're going to get us all killed with this love." Pausing, he looked at Sanchez and continued, "Burn Hernandez and his family. I want to make an example out of them."

Alejandro took a deep breath and said, "Let Rafael speak to Rico, and we don't kill the girl yet."

Looking at Rafael again, Alejandro said, "But brother, time is coming soon that we may be forced to. I want you to prepare yourself for that eventuality."

Bogota International Airport
11:05 a.m.

After racing to pick up Hernandez's family and rushing them to the airport, Aguilar and Timms watched them hurry down the walkway as they boarded the Líneas Aéreas Suramericanas flight to Florida.

Turning to Aguilar, Timms said, "Let's get to your place so we can get naked. I need that hard black body."

Grabbing the beauty by the arm, Aguilar began walking Timms back out of the airport to the taxi and said, "Do you mind an audience?"

"What?" Timms asked, looking at the man.

"There've been some other things going on, honey. I need to fill you in on a few details."

"You got a guest?"

"Yes, two and it will be three soon."

"Shit," Timms said, getting in the front passenger seat of the taxi as Aguilar got behind the wheel.

Leaning over, the beauty started unzipping Aguilar's pants. "Well, you'd better be able to drive while you're getting a blowjob then," she said.

"Dear God, I'll try my damnedest," Aguilar said, putting the taxi in gear and gritting his teeth. "Oh God, I love you," he groaned as he started towards La Ceja.

CHAPTER 34

We'll See Who Kills Whom

12:15 p.m., Monday, May 10, 1993

Reynolds was sitting on a stool at the kitchen counter pointing his MP5 at the stairwell where the door was propped open with a chair. His knees were against the heaviest wooden bedroom door that West had taken off and leaned up against the counter on the kitchen side. If a bullet was to reach him, it would have to go through the wall, the two cabinet sides, and the heavy door. If a bullet did penetrate the barriers, hopefully it would be slowed down to the point of not inflecting as much damage. Reynolds wasn't so much worried about being shot in the head as he was in the balls.

West was sitting on a chair behind two wooden doors leaned up against the back of the couch. Holding the MP5 on top of the couch, he said, "I think, we're good."

"Roger that," Reynolds said. "Bring on the hate."

West nodded as he heard the garage door start to open and a car pull up. Getting up from the chair, he quickly looked out the front window, turned, and said, "The cab's pulling in."

"Still cover that door. We don't know who's driving," Reynolds said, pulling the MP5 stock back against his shoulder and leaning down to place his cheek on the weapon.

Hearing the car's engine stop and multiple doors open, West said, "He's not alone," pointing the weapon at the doorway.

"Don't shoot. I have someone with me," Aguilar yelled.

"Pass phrase?" Reynolds yelled back down the stairs, still pointing the machine gun at the stairs with his finger on the trigger.

"The frog's ass is watertight!" Aguilar yelled, coming up the stairs. "Don't shoot."

Reynolds laid his weapon on the counter and said, "Come ahead."

Aguilar and Timms made it to the top of the stairs.

"Well, if it's not Miss Gas Company," Reynolds said with a smile while looking at the woman.

"Damn," West said, as he laid his weapon on the floor behind the couch.

"Jack, Nathan, this is CIA undercover operative Special Agent Brenda Timms. She's been covering Hernandez for over three years now. Brenda, this is Nathan West, and the big man is Jack Reynolds."

Both men walked up to the lady and shook hands. "Pleasure meeting you, Brenda," West said as Reynolds stood there and smiled.

"God, I am so glad to see you," Reynolds said.

"And why is that?" Timms asked.

"Well, because before you walked up those stairs, I was a little worried if the hardware was still going to work," he said and grinned from ear to ear.

"I'm happy I could have a positive change in your condition, Jack Reynolds. I hear you've had it kinda rough lately," Timms said with a smile.

"Yeah, but I now know I'm on the mend."

Bogota
2 a.m., Tuesday, May 11

A LOUD EXPLOSION ROCKED ONE OF THE apartment buildings in the West Lake community as the first floor of the three-story building burst into flames. An incinerating device had been thrown through one of the windows into the hallway. All the first-floor windows were blown out, feeding the fire that needed oxygen to rapidly spread from floor to floor. The occupants quickly awakened as the fire alarms blared on each floor. Families desperately woke the children up and tried getting them down the stairwells to safety. Many didn't make it as the toxic smoke filled every inch of the older building, causing many to become confused or unconscious. The flames that would completely destroy the building ultimately consumed those bodies.

Alex Sanchez slowly walked back to his black Mercedes. Before getting in, he listened to the panicked screams and cries for help grow louder. Ten people would die, among them seven children.

Carrera 78
9 a.m.

"We're family, Rico," Rafael said, standing in the living room. "I need the truth. Do you know anything about the raid at the ranch?"

"No, Rafael. By the grace of God, I'm not dead too. If I hadn't gone to work on the jet, I wouldn't be here, no matter what this crazy bastard says," Rico said, looking at Sanchez standing next to Rafael.

"You're a liar," Sanchez snarled. "I can see it in your eyes."

"You're crazy. Rafael knows I wouldn't do anything to hurt him or Alejandro."

"I'll kill you," Sanchez said.

"Enough, Alex, enough," Rafael said. "I believe Rico. We've known each other a long time, longer than I've known you," he added, turning to glare at Sanchez.

"You've been warned, Rafael. I can't protect you if you won't believe me," Sanchez said and walked away.

Rafael watched Sanchez go downstairs to the garage and then he turned to Rico. "How is she?"

"She's doing good, probably not back to normal but as normal as she can be."

"Ask her if I can speak to her."

Rico nodded and went into the bedroom, closing the door behind him. A few seconds later, he came out, walked to Rafael, and said, "Si, she'll speak to you."

Rafael took a deep breath, walked to the door, stood for a moment, and then went in, closing the door behind him. Pulling a chair up to the edge of the bed, Rafael looked at the scarred and battered women sitting up against the head of the bed and said, "I hope someday you can forgive me."

CIA Safe House
8 p.m., Thursday, May 13

OVER THE PAST TWO DAYS, TIMMS had assisted West in cooking some high-calorie meals for Reynolds—big plates of eggs, fried bacon and potatoes, and toast for breakfast; stacked sandwiches full of meat, lettuce, tomato, lots of mayonnaise, and soups for lunch; and for dinner, big plates of spaghetti with meatballs or stuffed shells loaded with three types of cheese and smothered in marinara sauce, and of course with Texas toast, loaded with butter and garlic. Reynolds had also started doing push-ups and sit-ups daily; he was getting stronger quickly.

Pushing himself back from the table, Reynolds patted his stomach and said, "Sunday, zero dark thirty, we hit the house. They may be drinking Saturday night. We'll use that to our advantage, and let's get Lopez back."

"You good?" West asked, looking at the big man, who now appeared to be pretty much back to his old self.

"Affirmative, it's time to kill some assholes," he said. Pointing around the table, he continued, "And nobody here kills Sanchez. He's mine."

"Damn straight," Aguilar said, smiling.

"Luis, we need some recon," West said. "Can you drive me by the place so I can get some eyes on the building?"

"Affirmative, whenever you want. I know the neighborhood and the roads."

"Midnight should be good enough," West replied.

"I want to go," Timms said.

"No way in hell, baby," Aguilar said. "Sanchez has seen you. You'd only be a bullet magnet."

"All right, I'll stay here and make eyes at Jack, so don't be gone too long," Timms replied.

"Take all the time you need," Reynolds said as he smiled at Timms and she tilted her head and batted her long eyelashes.

Carrera 78
11 p.m.

"Anything, Mateo?" Sanchez asked the big man with long black hair who was standing in the corner of the living room next to the bay window and looking out to the street below.

"No. But the hair on the back of my neck is starting to stand up like something's about to happen."

"I've got the same feeling," Sanchez said. "We need to kill Rico and Lopez and get out of this damn deathtrap."

"Yes, we have only one way out, Alex," Mateo said, glancing at his boss. "There's not even another building we can jump to from the windows."

"I know," Sanchez said. "Keep watching. I'll take over at midnight."

"Okay," the big man said. "I'll wake you up if you fall asleep."

"All right," Sanchez said, and he lay down on the couch across the room, facing the stairs.

CIA Safe House
11:30 p.m.

"Luis, how long does it take to get there?" West asked, putting the Smith & Wesson 9mm in the front of his belt and pulling the bottom of his black long-sleeve T-shirt over the wooden grips.

"Twenty-five, thirty minutes. You ready?"

"Let's go," West said as he started down the stairs to the taxi.

"Be careful, sweetheart," Timms said and gave Aguilar a kiss on the lips.

"Be back in a little while, honey. Get some sleep," Aguilar said and then headed towards the taxi.

"I'll be up when you get back," she replied, glancing back at Reynolds.

He nodded and said, "Me too."

Carrera 78
11:57 p.m.

I NEED TO PISS BEFORE I WAKE him up, Mateo thought. He turned and walked to the bathroom and closed the door. Lifting the seat, he pissed hard into the water. The sounds of the urine splashing in the toilet masked any noise from the yellow taxi as it slowed down in front of the building and then drove on.

Finishing, he flushed the toilet and walked back out of the bathroom to the couch.

"Alex," Mateo said, gently nudging the sleeping man's shoulder, "it's midnight."

Sanchez woke up and swung his feet off the couch to the floor. Rubbing his face with his hands he asked, "Anything?"

"No, it's been quiet. Not even a cat."

"All right. I'll take over until six. Then I'll need a couple hours of sleep."

"Okay, wake me when you need to," Mateo replied and lay down on the couch, pulling a blanket off its back and covering up.

AS THE TAXI GOT TO THE end of the block on Carrera 78, West asked, "How are most of these homes laid out? What's the floor plan? They all look alike from the outside."

Aguilar turned east onto Carrera 79 and headed back towards La Ceja, unknowingly driving past the sleeping Alejandro and Rafael Espinoza. "They are mostly exactly alike. That one had two basement doors, but only one of them will lead upstairs, and that's the one next to the garage."

"What's the other door used for?"

"It usually goes to ground-level storage, or some people use that room for a shop to sell knickknacks to make a little extra money."

"I see."

"How are your lock-picking skills?" Aguilar asked.

"A padlock?"

"Yes, that outside metal bar door will have a small padlock on it. The inside wooden door won't even be locked. Do you have a lock-picking set?"

"No. Do you have a couple of paper clips?" West asked.

"Yeah, got those at the house."

"That's all I need. It'll take me a minute or two; if I'm lucky, less than that."

"Old school shit, I like that," Aguilar said.

"Bring the master key just in case we need it," West said.

"Roger that."

1 a.m., Friday, May 14

We're sitting ducks here, Sanchez thought as he glanced out the window. Walking past the sleeping Mateo, he opened the door to the Customs agent.

"I need to kill you now," he said under his breath.

Lopez opened her eyes and stared at the man.

"Do you hear me, bitch?"

"Yes, I hear you, and we'll see who kills whom."

Sanchez scoffed and closed the door.

CHAPTER 35

Call Me a Bitch Now

Noon, Saturday, May 15, 1993

"Hello," Hayden said, answering his phone on St. Simons Island, Georgia.

"Buddy, it's Nathan."

"What's the latest? How's Jack?"

"He's good and we're hitting the house tonight."

"Dear God, you'll all be in my prayers."

"Thank you. I need a favor."

"Anything. What?"

"Does Bobby Taylor still work at the Glynco Jetport?"

"Yes, he does. You need a lift?"

"Yes, at about 0200 hours. I checked with Aguilar. There's an executive hangar at the north end of the Medellin Airport. We can run the gate there."

"I'll call him now. He'll be there waiting for you."

"If we don't show up by 0300 hours, tell him to beat feet."

"You just make sure you're there," Hayden said. "Bobby will be waiting. He's a former fighter pilot; he enjoys being shot at."

"Roger that."

"Let me talk to Jack."

West handed the phone to Reynolds who was standing next to West in the kitchen.

"Yeah."

"Jack, you up to this?" Hayden asked.

"Yeah, Buddy. I'm solid."

"Okay, kill those sons of bitches and get that agent back."

"Roger that," Reynolds said and gave the phone back to West.

"Thanks, Buddy. We'll talk soon," West said and hung up. Looking at Aguilar, West asked, "Do you have any small lights?"

"Yes, I've got two or three small Maglites here somewhere."

"Great, we're going to need them," Reynolds said. "And do you have any vests?"

"Yes, but I have only one," Aguilar replied.

"Well, that makes you the lead then," Reynolds said.

"Affirmative," Aguilar replied. "I'll tape my light to the 12-gauge barrel. You guys can tape them to the forearm of the MPs.

"Roger that," West said.

Carrera 79B
11:30 p.m., Saturday, May 15

"I'll be back after a while," Rafael said to Limon and Alejandro who were watching a movie on TV.

"Where you going?" Alejandro asked. "It's getting late."

Shrugging his shoulders, Rafael replied, "Just for a walk," and he opened the door to leave.

Alejandro started shaking his head as he watched his brother go out. "That poor bastard is so in love he can't stand himself."

"That's dangerous," Limon replied.

"Yes, it is."

Ten minutes later, Rafael unlocked the barred gate to get into the lower door of #29 on Carrera 78. He didn't bother to relock it.

Rico was standing in the kitchen getting a drink of water before he went to bed when he heard the outside barred door being unlocked and opened. A moment later, the stairs creaked, and then he watched the upstairs door open and the lovesick man walk into the living room. “Rafael, is something wrong?”

“No, I’m only here to check on her. Go to bed, Rico,” he said softly as he looked at Sanchez lying on the couch asleep in front of the TV that was still on with the volume turned down. Mateo was leaning in the corner holding his pistol.

Rafael nodded to Mateo, turned, and walked to Lopez’s bedroom. He opened the door and quietly walked in, closing the door behind him.

Mateo shook his head, slid the pistol back into his belt, and looked back out the window thinking, If someone stays close to the wall, we won’t be able to see them. He had seen only Rafael’s right shoulder as he came into the house.

“What do you want?” Lopez asked, sitting up in bed when she saw the man in the soft glow of the nightlight.

“I wanted to be near you. Can I sleep here on the floor?” he asked with a pleading in his voice.

Lopez looked at the man for several moments and then handed him the pillow she wasn’t using.

“Thank you,” Rafael said and lay down on the floor.

Lopez put her head back on her pillow.

Both had tears in their eyes.

CIA Safe House
1 a.m., Sunday, May 16

“LET’S GO OVER THIS ONE MORE TIME,” Reynolds said.

“Brenda will stay with the car after we get out one block up the street. She’ll watch for our egress to pick us back up. Nate will lead down the block, followed by Luis and then me. Nate will pick the lock, pull the steel door open, and Luis will take the lead with the double-aught buck loaded shotgun. We stack at the bottom of the stairs and again at the top if all is still quiet. Luis, then Nate, then me. So far so good?” Reynolds asked.

"Yes," West, Aguilar, and Timms replied.

"As we enter the upstairs, Luis goes straight ahead, West peals left, and I peal right. Let's hope there's some light still in the house. These small flashlights are almost useless, but that's all we have. Still good?" Reynolds asked.

"Yes," the others replied.

"We kill everyone in the house and get Lopez out. Timms will drive us to the airport and run the gate. We get to the jet, and Nate and Lopez catch a ride back to the States. The rest of us will come back here, and we start concentrating on helping Search Bloc, Customs, and DEA get Espinoza. Is everyone good with this?" Reynolds asked.

"Sounds like a plan," West said, and Aguilar and Timms nodded.

"All right, let's saddle up," Reynolds said.

Medellin International Airport
1:30 a.m.

"Medellin Control, this is Glynco Jet Service, November-zero-niner-Zulu, requesting permission to land straight in on runway zero-one," CIA pilot Captain Bobby Taylor said in the mic.

"Ten-four, November-zero-niner-Zulu, you're cleared to land runway zero-one," the tower replied.

"Ten-four, tower, will be taxiing to Executive Hangar on the north end of the field. Have a nice evening."

After landing and taxiing to the hangar, Taylor brought the jet to a stop, got out of his seat, and lowered the left side door. "Now we wait," Taylor said.

"Yeah," Buddy Hayden replied as he racked a live round into the M4 and looked out at the dimly lit tarmac.

Carrera 78, #29, Medellin
2 a.m.

The taxi slowed at the corner one block south of #29.

"I love you, Luis," Timms said as Aguilar and then Reynolds followed West out of the backseat.

"Love you too, baby. Be back in a few minutes," Aguilar whispered.

After the men got out, Timms pulled the car to the right side of the road where she had a clear view of the front of the house as it was lit up by the streetlights.

Quickly walking the two hundred feet to the house, West and Aguilar, in dark jeans and black, long-sleeve T-shirts, blended into the darkness. Reynolds almost glowed in his Dominion Energy slacks and white long-sleeve shirt. Nobody else's clothes fit him, and Sanchez had destroyed the only street clothes he had. The three stayed next to the buildings so no one upstairs could see them.

West frowned as he looked at the front of the building with the steel door already opened. Turning his head, West whispered to Aguilar, "Someone else is here."

Aguilar nodded as West silently opened the inner door. Aguilar took the lead. As the men entered the garage, they switched on the lights taped to their weapons. Softly walking to the bottom of the stairs past the black Mercedes, they made not a sound. Aguilar continued to point the 12-gauge pump shotgun up the stairs as West and Reynolds stacked behind him.

Holding the MP5 in his right hand, Reynolds squeezed West's left shoulder who in turn squeezed Aguilar's left shoulder, and he began leading the trio slowly up the stairs to the closed door.

MATEO WAS HAVING TROUBLE SLEEPING ON the couch. It was just too small for his large body, and he shifted constantly, keeping him partially awake. Sanchez had earlier moved a chair into the corner so he could sit and watch the street. In doing so, he could barely see the sidewalk, but he still had a full view of the street. Sanchez's eyes were very heavy as he struggled to stay awake.

Rico was lying on his bed fully clothed with his shoes still on in the bedroom at the end of the hall on the left. He knew it was a matter of time before the shooting started. He had already decided he was rolling off the bed and crawling under it at the first loud noise.

Hopefully someone checking the room and seeing the bed was made would not look under it.

Rafael was asleep on the floor in Lopez's room, first door on the right starting up the hallway.

The trio of agents had almost made it to the top step when the next-to-the-last step made a loud creaking sound. Sanchez didn't hear it, but Mateo immediately opened his eyes and stared at the door. He was sure the sound came from the steps; he had heard that step creak many times from his own weight. Pulling his Glock 9mm out of his belt, Mateo pointed it at the door. He squinted his eyes to see in the dim light provided by the TV. By lying on the couch, he was low enough to see slightly underneath the door. Maybe he was hearing things and it was nothing. Tilting his head to see better, he suddenly saw a flash of light in the crack underneath the door.

"Alex!" he yelled. He began firing through the door as it burst open and a load of double-aught buck from the shotgun hit him square in the face.

Seeing Aguilar drop to the floor in front of him, West sent a hail of bullets into the man on the couch where the shots were fired from and turned left in a crouch to cover the hallway.

Startled, Sanchez leaped from his corner chair half asleep and started firing wildly towards the stairs with the Beretta as Reynolds sprang around the door to his right. Seeing Sanchez, Reynolds filled the corner with a dozen 9mm slugs from the MP5. The firing from the corner stopped as Reynolds watched Sanchez fall flat on his face and not move.

Hearing the shots, Rico did exactly what he had planned. He rolled off the bed and crawled underneath it, trying not to make any sounds. Pulling the crucifix out of his shirt, he kissed it and clutched it next to his face. He closed his eyes, praying they wouldn't be able to hear him shaking.

"Agent Lopez," West yelled while keeping his position at the beginning of the hallway and pointing the MP5 in that direction.

"In here," he heard a female's voice say, coming from the first door on the right.

"Go," Reynolds yelled to West as he moved to cover the man who'd been shooting from the corner of the living room.

"Luis is down," West yelled, glancing back as he got up and kicked open the first door on the right.

"Dammit," Reynolds said, as he bent down to pick the weapon off the floor that the man had been firing and quickly returned to help Aguilar. Glancing at the man on the couch, Reynolds saw most of his head was gone. Reynolds rolled Aguilar over and could see he was having difficulty breathing with blood gushing from a hole in his throat. The tactical vest had stopped two rounds; the third bullet had hit above the vest in Aguilar's neck.

"Hang in there, Luis," Reynolds said, as he picked up his head and cradled it in his lap.

"Who are you?" West said, pointing the MP5 at the head of the tall man standing behind the far side of the bed with Lopez standing in front of him.

"Don't shoot him," Lopez said, holding her arms up.

"Rafael Espinoza," the man said.

"I know you," Lopez said. "Please don't shoot him. He saved my life."

"Pull up your shirt and do a 360," West demanded, still pointing the weapon at the man's head.

"I'm not armed," Rafael said as he did as ordered, pulling his shirt up and turning in a complete circle.

"Don't move," West said. He quickly left the room and kicked in the door across the hall to the bathroom. Nothing. Running down the hall he kicked open the door at the end of the hall. Shining the light around the room as he pointed the MP5, he could see the bed had not been slept in. He quickly returned to Lopez's room.

West walked up to Rafael and put the barrel of the MP5 underneath his chin. "You've got a temporary reprieve. You need to get right with Jesus and soon. You come out of this room and you die."

Rafael nodded.

West looked at Lopez. "You able to walk?"

"Yes."

"Coming out," West yelled, and he left the bedroom followed by Lopez. Kneeling down beside Aguilar and Reynolds, West asked, "How is he?"

"He's gone, Nate," Reynolds said, looking up.

"Dammit," West said.

"I'll carry him," Reynolds said. "Get the shotgun." He stood and pulled Aguilar's body up and over his right shoulder.

Lopez saw the Beretta lying on the floor, picked it up, and went to the man lying face down in the corner. Rolling the man over, she stood over him and said, "Call me a bitch now, Alex."

The almost-dead man coughed up a mouth full of blood and spit it at Lopez. "Bitch."

Lopez emptied the pistol into the man's chest and face. "Who killed whom?" she yelled and then turned and walked back to West and Reynolds.

"We go now!" Reynolds said. He started down the stairs with Aguilar over his shoulder, followed by Lopez carrying the Beretta.

West glanced around, picked up the shotgun, and hurried down the stairs behind them.

CHAPTER 36

Baby, Don't Die

Carrera 78, #29, Medellin
2:05 a.m.

THEY HAD BEEN IN THE HOUSE for less than two minutes. Reynolds, carrying Aguilar's body, Lopez, and West ran into the street.

Seeing several people come out of the house, Timms quickly started the taxi and gunned the engine, racing the car down the street to the group. As the taxi came to a screeching halt, West jerked the rear door open, and Reynolds began sliding the body onto the back seat.

"Nooo," Timms yelled and got out from behind the wheel and put her hands over her mouth, seeing the blood on Reynolds's white shirt and her partner and lover's limp body being put in the cab.

"Angelina front passenger seat, Brenda back seat," West barked as he helped Reynolds get the body in the car.

Lopez went around the front of the vehicle and got in the front passenger seat as Timms ran around the back of the car, jumped in the backseat, and guided Aguilar's head onto her lap. Reynolds pushed the body in further, raised Aguilar's legs, and slid in under them onto the backseat.

"Drive," Reynolds yelled at West, who shut the back door of the taxi and got in behind the steering wheel.

"Baby, don't die!" Timms screamed as she gently held the man's head and looked into the blank eyes of Luis Aguilar. Tears began to stream down her face.

West put the car in gear and gunned the engine as the car spun its rear tires and headed towards the Medellin Airport.

Tears swelled in everyone's eyes as Timms screamed again.

Rafael heard the tires squeal as the car drove away. Leaving the bedroom, he walked into the living room and looked at Mateo's and Sanchez's lifeless bodies. He turned and walked back to the end of the hall, entered the bedroom, and switched on the light. Not seeing anyone, he softly said, "Rico."

"Rafael?" came from under the bed.

Squatting down, Rafael looked underneath the bed and could see the terrified man clutching the cross. "Come out," Rafael said and stood back up.

"Is it safe?"

"Yes, they're gone. Come out," Rafael said.

Rico crawled out from under the bed and followed Rafael back down the hall. Rico glanced into the bedroom where Lopez had been kept. Walking past the living room and into the kitchen, he saw the bodies of Mateo and Sanchez. "So much death, Rafael. We are surrounded with so much death," Rico said, still clutching the crucifix and looking into the tearful eyes of his boss who now sat down at the kitchen table. Why do we continue to do this?" Rico asked as he sat down across from his cousin and boss.

Rafael looked at Rico and said, "I no longer will. Do you have paper and a pen?"

"Yes, Rafael."

"Get them for me."

Rico got up and returned to his bedroom where he opened the desk drawer and took out a large pad and pen. Returning to the kitchen, he handed them to Rafael.

"I'm the legal owner of the jet," Rafael said. "I'm transferring full ownership to you." He wrote out a bill of sale for the jet, signed, and dated it. Handing it to Rico, Rafael said, "You must leave Colombia. Take Sanchez's car, drive to Bogota, get the jet, and leave."

"Rafael, I don't know what to say. What will you do?"

"I don't know yet, but you leave. Go somewhere and start over."

Both men stood up and embraced.

"Thank you," Rico said. Walking to Sanchez's body, he took the Mercedes car keys out of the man's front pants pocket and went down the stairs to the garage.

Medellin Airport
2:15 a.m.

"HOLD ON," WEST SAID AND THEN SHOVED THE GAS PEDAL to the floor and drove the taxi though the airport's north-end gate. With a loud crash, the metal pipes and cyclone fencing of the gate were thrown off to the sides of the fence and out of the car's path. Racing around the end of the large hangar, West could see the CIA Learjet with the steps lowered. He slid the car to a stop at the bottom of the steps, put it in park, and jumped out.

"We need a hand," West yelled to Taylor, who hurried down the stairs and followed West to the back door of the taxi as West opened it and helped Reynolds slide out from underneath Aguilar's legs.

"What happened?" Taylor asked as Reynolds pulled the body out.

"KIA. Get me a blanket," Reynolds said. He carried the body up the steps and into the jet, followed by Taylor and West.

"God dammit," Hayden said, standing to the side to allow Reynolds carry the body to the back of the jet and place it in one of the seats.

"Here," Taylor said, handing a small blue flight blanket to Reynolds, who placed it over the body, tucking it over Aguilar's head so the blanket wouldn't fall off.

Lopez helped Timms out of the car, up the steps, and into the jet as they watched Reynolds cover the body. "I'm so sorry," Lopez said and hugged Timms while both cried.

"He was such a good man," Timms said, looking at Lopez as tears streamed down their faces.

"Wheels up, Bobby," West said.

"Yes, let's get the fuck out of here," Hayden said.

Turning to face Hayden, Reynolds said, "I'm not leaving. You get the two women and Nate back to the States. I'm staying to help the new DEA agent that's now here."

"I'm staying too," Timms said as she wiped the tears from her face. "I'm seeing that Luis didn't die in vain. I'm staying until Alejandro's dead."

Reynolds looked at the woman and said, "Get in the car if you're staying. We leave now before the police show up."

After shaking hands with Hayden, West, and Taylor, Reynolds turned to Lopez, gave her a hug, and said, "Can I have my Beretta back?"

Pulling the pistol from her jeans, she handed it to the big man. "I didn't know it was yours. It's what Sanchez has been carrying."

"Yeah, I told him I'd get it back."

"Thank you," Lopez said.

Reynolds nodded and followed Timms down the steps to the car.

"Be careful, Jack," West said.

"I'll be in touch, Nate. You watch for it," Reynolds said.

He and Timms got in the car and drove out through the busted gate.

"Light this candle, Bobby," Hayden said as he pushed the control to raise the steps and secure the door.

"Yes, sir," Taylor replied. Now in the left seat, he increased throttle, began to turn the jet around, and taxied back towards the runway.

West and Lopez took seats beside each other and fastened their seat belts tightly. Hayden went into the cockpit and buckled up in the right-side seat.

"Medellin Tower, this is November-zero-niner-Zulu, requesting immediate departure runway one-niner," Taylor said into the mic.

"Negative, November-zero-niner-Zulu. Authorities are requesting you hold your position. They're on their way to your location now."

Continuing to taxi to the end of the runway, Hayden smiled as Taylor turned the jet to face the south and said, "Thank you, Medellin Tower. Have a good evening." He pushed the throttle handles forward all the way to maximum thrust. The Lear Jet began to scream down the runway and leaped into the air as flashing lights on the airport security vehicles could be seen arriving at the Executive Hangar.

West glanced back at the blanket-covered body and then continued to look straight ahead.

Lopez reached over and squeezed his hand saying, "I'm so sorry about your friend. Thank you."

West nodded, looked at Lopez, and said, "He died a warrior. He died an honorable death. He would have wanted it that way."

Medellin
July 1993

ROBERTO ESCOBAR (RAFAEL ESPINOZA) TURNED HIMSELF in to the authorities of Search Bloc. He knew his life was over unless he did. However, he never told anything that would give away the hiding locations of his brother. Roberto would spend the next thirteen years in prison.

Lewisburg, West Virginia
August 9, 1993

AT THE AGE OF THIRTY-EIGHT, NATHAN WEST BEGAN his first year at the West Virginia School of Osteopathic Medicine (WVSOM). He tried to put that shadowy world of death behind him. But it was hard, and for the first time in his life, he found it difficult to sleep. He wasn't sure who he was any longer. Which man was it that sat in those classes day after day and tried to absorb all that was thrown at him and his classmates?

His maturity must have shown through since his classmates elected him to be the freshman class president of the Class of 1997. Still, he struggled to fit into that new world of good but naïve people.

He often sat in class, looked around the room, and thought, They have no idea what really goes on in this world or that a new star has been added to the white marble wall in Langley.

Monday, November 29, 1993

West was sitting in class when Dr. Jim Stoogey, dean of WVSOM, entered the large room and briefly spoke to the instructor of the class, Dr. Robert Forester. Dean Stoogey then turned and left the room.

After the class was concluded, Dr. Forester said, "Hey, Nate, Dr. Stoogey would like to speak to you."

West nodded and said, "Thank you, Dr. Forester." He walked out of the classroom and turned to the left in the main hall. Going up the hallway a short distance, he knocked on Dean Stoogey's door and entered.

"Good morning," Margret, Stoogey's secretary said.

"Good morning. Dr. Stoogey would like to speak to me."

"Yes, come with me," she said, got up from behind her desk, and opened the door to Stoogey's office. "Dr. Stoogey, Mr. West is here."

"Yes, come in, Freshman Class President. Have a seat," the white-haired, gruff dean directed.

"Yes, sir," West said and sat down in the chair in front of the dean's desk.

"I got a strange phone call, and the person said the message was for you."

"Yes, sir. What was the message?"

"It was about a frog's ass or something," Stoogey said, looking intently at West. "Just so you know, I don't have time to be running around and trying to find the freshman class president for horseshit."

"Yes, sir. Sir, do you know specifically what the message was because that makes no sense to me."

"I didn't take the phone call; Margret did."

"Can I speak to her?"

"Why not? You're the freshman class president," Stoogey said sarcastically. "Margret, step in here, please," Stoogey said loudly towards the door.

The door opened, and the secretary walked into the room.

"What did the caller actually say, do you recall?" Stoogey asked.

"Yes, sir. The man said to tell Nathan West the frog's ass is watertight."

Stoogey looked at West.

"Sir," West said, "I apologize for the inconvenience, but that must have been a prank phone call."

"You're not going to cause me any more problems are you, Freshman Class President?"

"No, sir. I need to get back to class."

"Get the hell out of my office, West."

"Yes, sir."

Standing, West turned to walk past the smiling secretary and out of the office.

"Nathan," Stoogey said.

Pivoting, West said, "Yes, sir?"

"Tell your dad I said hello."

"Yes, sir. I will," West said and left the dean's office.

West returned to the class that was already underway. Sitting down, he looked around and thought, They have no idea.

Medellin
December 2, 1993

PABLO ESCOBAR (ALEJANDRO ESPINOZA) and his bodyguard, Limon, were shot and killed by members of Search Bloc after a short chase and firefight across the roof of his home on Carrera 79B. With recently provided information that he was somewhere close to the Girardot Estadio, DEA Special Agent Javier Pena (Julio Piniella), with assistance from Customs, Delta Force, and agents of the CIA Clandestine Service, was able to track Escobar to that area and kill the most famous drug smuggler ever known as he was running across the rooftops towards Carrera 78.

EPILOGUE

THIS IS A FICTIONAL STORY based on actual events. The Special Activities Center of the Central Intelligence Agency sends brave men and women throughout the world to fight dangers that few are aware of. These members risk their lives daily in their attempt to make this country and the world a safer place. Some die in obscurity, and their names are never known. Each of their sacrifices is honored by a single engraved star in the white marble at the CIA Memorial Wall in Langley. There are currently 139 stars.

ABOUT THE AUTHOR

On May 31, 1997, in Lewisburg, West Virginia, Dr. Norman Wood graduated from the West Virginia School of Osteopathic Medicine with honors. He was joined on the stage by his father, Dr. Norman Wood Sr., and his brothers, Dr. Ralph Wood, Dr. Victor Wood, and Dr. Gregory Wood. He had been elected the freshman class president in 1993 and later the student government president. He was presented with the Dr. Roland P. Sharp President's Award and Foundation Award of Excellence for Student Achievement. Dr. Wood is a former special agent and former West Virginia State Trooper. He is credited with making the largest drug seizure in US history in 1988 as undercover Special Agent Tony Davis for the US Customs Service in San Francisco.

Dr. Norman Wood's graduation from the West Virginia School of Osteopathic Medicine with honors, May 31, 1997. *Left to right*: Dr. Victor Wood, Dr. Norman Wood Sr., Dr. Norman Wood Jr., Dr. Gregory Wood, and Dr. Ralph Wood.

Made in the USA
Middletown, DE
07 August 2023

36296321R00146